*Tahira Naqvi* was educated in Pakistan and the United States, and has been teaching writing at Western Connecticut State University since 1984. She has been translating Urdu fiction for journals and periodicals in Pakistan and abroad for many years, and has translated many of Urdu's well-known writers, including Manto (*Another Lonely Voice: The Life and Works of Saadat Hasan Manto*); Ismat Chughtai, Ahmed Ali and Prem Chand. The author of many short stories herself, she is currently completing work on her first novel.

*Syeda S Hameed* was educated in Delhi, the United States and Canada, and has taught English at Lady Sri Ram College (Delhi) and the University of Alberta (Canada). She has been translating from Urdu to English for some time, and among her translated works are Mohammad Yunus' *Letters from Prison*; S M H Burney's *Iqbal: Poet Patriot of India*; and Khan Abdul Wali Khan, *Facts are Facts*. She is currently translating the autobiography of Sheikh Abdullah into English; she has also edited the four centenary volumes of Maulana Abul Kalam Azad, *India's Maulana*.

# The Quilt
# and Other Stories

## Ismat Chughtai

*Translated by Tahira Naqvi
and Syeda S Hameed*

The Women's Press

First published in Great Britain by
The Women's Press Limited 1991
A member of the Namara Group
34 Great Sutton Street
London EC1V 0DX

First published in 1990 by
Kali for Women
A 36 Gulmohar Park
New Delhi 110 049

British Library Cataloguing in Publication Data
Chughtai, Ismat
    The quilt and other stories.
    1. Urdu fiction. Short stories
    I. Title
    891.43937

    ISBN 0-7043-4277-4

Printed and bound in Great Britain by
BPCC Hazell Books
Aylesbury, Bucks.
Member of BPCC Ltd

# Contents

|  | *Introduction* | *vii* |
|---|---|---|
| 1. | The Veil (*Ghunghat*) | 1 |
| 2. | The Quilt (*Lihaaf*) | 7 |
| 3. | Sacred Duty (*Muqaddas Farz*) | 20 |
| 4. | The Eternal Vine (*Amar Bel*) | 39 |
| 5. | Kallu (*Kallu*) | 55 |
| 6. | Chhoti Apa (*Chhoti Apa*) | 65 |
| 7. | The Rock (*Chatan*) | 73 |
| 8. | The Wedding Shroud (*Chauthi ka Jora*) | 91 |
| 9. | The Mole (*Til*) | 110 |
| 10. | A Morsel (*Niwala*) | 127 |
| 11. | By the Grace of God (*Allah ka Fazl*) | 142 |
| 12. | Poison (*Zehr*) | 152 |
| 13. | A Pair of Hands (*Do Haath*) | 162 |
| 14. | Aunt Bichu (*Bichu Phupi*) | 176 |
| 15. | Lingering Fragrance (*Badan ki Khushboo*) | 190 |
|  | *Glossary* | 225 |

# Introduction

ONE OF Urdu's boldest and most outspoken women writers, Ismat Chughtai played an important role in the development of the modern Urdu short story as we know it today. Not only did she make strides in the areas of style and technique, she also led her female contemporaries on a remarkable journey of self-awareness and undaunted creative expression. One must not forget that in the India of the Thirties and Forties, writing by and about women was tentative; it was generally held that literature had no place in women's lives. Making a break with tradition, Ismat proved that this was a fallacy.

In 1944 she stepped into the realm of Urdu fiction with her story *Lihaaf* (The Quilt), with such force that she confounded her readers as well as her male counterparts. Since boldness and unconventionality were not characteristics generally associated with women in those days, many of her critics went so far as to suggest that these new stories came from a man's pen, that 'Ismat Chughtai' was a pseudonym for a male writer. In the introduction to *Choten* (Wounds), Krishan Chander says that "as soon as Ismat's name is mentioned, male short-story writers get hysterical, they are embarrassed, they experience mortification."[1] When face to face with the Ismat who blushed at the mention of the mysteriously suggestive ending to her story, *Lihaaf*, Manto, her contemporary and later her friend and harshest critic, was disappointed. "She's a woman after all," he thought in dismay. But when he got to know her better and became familiar with her work, he was compelled to change his opinion. He states in *Ganje Farishte* (Bald Angels), that Ismat was indeed a woman first and foremost, but that in order to fully develop one's art one must remain true to one's basic nature. "If she were not a woman," he continues, "one would never have seen such smooth, sensitive stories like *Bhul Bhulaiyan* (Mazes), *Til* (The Mole), *Lihaaf* and *Gainda* (The Marigold), in her collections.[2]

Ismat Chughtai was born on August 15, 1915, into a middle-class family in Badayun. She was the youngest of six brothers and four sisters. Her father, Mirza Qaseem Beg, was an honest civil servant who rose to the position of deputy collector through his own merit and hard work. Ismat attended the local municipal school, the cantonement school having been disregarded owing to its policy that girls wear frocks, a practice contrary to the Chughtai family tradition.

Since her sisters got married when Ismat was very young, the better part of her childhood was spent in the company of her brothers, a factor she has admitted contributed greatly to the frankness in her nature and subsequently her writing. As she describes it:

> We are all frank, my father, my brothers, all of us. We never used to sit in separate groups . . . my father was very progressive and broad-minded. He believed in education and gave me equal chances with my brothers . . . I never had the feeling I should be shy and nervous. Be-

cause of that upbringing, I'm this way.[3]

Her brother, Mirza Azim Beg Chughtai, already an established writer while Ismat was still a young girl, was her first teacher and mentor. At his bidding, Thomas Hardy was the first novelist she "consumed"; others followed, as did lessons in translation, both from Urdu to English and vice versa. Later, after she had read her brother's short stories, she began experimenting with fiction herself. The romantic works of Hajab Ismail, Majnun Gorakhpuri and Niaz Fatehpuri filled her head with adventurous ideas and she imagined herself a heroine in a story. Writing in secret, she produced melodramatic stories that would have been regarded as "dirty" and she knew she would be severely reprimanded if they were discovered. She soon realized that what she had written so far was below par and ineffective, so she tore everything up and embarked on a course of serious study. The works of Dostoyevsky and Somerset Maugham had a great impact on her and she also developed a special fondness for Chekhov. And it was O' Henry, she claims, from whom she learned the conventions of storytelling. Of the serious Urdu writers, Prem Chand was her favourite and understandably so. Having been influenced by Dickens, Tolstoy and later Gandhi, Munshi Prem Chand was the first Indian to write cohesive European style Urdu fiction.[4]

With college came the beginning of a new life for Ismat, and writing took a back seat to education. "The world changes after B.A.," she says in the introduction to *Guftagu* (The Conversation), a collection of her short stories. "One grows so much in four years." Beginning with Greek drama, continuing with Shakespeare down to Ibsen and Bernard Shaw, she read voraciously.[5] Finally, when she was twenty-three, Ismat decided she was ready to write seriously; she was certainly old enough, she told herself, and had read the best there was in fiction, Urdu as well as English. Her first story, *Fasadi* (The Troublemaker), was published in *Saqi*, a literary journal of considerable repute. Its readers were perplexed; they wondered why Azim Beg Chughtai had "changed" his name. The man himself was not aware that his little sister, "Munee", had become a writer and had published a short story.

In 1936, while she was completing her B.A., she attended the first meeting of the Progressive Writers Movement in Lucknow, at which Munshi Prem Chand was also present. Here she met Rashid Jahan for the first time. A doctor by profession and "a woman of a particularly strong-willed, liberated sort," Rashid Jahan also wrote stories and radio plays, which appear in the collection titled *Aurat aur Digar Afsane* (Woman and Other Stories), and was the only woman who left a lasting impression on Ismat.[6] Explaining her fascination with Rashid Jahan and the extent to which she was influenced by her, Ismat says: "She spoiled me because she was very bold and used to speak all sorts of things openly and loudly, and I just wanted to copy her. She influenced me a lot; her open-mindedness and free thinking."[7]

After completing her B.A. Ismat went on to obtain a B.T. and became the first Muslim woman to have both B.A. and B.T. degrees. For some time she held the post of principal at the Girls' College in Bareilly and, while she was here, her father passed away. The next few years were spent in Jodhpur from where she went on to Bombay as Inspectress of Schools.

In Aligarh Ismat met Shahid Latif, her future husband. He was completing his Masters degree at the time and the two developed a close friendship. Later he became a film director and it wasn't until Ismat was twenty-nine that she married him. "It was just friendship," she says, "and love or romance didn't have any part in it." Because they were often seen in each other's company, people presumed they were going to be married. "And then we don't know what happened, maybe there was such a scandal, but we found ourselves married".[8] Her brother, Azim Beg Chughtai, vehemently opposed the match, perhaps because he disapproved of Shahid Latif's association with films.

In 1942, two months before she got married, Ismat wrote *Lihaaf*, which proved to be a breakthrough in Urdu short story writing. A frustrated housewife, whose nawab husband has no time for her, finds sexual and emotional solace in the companionship of a female servant. The narrator of the story is a woman remembering a childhood experience. Because of this we get a viewpoint which is utterly refreshing since a child may naively and artlessly say things an adult may not. The lesbian relationship between the begum and her maidservant is vividly drawn, but since we are looking at it from a nine-year-old's eyes, there is none of the awkwardness that would have accompanied an adult's perception of what went on between the two women.

When *Lihaaf* was published two months later, a storm of controversy broke out. Readers and critics alike openly and unequivocally condemned Ismat and her story. Charged with obscenity, she was submitted to a trial in Lahore. Here she had occasion to spend a great deal of time with Manto who was among the few who supported her and who was being similarly charged for his story, *Thanda Gosht* (Cold Meat). The trial lasted for two years; the court could not find any "four-letter words" in the story and finally the case against Ismat was dismissed. According to her own accounts the story is based on fact. As a child she had heard the women in her household giggle and whisper tales about a begum and her female servant. "My brother and I hid under a takht while the women gossiped and as soon as someone caught a glimpse of us, we were told to make ourselves scarce. This led us to believe that the women were talking about forbidden subjects, and although in the beginning what they were saying didn't make sense to us, gradually we began to understand."[9] Ismat's recollection explains the viewpoint in the story and also throws light on the enigmatic last sentence: "What I saw when the corner of the quilt was lifted I will never tell anyone, not even if someone gives me a lakh of rupees." At the time she wrote the story her knowledge regarding the subject of lesbianism was meagre; what she couldn't "tell" was actually what she didn't know.

Although *Lihaaf* set the tone for all of Ismat's later work and established her not only as a mature writer but as someone who was of the same standing as Manto, Krishan Chander, Ahmed Ali, Rajinder Singh Bedi, Ahmed Nadeem Qasmi and others, it also became a focal point of recognition for Ismat's work in popular terms. However, readers of Urdu fiction have a tendency to ignore the fact that Ismat is more than *Lihaaf*, much more. She is also *Kallu*, *Chauthi ka Jora* (The Wedding Shroud), *Hindustan Chor Do* (Leave Hindustan), *Do Haath* (A Pair of Hands), *Terhi Lakir* (The Crooked Line — one of her best novels), and so many others.

Ismat, like her contemporaries, was influenced a great deal by European fiction, especially the works of late-nineteenth century Russian writers. She and others in her class became involved with a new kind of writing which, although it was linked with social themes, was neither didactic nor entirely political in its overtones. A socialist outlook, accompanied by the use of non-traditional techniques to tell a story, gained strength. Having been greatly influenced by Freud's theories of psychosexual development, the new writers also wrote freely and openly about certain aspects of human sexuality, but, as in the case of Ismat, with sincerity and intelligence. In addition to changes in subject matter and tone, a new language evolved, a style that did not waste time mincing words or tip-toeing around the real issues. This was a style that was bold, innovative, rebellious and explicitly realistic in its representation and analysis of character and the human condition.

Ismat began writing at a time when the voices of women writers were still muffled. Tradition and ethical mores held a tight grip on society and any attempt on the part of women to write poetry and fiction was viewed as "intellectual vagrancy".[10] However, despite this taboo, certain women succeeded in making themselves heard; Begum Yaldram, Hajab Ismail and Begum Nazar Sajjad, for example. Although their fiction had gained considerable popularity, these early works by women were largely romances or were instructional and reformist in nature, the characters and subject matter remaining stilted and unbelievable. Ismat herself was affected initially by Hajab Ismail's overly- romanticized themes and larger-than-life characters, but she soon broke free from this influence.

Motivated by the initiative that Ismat's dramatic entry into the world of literature provided, other women writers also came forward valiantly, and many more voices arose to join hers. Qurratulain Hyder, Mumtaz Shireen, Hajira Masroor, Khadija Mastoor, Razia Sajjad Zaheer, Tasneem Salim, Sarla Devi, Sadiqa Begum and Shakila Akhtar were some of the most notable among them.

In her writing Ismat concentrated on what she was most familiar with. Having lived in a family where there was no dearth of mothers-in-law, aunts, uncles, cousins, servants and a whole network of neighbours (*muhalle wale*), she was able to portray these characters vividly and realistically when she used them in her stories. That she frequently drew her fiction from actual events she had been a part of, either directly or indirectly, explains the intense realism we meet with in her work. Many of her stories are clearly autobiographical: *Bichu Phupi* (Aunt Bichu) and *Kunwari* (The Virgin), for instance, but the story loses nothing in terms of fictive value or drama on account of that fact. In her best novel, *Terhi Lakir*, the period spanning the narrator's childhood comes very close to Ismat's own childhood. Several of the characters appearing later in the book are fashioned after people she knew in real life, many of these women being close friends who were not at all happy at finding themselves in Ismat's novel.

Many of Ismat's critics have accused her of being limited in her choice of subject matter. Perhaps that is true. She wrote only of what she knew well. But within these limits she perfected her art. The bulk of her work reflects a deep and abiding preoccupation with themes directly related to women and their cultural status and role in Indian society. Stressing the struggles of women against the oppressive social institutions of her time, she brings to her fiction an understanding and perception of the female psyche that is unique to her alone; no other writer approaches the subject of women in the same sympathetically probing, sharply cognizant and readable way that she does. One cannot discredit anything she offers, whether it be the behaviour of a sexually-frustrated housewife in *Lihaaf*, or the futility and despondency experienced by Madan, the film star in *Kunwari*, who seeks but cannot find respectability.

The world of Ismat's fiction is inhabited by people who come from the middle class, much as she did. Their circles of familiarity include, as hers did, not only relatives, close and distant, but also the entire servant class (*Kallu*), sweepers and sweepresses (*Do Haath*), not forgetting an assortment of neighbours. Perceived as a societal network, this world teems with stories that can be told from diverging viewpoints, offering unlimited variety, colourful and strikingly interesting, to say the least.

Ismat depicts her characters realistically, using language that is so direct, colloquial and down to earth that her characters remain characters no longer, becoming instead people, real people we see every day and know well. Kubra's mother in *Chauthi ka Jora*, struggling to find a suitable husband for her older daughter, is no stranger to us; Bichu Phupi, on the warpath with her brother and his family, but undeniably woman and sister in the end, could be anyone's estranged aunt, and Gori, the dark, sultry temptress in *Do Haath*, and Rani in *Til* we have frequently encountered among the cleaning women in our households when we were children. And the fact of their familiarity doesn't bore us, doesn't render them banal; no, we read on avidly to find out how they fare and what fate awaits them.

In large part it is Ismat's diction, her unique and rich idiom that pulls us along. "Not only does her story appear to be running," says Krishan Chander, "but the sentences, images, metaphors, the sounds and sensibilities of the characters and their feelings—all seem to be moving together and forward with the intensity of a storm."[12] Although some of the energy is lost in translation as it always will be, the following passage from *Kunwari*, is an example of the force Krishan Chander is talking about:

> During her association with Sunder, Madan had stopped using profanities altogether. Sunder's love had been like a balm for her bleeding sores and had obstructed the passage of filth. As soon as he dropped from view, the freshly sutured wounds gaped open again and pus flowed from them once more. My heart sank when I saw the old curses falling from her lips. Angered, Madan was like a string of snappers.[13]

From the point of view of richness of metaphor and simile, the power of the idiom, and the ease and facility with which images fall into place, soundlessly and with absolute clarity, the quality of Ismat's language surpasses that of any of her contemporaries.

Of the early writings by Ismat's contemporaries, many reveal shortcomings in the areas of style and subject matter that one generally attributes to professional and literary incipience. In Ismat's earliest stories, however, one observes a forceful viewpoint and a mature handling of subject matter that is surprising, when one takes into account the fact that she was a lone voice at the time, a woman severing her ties with tradition, both in literary and social terms. In reviewing Ismat's skill as a writer, Ehtesham Hussain, a leading critic of Urdu literature, has this to say about her art:

> Ismat's undaunted intelligence and her power of expression were so well integrated that from the very beginning her stories caught everyone's attention. It is true that at first she too probed only some of society's ills, scraped wounds, poured salt over them, and left her readers in a quandary. But it did not take her long to become aware of the truth about her writing and soon she was able to strike an effective balance between her themes and her subject matter.[14]

We can also view Ismat's stories as socio-cultural data. A thorough study of her fiction will reveal valuable facts about the social and cultural aspects of life in U.P. Muslim families. Class consciousness, styles in clothing, cooking habits, foods, elements of social exchange, customs regarding such important events as birth, marriage and death—we can examine them all simply by perusing Ismat's fiction. For example, in *Chauthi ka Jora* we observe the tradition of matchmaking at work. It would be incorrect to say the tradition is outdated; in India and Pakistan there are still households where the process of marriage continues to take a somewhat similar, if not the same, route. Kubra, the young woman who is to be married, stays in hiding while her younger sister is sent out by the mother and her old friend to "play jokes" on the cousin who is, without his knowledge, being viewed by all the women in that household as a prospective groom. The idea is to engage his attention indirectly in this manner and prod him into delivering a proposal for the woman he has never seen, and will never see unless he marries her. One may also learn in the same story how the Muslim shroud is prepared, how the cloth is squared and measured and ripped by hand, without the use of scissors. In *Niwala* (A Morsel), we come across more matchmaking, this time of a different nature. We also get a rare glimpse of life in a Bombay *chal*. *Muqaddas Farz* (Sacred Duty), brings us face to face with secularism as a way of life in present day India. The young no longer care whether they are Muslims or Hindus. Representative of a new age, they are content to be just Indians. And in *Ghunghat* (The Veil), we are confronted with a woman whose loyalty to the institution of marriage tragically consumes her entire life, a phenomenon deeply engrained in the very fibre of our culture.

For anyone studying the development of Urdu, Ismat's language provides ample opportunities to unravel the idiom that was once an integral part of the Urdu vernacular. Here are some examples from *Amar Bel*:

> But in opposition to these five Pandus, Aunt Imtiazi held the power of a hundred Kurus.
>
> . . . her body was like kneaded dough coated with butter.
>
> . . . her pale skin reminded one of gold which a dishonest goldsmith had adulterated with silver . . .
>
> The very hands he had once compared to un-

opened jasmine buds he now perceived as the dangerous claws of a red falcon threatening to scratch out his eyes.

*Kaliyan* (Buds), Ismat's first collection of short stories and *Choten*, her second, were published in Azim Beg Chughtai's lifetime. Her other books are: *Aik Bat* (A Word; short story collection), *Terhi Lakir* (Crooked Line; novel), *Chui Mui* (The Sensitive One; short story collection), *Ziddi* (The Stubborn One; novella), *Masooma* (The Innocent; novella) *Dhani Bankpan* (Green Elegance; short stories), *Do Haath* (short stories), *Hamlog* (We People; essays and stories), *Shaitan* (The Devil; plays), *Saudai* (The Madman; novel), *Aik qatra-e-khun* (A Drop of Blood). In addition, Ismat has produced scripts of five films in which she collaborated with her late husband, Shahid Latif, and has made five films independently.

Ismat had two daughters by Shahid Latif. A widow now, she lives in Bombay. A few years ago she was asked why she had not written her autobiography. "I've written it, I've written a lot," she replied. When asked why she had not published it, she had this to say: "Why should I publish it right now? It will be published when I'm dead. Why should I die just yet? At this moment I'm telling you the truth, but it isn't necessary that I speak the truth in my autobiography; you no longer remain objective when you write an autobiography, you begin to think of your own reputation."

TAHIRA NAQVI

# NOTES

[1] Krishan Chander wrote the Foreword to Ismat's first collection of short stories, *Choten*. In it he explained that what he was writing about her was motivated by the desire on the part of male short story writers to eradicate the feelings of "mortification" they experienced in her literary presence.

[2] This quote is from *Ganje Farishte* (Lahore, Maktaba-e-shero adab, 1984), Saadat Hasan Manto's collection of essays on well-known literary and film personalities. In a similar essay Ismat wrote about Manto after his death, she called him *mera dost, mera dushman* (my friend, my enemy).

[3] *Guftagu* is a short interview with Ismat Chughtai, functioning as a foreword to her collection of short stories titled, *Kharid lo* (Lahore, Raffat Publishers, 1982).

[4] *The Life and Works of Saadat Hasan Manto: Another Lonely Voice* (Lahore, Vanguard Publishers, 1985), pp. 23-27. This book contains a lengthy monograph by Dr. Flemming who teaches at the University of Tucson, Arizona. The stories have been translated by Tahira Naqvi.

[5] *Lady Killer*, a collection of short stories by Ismat Chughtai.

[6] Carlo Coppola, "The All-India Progressive Writers' Association: The European Phase," *Marxist Influences and South Asian Literatures*. Carlo Coppola, (ed.) Vol 1, Occasional Papers No. 23, South Asia Series (East Lansing: Michigan State University, Asian Studies Center), 1.

[7] Tahir Masud, "Ismat Chughtai" from *Ye suratgar kuch khabun ke*, a collection of interviews, p. 344. This interview took place during Ismat's second visit to Pakistan some years ago.

[8] *Guftagu*, p. 1.

[9] *Lady Killer*, p.5.

[10] *Lihaaf, Ismat Chughtai ke behtreen afsane*, (Lahore, Chaudhry Academy, 1979) p.257.

[11] Mahmud Wajid, *Ismat ke afsanon men riwayat aur tajurba* (Tradition and Experience in Ismat's Short Stories), Jamil Akhtar (ed.)*Alfaz*, Ismat Chughtai Issue (Karachi, 1985), 16.

[12] Azhar Qadri, *Ismat Chughtai ka ahang-e-fan* (The Style of Ismat's Art), *Alfaz*, p. 12.

[13] Ismat Chughtai, *Kunwari*.

14*Ismat Chughtai ke behtreen* . . . p.12
15*Ye suratgar kuch khabun ke*, p. 361.

# The Veil

SEATED on a divan covered with a white sheet, her hair whiter than the wings of a heron, grandma looked like an awkward mass of marble; it seemed as though there was not a single drop of blood in her body. White had crept up to the edges of her grey eyes which, lustreless, reminded one of casements that were barred, of windows hiding fearfully behind thick curtains. Her presence, shrouded in what could be likened to a stationary cloud of finely ground silver, was dazzling, and a snowy-white, blinding radiance seemed to emanate from her person. Her face shone with the glow of purity and chastity. This eighty-year-old virgin had never known the touch of a man's hand.

She was like a bouquet of flowers at thirteen with hair that fell below her waist and a complexion that shimmered with youthful silkiness and translucence. But her youth had been ravaged by time; only the softness now remained. Her beauty was of such renown in those days that her parents, afraid she might be whisked away by jinns, couldn't sleep at night. Indeed, she didn't appear to be of this world.

At fourteen she became engaged to my mother's uncle. He was as dark as she was fair, although otherwise he was exceedingly well-proportioned and manly in appearance: what a sharply delineated nose he had, just like the blade of a sword, hooded eyes that were ever watchful, his teeth a string of pearls. But he was unusually sensitive about his inky complexion.

During the engagement celebrations everyone began teasing him.

"Dear, oh dear, the bride will be tarnished by the groom's touch!"

"It will be like an eclipse of the moon."

Kale Mian was a stubborn, immature, seventeen-year-old at the time. Terrified by all this talk about his bride-to-be's beauty, he ran away to his maternal grandfather's house in Jodhpur. There, hesitatingly, he admitted to his friends that he didn't want to get married. In those days defiance was dealt with severely and a beating or two was not at all uncommon. Under no circumstances could an engagement be terminated; such an act would bring eternal shame upon the family.

And what was wrong with the bride-to-be, anyway? Just that she was exceedingly beautiful? The world idolized beauty and here he was, manifesting extreme bad taste by spurning it.

"She's arrogant," he confessed diffidently.

"How do you know?"

There was no proof, but beauty is known to beget arrogance and it was impossible that Kale Mian should submit to arrogance; he was not accustomed to submitting to the will of others.

A concerted effort was made to explain to him that once she was his wife, Goribi would become his possession and comply with his every wish. She would say 'day' if he wanted her to, 'night' if he wished it thus; she would sit wherever he made her sit, and stand up if he ordered her to do so. Some physical force was also employed to coerce Kale Mian into returning home and finally the wedding took place.

The women singing wedding songs sang of a fair bride and a dark groom. As if that were not enough to incense Kale Mian, someone recited a poem in which a stinging allusion was made to his dark complexion. This proved to be the last straw. However, nobody took his indignation seriously, and, presuming that he was in tune with the spirit of fun that prevailed, continued to jokingly tease him.

When, like a sword out of its sheath ready for attack, he entered the bridal chamber and saw the bride who was enmeshed in glittering red flowers, he broke out in a sweat. Her pale, silken hands made his blood boil, and he was overcome by an overpowering desire to grind in his blackness with her whiteness so that the difference between them would be obliterated forever.

The bride bent over as he extended his hands towards her veil.

"All right then, you lift the veil yourself," he said.

The bride dropped her head lower.

"Lift your veil!" he ordered her sharply.

The bride was all rolled up like a ball now.

"Ohhh! Such arrogance! Hunh!" The bridegroom slipped his shoes under his arm, jumped out of the window which opened on to the garden, made directly for the station and from there, to Jodhpur!

The women in the family knew the bride had not been touched and it was not long before the news reached the men. Kale Mian was interrogated.

"She is defiant," he proclaimed.

"How do you know that?"

"I told her to lift her veil and she ignored my

request."

"You fool! Don't you know a bride does not lift her own veil? Why didn't you do it yourself?"

"Never! I have sworn. If she will not lift her veil, she can go to hell!"

"You are stupid to ask her to lift her veil herself; next thing you know you will be wanting her to take the initiative for everything else. What a damned stupid idea!"

There was no question of divorce in those days. Once married you stayed married. Kale Mian disappeared for seven years, but he continued to send money to his mother. Goribi, his bride, was suspended between her parents' home and that of her in-laws.

Her parents were deeply shocked by the tragedy that had befallen their only daughter. They were hurt; what was wrong with the girl that the bridegroom had not touched her? Who had heard of such injustice?

In order to prove his manhood Kale Mian indulged in all the vices that were available to him; he consorted with prostitutes and homosexuals and, among other things, spent time as a pigeon- fancier; all this while Goribi quietly smouldered away behind her veil.

When his mother fell seriously ill, Kale Mian came home. Considering this to be a stroke of good fortune, the elders made another attempt to bring the bride and groom together. Once again Goribi was clothed in bridal attire. But Kale Mian said, "I've sworn on my mother's life I will not lift her veil."

Everyone reasoned with Goribi: "Now, girl, this is going to affect your whole life. Set your modesty aside, stir up some courage, and raise your veil yourself. There is nothing indecent about this—he is your husband, your earthly God. It's your duty to obey him. Your freedom lies in doing as he says."

Once again the bride was adorned, the nuptial bed was decorated, pulao and sweet rice were cooled, and once more the bridegroom was pushed into the bridal chamber. Goribi was a flowering beauty of twenty-one now; she exuded the warmth of womanhood, her eyelids drooped heavily, her breath came fast. For seven years she had dreamt of this particular night, friends had whispered secrets that made her heart beat wildly. As soon as Kale Mian's eyes fell upon the bride's henna-covered hands and feet he felt emotion take control of him. His bride sat before him, not an unopened bud of fourteen, but a full-blown bouquet. Desire melted him; the night was sure to be filled with delights. Restive, his experienced body yearned for her like a tiger anticipating its prey. Although he had never seen her face, an image of this wondrous bride had tormented him even when he was with other women.

"Lift your veil," he said tremulously.

There was not the slightest movement.

"Lift your veil," he murmured in a pleading, tearful voice.

The silence remained unbroken.

"If you don't do as I say I am never going to show you my face again!"

The bride did not stir.

Kale Mian knocked the bedroom window open with a jab of his fist and jumped out into the garden.

Gone that night, he never returned to her.

Goribi, the untouched bride, waited thirty years for him. Gradually, nearly all the elders in her family died. It was while she was staying with an old aunt of hers in Fatehpur Sikri that she learned about the bridegroom's return.

After leading a life of indiscriminate debauchery, Kale Mian had returned home burdened with disease. On his deathbed he requested that Goribi come to him so that he could die in peace.

When she received Kale Mian's message, Goribi leaned against a pillar for a long time, unmoving and silent. Then she went to her old trunk, took out her tattered wedding suit and put it on, applied bridal oil to some of her grey hair and, her long veil cradled between her hands, she arrived at the side of the dying patient.

"Lift your veil," Kale Mian whispered convulsively.

Goribi's trembling hands reached up toward her veil, and fell.

Kale Mian had taken his last breath.

That very moment Goribi calmly sat down on the floor beside his bed, smashed her glass bangles against the bedpost, and instead of the bridal veil, pulled the white veil of widowhood over her head.

*Translated by Tahira Naqvi*

# The Quilt

IN the depth of winter whenever I snuggle into my quilt, its shadow on the wall seems to sway like an elephant. My mind begins a mad race into the dark crevasses of the past; memories come flooding in.

Begging your pardon, I am not about to relate a romantic incident surrounding my own quilt—I do not believe there is much romance associated with it. The blanket, though considerably less comfortable, is preferable because it does not cast such terrifying shadows, quivering on the wall!

This happened when I was a small girl. All day long I fought tooth and nail with my brothers and their friends. Sometimes I wondered why the hell I was so quarrelsome. At my age my older sisters had been busy collecting admirers; all I could think of was fisticuffs with every known and unknown girl or boy I ran into!

For this reason my mother decided to deposit me with an 'adopted' sister of hers when she left for Agra. She was well aware that there was no one in that sister's house, not even a pet animal, with whom I could engage in my favourite occupation! I guess my punishment was well deserved. So Mother left me with Begum Jan, the same Begum Jan whose quilt is imprinted on my memory like a blacksmith's brand.

This was the lady who had been married off to Nawab Sahib for a very good reason, courtesy her poor but loving parents. Although much past his prime, Nawab Sahib was noblesse oblige. No one had ever seen a dancing girl or a prostitute in his home. He had the distinction of not only performing the Haj himself, but of being the patron of several poor people who had undertaken the pilgrimage through his good offices.

Nawab Sahib had a strange hobby. People are known to have irksome interests like breeding pigeons and arranging cockfights. Nawab Sahib kept himself aloof from these disgusting sports; all he liked to do was keep an open house for students; young, fair and slim-waisted boys, whose expenses were borne entirely by him. After marrying Begum Jan, he deposited her in the house with all his other possessions and promptly forgot about her! The young, delicate Begum began to wilt with loneliness.

Who knows when Begum Jan started living? Did her life begin when she made the mistake of being born, or when she entered the house as the Nawab's new bride, climbed the elaborate four-poster bed and started counting her days? Or did it begin from the time she realised that the household revolved around the boy-students, and that all the delicacies produced in the kitchen were meant solely for their palates? From the chinks in the drawing-room doors, Begum Jan glimpsed their slim waists, fair ankles and gossamer shirts and felt she had been raked over the coals!

Perhaps it all started when she gave up on magic, necromancy, seances and whatnot. You cannot draw blood from a stone. Not an inch did the Nawab budge.

Broken-hearted, Begum Jan turned towards education. Not much to be gained here either! Romantic
novels and sentimental poetry proved even more
depressing. Sleepless nights became a daily routine.
Begum Jan slowly let go and consequently, became a
picture of melancholy and despair.

She felt like stuffing all her fine clothes into the
stove. One dresses up to impress people. Now, neither
did Nawab Sahib find a spare moment from his preoccupation with the gossamer shirts, nor did he allow
her to venture outside the home. Her relatives, however, made it a habit to pay her frequent visits which
often lasted for months, while she remained a prisoner
of the house.

Seeing these relatives on a roman holiday made
her blood boil. They happily indulged themselves
with the goodies produced in the kitchen and licked
the clarified butter off their greedy fingers. In her
household they equipped themselves for their winter
needs. But, despite renewing the cotton filling in her
quilt each year, Begum Jan continued to shiver, night
after night. Each time she turned over, the quilt assumed ferocious shapes which appeared like shadowy
monsters on the wall. She lay in terror; not one of the
shadows carried any promise of life. What the hell
was life worth anyway? Why live? But Begum Jan was
destined to live, and once she started living, did she
ever!

Rabbo came to her rescue just as she was starting
to go under. Suddenly her emaciated body began to
fill out. Her cheeks became rosy; beauty, as it were,
glowed through every pore! It was a special oil massage that brought about the change in Begum Jan.
Begging your pardon, you will not find the recipe for

this oil in the most exclusive or expensive magazine!

When I saw Begum Jan she was in her early forties. She sat reclining on the couch, a figure of dignity and grandeur. Rabbo sat against her back, massaging her waist. A purple shawl was thrown over her legs. The very picture of royalty, a real Maharani! How I loved her looks. I wanted to sit by her side for hours, adoring her like a humble devotee. Her complexion was fair, without a trace of ruddiness. Her black hair was always drenched in oil. I had never seen her parting crooked, nor a single hair out of place. Her eyes were black, and carefully plucked eyebrows stretched over them like a couple of perfect bows! Her eyes were slightly taut, eyelids heavy and  eyelashes thick. The most amazing and attractive part of her face were her lips. Usually dyed in lipstick, her upper lip had a distinct line of down. Her temples were covered with long hair. Sometimes her face became transformed before my adoring gaze, as if it were the face of a young boy. . . .

Her skin was fair and moist, and looked like it had been stretched over her frame and tightly stitched up. Whenever she exposed her ankles for a massage, I stole a glance at their rounded smoothness. She was tall, and appeared taller because of the ample flesh on her person. Her hands were large and moist, her waist smooth. Rabbo used to sit by her side and scratch her back for hours together — it was almost as if getting scratched was for her the fulfillment of life's essential need. In a way, more important than the basic necessities required for staying alive.

Rabbo had no other household duties. Perched on the four-poster bed, she was always massaging Begum Jan's head, feet or some other part of her anatomy.

Someone other than Begum Jan receiving such a quantity of human touching, what would the consequences be? Speaking for myself, I can say that if someone touched me continuously like this, I would certainly rot.

As if this daily massage were not enough, on the days she bathed this ritual extended to two hours! Scented oils and unguents were massaged into her shining skin; imagining the friction caused by this prolonged rubbing made me slightly sick. The braziers were lit behind closed doors and then the procedure started. Usually Rabbo was the only one allowed inside the sanctum. Other servants, muttering their disapproval, handed over various necessities at the closed door.

The fact of the matter was that Begum Jan was afflicted with a perpetual itch. Numerous oils and lotions had been tried, but the itch was there to stay. Hakims and doctors stated: It is nothing, the skin is clear. But if the disease is located beneath the skin, it's a different matter.

These doctors are mad! Rabbo used to say with a meaningful smile while gazing dreamily at Begum Jan. "May your enemies be afflicted with skin disease! It is your hot blood that causes all the trouble!"

Rabbo! She was as black as Begum Jan was white, like burnt iron ore! Her face was lightly marked with smallpox, her body solidly packed; small, dextrous hands, a tight little paunch and full lips, slightly swollen, which were always moist. A strange and bothersome odour emanated from her body. Those puffy hands were as quick as lightning, now at her waist, now her lips, now kneading her thighs and dashing towards her ankles. Whenever I sat down with Begum

Jan, my eyes were rivetted to those roving hands.

Winter or summer, Begum Jan always wore kurtas of Hyderabadi *jaali karga*. I recall her dark skirts and billowing white kurtas. With the fan gently rotating on the ceiling, Begum Jan always covered herself with a soft wrap. She was fond of winter. I too liked the winter season at her house. She moved very little. Reclining on the carpet, she spent her days having her back massaged, chewing on dry fruit. Other household servants were envious of Rabbo. The witch! She ate, sat, and even slept with Begum Jan! Rabbo and Begum Jan—the topic inevitably cropped up in every gathering. Whenever anyone mentioned their names, the group burst into loud guffaws. Who knows what jokes were made at their expense? But one thing was certain — the poor lady never met a single soul. All her time was taken up with the treatment of her unfortunate itch.

I have already said that I was very young at that time and quite enamoured of Begum Jan. She, too, was fond of me. When mother decided to go to Agra she had to leave me with somebody. She knew that, left alone, I would fight continuously with my brothers, or wander around aimlessly. I was happy to be left with Begum Jan for one week, and Begum Jan was equally pleased to have me. After all, she was Ammi's adopted sister!

The question arose of where I was to sleep. The obvious place was Begum Jan's room; accordingly, a small bed was placed alongside the huge four-poster. Until ten or eleven that night we played Chance and talked; then I went to bed. When I fell asleep Rabbo was scratching her back. "Filthy wench," I muttered before turning over. At night I woke up with a start.

It was pitch dark. Begum Jan's quilt was shaking vigorously, as if an elephant was struggling beneath it.

"Begum Jan," my voice was barely audible. The elephant subsided. "What is it? Go to sleep." Begum Jan's voice seemed to come from afar.

"I'm scared." I sounded like a petrified mouse.

"Got to sleep. Nothing to be afraid of. Recite the *Ayat-ul- Kursi*."

"Okay!" I quickly began the Ayat. But each time I reached *"Yalamu Mabain"* I got stuck. This was strange. I knew the entire Ayat!

"May I come to you, Begum Jan?"

"No child, go to sleep." The voice was curt. Then I heard whispers. Oh God! Who was this other person? Now I was terrified.

"Begum Jan, is there a thief here?"

"Go to sleep, child; there is no thief." This was Rabbo's voice. I sank into my quilt and tried to sleep.

In the morning I could not even remember the sinister scene that had been enacted at night. I have always been the superstitious one in my family. Night fears, sleep-talking, sleep-walking were regular occurrences during my childhood. People often said that I seemed to be haunted by evil spirits. Consequently I blotted out the incident from memory as easily as I dealt with all my imaginary fears. Besides, the quilt seemed such an innocent part of the bed.

The next night when I woke up, a quarrel between Begum Jan and Rabbo was being settled on the bed itself. I could not make out what conclusion was reached, but I heard Rabbo sobbing. Then there were sounds of a cat slobbering in the saucer. To hell with it, I thought and went off to sleep!

Today Rabbo has gone off to visit her son. He was

a quarrelsome lad. Begum Jan had done a lot to help him settle down in life; she had bought him a shop, arranged a job in the village, but to no avail. She even managed to have him stay with Nawab Sahib. Here he was treated well, a new wardrobe was ordered for him, but ungrateful wretch that he was, he ran away for no good reason and never returned, not even to see Rabbo. She therefore had to arrange to meet him at a relative's house. Begum Jan would never have allowed it, but poor Rabbo was helpless and had to go.

All day Begum Jan was restless. Her joints hurt like hell, but she could not bear anyone's touch. Not a morsel did she eat; all day long she moped in bed.

"Shall I scratch you, Begum Jan?" I asked eagerly while dealing out the deck of cards. Begum Jan looked at me carefully.

"Really, shall I?" I put the cards aside and began scratching, while Begum Jan lay quietly, giving in to my ministrations. Rabbo was due back the next day, but she never turned up. Begum Jan became irritable. She drank so much tea that her head started throbbing.

Once again I started on her back. What a smooth slab of a back! I scratched her softly, happy to be of some assistance.

"Scratch harder, open the straps," Begum Jan spoke. "There, below the shoulder. Ooh, wonderful!" She sighed as if with immense relief.

"This way," Begum Jan indicated, although she could very well scratch that part herself. But she prefered my touch. How proud I was!

"Here, oh, oh, how you tickle," she laughed. I was talking and scratching at the same time.

"Tomorrow I will send you to the market. What

do you want? A sleeping-walking doll?"

"Not a doll, Begum Jan! Do you think I am a child? You know I am . . ."

"Yes . . . an old crow. Is that what you are?" She laughed.

"Okay then, buy a *babua*. Dress it up yourself, I'll give you as many bits and pieces as you want. Okay?" She turned over.

"Okay," I answered.

"Here." She was guiding my hand wherever she felt the itch. With my mind on the *babua*, I was scratching mechanically, unthinkingly. She continued talking. "Listen, you don't have enough clothes. Tomorrow I will ask the tailor to make you a new frock. Your mother has left some material with me."

"I don't want that cheap red material. It looks tacky." I was talking nonsense while my hand roved the entire territory. I did not realize it but by now Begum Jan was flat on her back! Oh God! I quickly withdrew my hand.

"Silly girl, don't you see where you're scratching? You have dislocated my ribs." Begum Jan was smiling mischievously. I was red with embarrassment.

"Come, lie down with me." She laid me at her side with my head on her arm. "How thin you are . . . and, let's see, your ribs," she started counting.

"No," I protested weakly.

"I won't eat you up! What a tight sweater," she said. "Not even a warm vest?" I began to get very restless.

"How many ribs"? The topic was changed.

"Nine on one side, ten on the other." I thought of my school hygiene. Very confused thinking.

"Let's see", she moved my hand. "One, two,

three . . ."

I wanted to run away from her, but she held me closer. I struggled to get away. Begum Jan started laughing.

To this day whenever I think of what she looked like at that moment, I get nervous. Her eyelids became heavy, her upper lip darkened and, despite the cold, her nose and eyes were covered with tiny beads of perspiration. Her hands were stiff and cold, but soft as if the skin had been peeled. She had thrown off her shawl and in the *karga* kurta, her body shone like a ball of dough. Her heavy gold kurta buttons were open, swinging to one side.

The dusk had plunged her room into a claustrophobic blackness, and I felt gripped by an unknown terror. Begum Jan's deep dark eyes focussed on me! I started crying. She was clutching me like a clay doll. I started feeling nauseated against her warm body. She seemed possessed. What could I do? I was neither able to cry nor scream! In a while she became limp. Her face turned pale and frightening, she started taking deep breaths. I figured she was about to die, so I ran outside.

Thank God Rabbo came back at night. I was scared enough to pull the sheet over my head, but sleep evaded me as usual. I lay awake for hours.

How I wished Ammi would return. Begum Jan had become such a terrifying entity that I spent my days in the company of household servants. I was too scared to step into her bedroom. What could I have said to anyone? That I was afraid of Begum Jan? Begum Jan, who loved me so dearly?

Today there was another tiff between Begum Jan and Rabbo. I was dead scared of their quarrels, because they signalled the beginning of my misfortunes! Begum Jan immediately thought about me. What was I doing wandering around in the cold? I would surely die of pneumonia!

"Child, you will have my head shaven in public. If something happens to you, how will I face your mother?" Begum Jan admonished me as she washed up in the water basin. The tea tray was lying on the table.

"Pour some tea and give me a cup." She dried her hands and face. "Let me get out of these clothes."

While she changed, I drank tea. During her body massage, she kept summoning me for small errands. I carried things to her with utmost reluctance, always looking the other way. At the slightest opportunity I ran back to my perch, drinking my tea, my back turned to Begum Jan.

"Ammi!" My heart cried in anguish. "How could you punish me so severely for fighting with my brothers?" Mother disliked my mixing with the boys, as if they were man-eaters who would swallow her beloved daughter in one gulp! After all who were these ferocious males? None other than my own brothers and their puny little friends. Mother believed in a strict prison sentence for females; life behind seven padlocks! Begum Jan's "patronage", however, proved more terrifying than the fear of the world's worst goondas! If I had had the courage I would have run out on to the street. But helpless as I was, I continued to sit in that very spot with my heart in my mouth.

After an elaborate ritual of dressing up and scenting her body with warm attars and perfumes, Begum Jan turned her arduous heat on me.

"I want to go home!" I said in response to all her suggestions. More tears.

"Come to me", she waxed. "I will take you shopping."

But I had only one answer. All the toys and sweets in the world kept piling up against my one and only refrain, "I want to go home!"

"Your brothers will beat you up, you witch!" She smacked me affectionately.

"Sure, let them," I said to myself annoyed and exasperated.

"Raw mangoes are sour, Begum Jan," malicious little Rabbo expressed her views.

Then Begum Jan had her famous fit. The gold necklace she was about to place around my neck, was broken to bits. Gossamer net scarf was shredded mercilessly. Hair, which were never out of place, were tousled with loud exclamations of "Oh! Oh! Oh!" She started shouting and convulsing. I ran outside.

After much ado and ministration, Begum Jan regained consciousness. When I tiptoed into the bedroom Rabbo, propped against her body, was kneading her limbs.

"Take off your shoes," she whispered. Mouse-like I crept into my quilt.

Later that night, Begum Jan's quilt was, once again, swinging like an elephant. "Allah", I was barely able to squeak. The elephant-in-the quilt jumped and then sat down. I did not say a word. Once again, the elephant started convulsing. Now I was really confused. I decided, no matter what, tonight I would flip the switch on the bedside lamp. The elephant started fluttering once again, as if about to squat. Smack, gush, slobber — someone was enjoying a feast. Suddenly I understood what was going on!

Begum Jan had not eaten a thing all day and Rabbo, the witch, was a known glutton. They were polishing off some goodies under the quilt, for sure. Flaring my nostrils, I huffed and puffed hoping for a whiff of the feast. But the air was laden with attar, henna, sandalwood; hot fragrances, no food.

Once again the quilt started billowing. I tried to lie still, but it was now assuming such weird shapes that I could not contain myself. It seemed as if a frog was growing inside it and would suddenly spring on me.

"Ammi!" I spoke with courage, but no one heard me. The quilt, meanwhile, had entered my brain and started growing. Quietly creeping to the other side of the bed I swung my legs over and sat up. In the dark I groped for the switch. The elephant somersaulted beneath the quilt and dug in. During the somersault, its corner was lifted one foot above the bed.

Allah! I dove headlong into my sheets!!

What I saw when the quilt was lifted, I will never tell anyone, not even if they give me a lakh of rupees.

*Translated by Syeda Hameed*

# Sacred Duty

THE tiny fragment of paper fell from Siddiqi Saheb's hands and fluttered to his lap like a dying moth. He brushed it off hastily, as if it had poisonous fangs that might get embedded in his very being.

Outside, seated on a pile of rugs, his wife supervised the hanging of chandeliers and coloured lanterns. She was also reading congratulatory telegrams that had arrived from abroad, and from Delhi and elsewhere in the country. The wedding of their darling daughter, Samina, who had recently passed her B.Sc. with the highest honours, was only a day away.

The young man, the groom-to-be, was employed in Dubai, received a monthly salary of twelve thousand, had free board and lodgings, and was allowed one pre-paid vacation very year. Progress in the Middle East had brought good fortune to so many single women; this shower of wealth had provided relief to any number of families. From a well-to-do family of good standing, the young man had no one to hassle him for a share in his income. The match had been arranged over the phone. He was not all that good looking, also just a trifle short, but does a girl have to put up her husband for rent? One doesn't bother with a man's physical attributes, it's his qualities that count. And in this case qualities numbered twelve thousand,

and total comforts even more.

Their daughter was like a flower. She had wanted to continue her education, but an opportunity like this doesn't come one's way every day, so the girl was silenced with a few words of censure. What was to be gained by going on to get an M.Sc., or becoming a doctor?

At first she was just quiet, but then she became unusually uncommunicative. These girls are such co-quettes, the mother reflected, putting aside the letter she had been reading. Well, it was settled: she would visit her daughter in Dubai in the month of Khali and, on her way back, God willing, be blessed with the opportunity of performing Haj.

At that very moment, suspended in a state of semi-consciousness, Siddiqi Saheb observed with glassy vision the minute fragment of paper which had pulled his world from a great height and flung it mercilessly into an abyss.

> Papa, Mummy — I'm terribly sorry, but I can't go through with this marriage. I'm leaving with Tashar Trivedi to go to his parents' home in Allahabad. We've been married in a civil cere-mony. I will consider myself privileged if you decide to forgive me.
>
> Your daughter, Samina Trivedi

May God preserve us! It was true that Siddiqi Saheb was a progressive; allowing girls to obtain a higher education and letting them marry whomever they pleased — he certainly believed in all of this. He also attended Eid prayers regularly, had been living a life of quiet respectability as a member of an en-lightened social class, and had never been involved in a dispute over religious convictions. But that wasn't going to stop his blood from boiling if his daughter strayed.

When his wife heard the news she almost fainted. *There's only one thing to do: let's go to Allahabad and shoot them both!* But the mention of the word 'gun' caused Begum Siddiqi to become deeply agitated. Ahhh, their beautiful, their only daughter! God's curse upon the rogue! How charming and harmless he had seemed during those Sunday visits to their house, how he appeared always to be having a good time, and how he and Samina bickered! Where did this blasted love come from, anyway? Such wicked children these days, sneaking off behind your back to get married — and no one had the slightest inkling. How he had flattered her, called her Mummy — indeed he had succeeded in making her his 'Mummy' after all, the wretch! Such a good-for- nothing generation! *No, we have nothing against Hindus:* Did one ever bother with who was Christian and who was Hindu at Papu's Sunday get-togethers? Just think of all the silly nicknames those women had. Pami Deshmukh, for example — was she Razak Deshmukh's wife or Chandra Deshmukh's? And what about Lily? Begum Siddiqi had thought Lily was Christian all along, until she discovered that she was really Laila Razdan. And wasn't it confusing with all those Razdans? Tirmila Razdan, for example, who called herself Nikki, always swore in English and liberally sprinkled her conversation with "Shut up!" and "Hell!" (and was sure to get there) was from an upstanding Shia family; as for Razdan Saheb — *Mohammad* Razdan Saheb — he had performed Haj thrice already. As a matter of fact, Nikki had too. What fabulous saris she had brought back from Haj this time, and all those cosmetics! She brought a gift of the holy water of Zamzam in phials along with a little snippet of the Ka'aba covering; with what cunning she must have used her nail scissors to snip off that swatch! The folds were thick and heavy, she had explained, so no one could tell the difference.

Husband and wife sat late into the night, calling people on the phone and sending telegrams, telling all those who had been invited to the wedding that the girl had come down with a severe attack of pneumonia: *She's in intensive care, the wedding has been postponed for the time being. If she lives, we'll see.*

But there wasn't even a well-sharpened knife in the house with which they could kill their daughter and son-in-law. *Forget the gun.* Getting a license would be such a bother, although, who knows, perhaps if they had tried they might have been successful in procuring one quickly; after all, Allah had blessed them with good connections. But by the time a gun was obtained a child would have been born. The thought of a child made their blood curdle.

*Well, Allah has given us two hands; at least the girl's neck can be wrung. First a good hiding place behind some bushes will have to be found. But are there any bushes there? Perhaps the villains live in a neighbourhood devoid of decent shrubbery.* This was a case of demanding that the river be full before one jumps into it to drown. If fate had been on our side, our daughter would not have run off, would not have blackened our faces thus.

But it would not be fair if Tashar, the ruffian who seduced their innocent daughter, were allowed to go unpunished. *Perhaps it will help to have the screwdriver sharpened. The tool-sharpener used to appear at the front gate every day; what a shame he had been threatened with police action and asked to set up shop elsewhere. What a dreadful grating noise he made when he sharpened a blade! As though a handful of sand had been thrust between your teeth.*

This was not something that could be shared with friends. But Jawad Jaffrey, who had a very successful practice in Allahabad, was like a member of the family. They called him on the phone and asked for advice. He promised to be with them around tea-time the following day.

And then a bomb exploded.

A newspaper sent to the girl's parents from Allahabad was splashed with pictures of Samina and Tashar's wedding. A civil ceremony had not sufficed. Sethji, Tashar's father, had arranged a religious ceremony complete with a *havan* and pandit. And pictures were taken, snapshots of the girl changing her faith, taking a dip in the holy waters of the Ganga in Banaras (she had been flown there), and finally a picture in which she appeared with Tashar, smiling coquettishly at him like a hussy.

Siddiqi Saheb's uncontrolled fury very nearly caused him to have a heart attack. But Jawad Saheb's timely arrival averted such a dreadful catastrophe. Tashar's father had indeed played it dirty. The man was a staunch Mahasabhi, and by printing those photographs with such aplomb he had succeeded in sprinkling salt over Siddqi Saheb's wounds.

Now the entire family would have to be blown up with a bomb: but how? *I, Siddiqi, who finds even the fireworks at Diwali and Shab-barat disturbing, have been shattered by this explosion. This is a nation of Hindus, after all.* Ah, such fine positions were offered to him in Pakistan, but he had been so full of the progressive spirit then — such stupidity!

"I can't leave my country, I will be buried in the earth that gave me life," he had said, using the Hindi word *janam*. Remembering now, he swore angrily. *That's a Hindi word, inappropriate for someone who is the product of a highly-principled, truly Muslim family.*

Jawad Saheb pacified him with great difficulty, calmed him down a little. Then the two friends convened behind closed doors for hours. Later the scheme was spelled out to the girl's mother. She expressed delight: What a crafty man, she said in praise of Jawad Saheb who, although a Jaffrey Shia, had nonetheless shared years and years of friendship with Siddiqi Saheb. History might look askance at a Siddiqi-Jaffrey alliance, but the association between these two men had remained untouched by discord. Faith and friendship do clash sometimes, but love and friendship generally succeed in emerging victorious. However, the contradiction can be tragic; how often do love and friendship serve to destroy principles!

Siddiqi Saheb told the driver to wait and rang the bell.

In a few minutes his beloved daughter Samina clung to him, shedding tears of joy; disobeying her parents deeply distresses a daughter, she can't be at peace with herself until she is forgiven. It was while she was under her parents' roof that Tashar's love had become a part of Samina's life. Would Tashar have been able to woo her in her own home if her parents had not been so liberal?

And Tashar stood nearby, grinning sheepishly. He had not approved of the newspaper stunt his father had pulled. But he was the only brother of four sisters, and one day he would take charge of his father's business. He was reminded of his duty again and again.

His sisters, all of them younger than he, were now well-settled. A long time ago the youngest had fallen in love with a dark-skinned Christian professor. Sethji had the young man cleverly whisked off to England on a government scholarship. Making a hasty retreat from the battlefield of love, the fellow hadn't even bothered to look back.

Sethji, an important man, was reputed to be a successful promoter of politicians. Although he never accepted a position himself, many of his proteges adorned the assembly and various committees. He was viewed as a very successful "king-maker". And despite the fact that he was not affiliated with any particular group, he was always found firmly positioned behind the winning party. He played a role in both the rise and the fall of the masses — his was a multi-faceted personality.

Jawad Saheb's advice to Siddiqi Saheb, whatever it had been, transformed him. His heart beat within his chest with a new rhythm; in very correct and proper Hindi, studded like diamonds with impressive words from Sanskrit, Siddiqui Saheb thanked Sethji for removing a great weight from his shoulders, that of an unwed daughter — for seven generations the debt could not be paid. All faiths are sacred, he said, and the truest faith consists of the love and respect a father-in-law bestows upon his daughter-in-law. Endowing a daughter-in-law with one's faith together with one's son was indeed commendable. And Ganga was the mother of all, regardless of who was Christian, or Hindu, or Muslim; her pure waters didn't question faith — Brahmin and Untouchable, she invited everyone to drink from her cup.

"Sayed Saheb," he said to Sethji, now using honorific titles, "I'm a human being, I've inherited my religion and accumulated knowledge from the written word: your Bhagwan and my Allah are two names for the same power."

Siddiqi Saheb quoted extensively from the Bible and the Gita, as well as the Quran. Sethji was very impressed. His wife requested a neighbour to cook an elaborate non-vegetarian, roast chicken dinner for their guest; the family bustled with excitement. Sethji's son's father-in-law, a man of great means and even greater principles, had come to bless his daughter — how liberally he passed out those fifty-rupee bills to the servants! Siddiqi Saheb attended many dinners thrown in his honour, but he refused to eat meat; meat weakens faith, he proclaimed repeatedly.

People said, "Listen, he's only half a Muslim, how long can he last?"

"You have enjoyed the fulfillment of your wishes," Siddiqi Saheb told Sethji, "now you must allow me to pay my debt to our family and friends. Samina's mother cries incessantly, although the pictures helped lessen her grief somewhat." (Actually his wife had suggested they tear up the pictures and throw them into the kitchen fire.)

Sethji's wife was a little reluctant to hand over the diamond necklace and earrings to her daughter-in-law at the time of her departure. Sethji admonished her: "Don't be of such small heart; our son's father-in-law is a man of wealth and principles. Didn't you see how gracefully he accepted our unfairness? And here you are, worrying about a few pieces of glass."

With great pomp and show Siddiqi Saheb

returned to Delhi with his daughter and son-in-law. Instructions had already been left with friends and relatives who were present at the railway station, laden with bouquets and garlands. Jawad Saheb had accompanied Siddiqi Saheb from Allahabad for good luck.

The girl's mother seethed with fury. She suggested, "Kill the boy and throw his body in the lawn so he can turn into compost."

"Are you out of your mind? Just be patient and see what happens. Tashar is Samina's husband now. Proposal and acceptance, whether it be in our language or any other, has already taken place — they are now husband and wife. And both are dear to us."

That evening the marquee was set up again and invitations went out to all the important people in the city.

Tashar became agitated when he was told to convert. Fearfully he glanced first at Siddiqi Saheb and then at Jawad Saheb, mentally planning an escape route through the window, no doubt.

"Papa, what's this nonsense? First it was Papaji who forced me to become Hindu, telling me to recite all kinds of holy hymns that sounded like gibberish, and now you've started this farce. We refuse to be part of your games. As soon as we return to Allahabad we'll be forced to dip again, have more photographs taken, and . . ." The girl's mother began to cry at this point, and Siddiqi Saheb floundered.

"There's only one way out," he said, clasping his wife's hand, "let's go and drown ourselves in the Jamuna."

"How can you drown, Papa, you know how to swim. You'll probably let Mummy drown and come out of the water yourself, all nice and clean for your girlfriend, Miss Farzana."

"Sami, be quiet!" Tashar scolded Samina. "Papa, I mean Siddiqi Saheb, I'm ready to be a Muslim."

"Shut up, you fool! I'm not ready to be re-converted. Don't you remember how your mother lovingly put the mangal sutra around my neck? These are diamonds, you know. Look, don't you think it's pretty?"

"You can wear the mangal sutra as a Muslim, too!" Tashar retorted angrily.

"Woe is me! Kill them both and bury them." It was the mother. "What an ungrateful daughter. He's ready to be a Muslim, and this miserable creature has decided to be troublesome!"

"Sami, will you be quiet or not?" Tashar admonished Samina again. "When I opposed Papaji you threatened to jump out of the window. Do you know there's a mouse hole under the window? The big mouse in there would have been surprised out of its hole if you had jumped, scaring you out of your wits!"

Someone said, "My word, the maulvi saheb has been waiting a long time to make the conversion. He hasn't even accepted a cup of tea, says he'll have a complete breakfast after he has performed his sacred duty. What a greedy man!"

"I'm ready, and two smacks across her face will bring her to her senses. Darling, did you lose anything by becoming Hindu? There's no need to be so pigheaded."

"Ohh . . . and what about the *arti*, and the lovely mangal sutra you gave me? But I must say, you wear such dirtly socks—I could smell your feet when I bent down to touch them."

"What is all this nonsense!" Siddiqi Saheb roared in anger. "Everything is a big joke for you! Tashar, get ready to submit to the honour." (He used the word *musharraf*, which means 'one who receives the honour'.)

"Musharraf? That Musharraf Hamidullah who is a lowdown thief and a crook? Always cheated in every exam. Sami, remember he pulled out a knife once when Sir caught him redhanded?"

"You're the spoilt son of a rich man, and he's the son of a poor orderly — what a crime! Have you ever wondered how he manages to survive, you bloody capitalist!"

"Look, Mummy, she's rude to me again. I'm going to hit her now."

"They have perished, those who would raise their hands to hit. Unh!" Mummy responded bitterly. Then, "How long is this to continue?" she asked. "Oh dear, I forgot the pudding in the oven." She ran towards the kitchen.

"Look here, these kids are driving me out of my mind — Jawad, help me please . . ." Siddiqi Saheb turned to Jawad.

"Well, what do you suggest?" Jawad, who had been quietly listening all this time, said smilingly. "I've followed your advice until now. What should I do next?"

"Look," Tashar interjected, "you had better convert me right away. I've booked seats for the matinee. We have to be there at three."

"The maulvi still hasn't eaten anything, you should skip the matinee. There's an at-home in the evening."

"But that's at eight!"

Every move made by Siddiqi Saheb was being repulsed.

"Listen to me, children," Jawad Saheb said, clearing his throat.

"Yes, Uncle," Tashar answered respectfully.

"Did you have a civil ceremony?"

"Yes, sir. The certificate is in a safe in Allahabad."

"Did you read the forms carefully before signing them?"

"Yes, I read them, but Samina was too upset to bother. I asked her to sign quickly so we could get out of there."

"How could I sign quickly with such a terrible pen? You can buy hundreds of shoes, but you can't get a decent pen."

"Do you see how rude and disrespectful she is? And we've been married twice, first in a civil ceremony, then a Hindu one. I had refused, but she thought it would be very romantic to be led around the sacred fire. She opposed everything I said just so she could win over my parents."

"Yes, it was romantic like a wedding in a fishing village, with the pandit muttering holy words that sounded like 'shutrum, shutrum', and Papaji, your father, pouring all that real ghee over the fire; it reminded me of carrot halwa when it's being fried — sugary sweet!"

"Ugh! Have you ever smelled real ghee over a burning funeral pyre?"

"You stupid fool, shut up!" Samina folded a newspaper and pounded his head with it.

"Oh, God! This is ridiculous." It was Siddiqi Saheb.

"Let me handle this," Jawad Saheb interjected in

a gentle voice.

"What a disaster! Will this *khachar-khachar* go on forever?" the mother asked as she came back into the room.

"Listen to me, children, and don't interrupt with any of your wisecracks this time. I'm going to ask you a very important question: Before the civil ceremony started, did you read the bit in the form which states that neither of you belongs to any particular faith?"

"No, I don't recall that I did, Uncle, but it doesn't matter. From the very beginning I've done whatever Mataji and Papaji have told me to do and, as a matter of fact, I never really thought much about questions of faith. Religion is for the elderly. In the convent we were exposed to Jesus, in Mathura, Krishanji reigned supreme, and once I accompanied Musharraf to a shrine where, imitating him, I lifted my hands together and moved my lips."

"You mean you've never thought seriously about Allah or Bhagwan?"

"Hmm. What about Dilip Kumar, the actor? Have you ever thought about him?" Siddiqi Saheb's tone was sarcastic.

"Well, Mataji was his fan at one time; personally I prefer Amit, Mithun and . . ."

"That's enough! Now listen, this means that no other proceeding has any meaning unless your civil marriage is dissolved first."

"So the Hindu ceremony was no good?" Tashar asked excitedly.

"Nonsense! It's no use your harping on that ceremony, Tushi. You can divorce me if you want, but you're not going to get back the mangal sutra."

"Oh, what a greedy girl! Here we are , discussing

such serious matters, and all she can think of is this mangal sutra! Tell me honestly, if Mataji had not shown you the mangal sutra and the rest of the jewellery first, would you have agreed to the Hindu ceremony?"

"You're mean, Tushi. Do you think I'm so greedy, you villain? Papa, marry me off to anybody, I don't care who. I called this man my protector, touched his smelly feet ... this ... this ... oh my God!" Samina clenched both fists and ran towards Tashar.

Bloodshed would have ensued if Siddiqi Saheb's wife had not threatened them with an attack of hysteria.

"Jawad," Siddiqi Saheb remarked, "I don't agree with this new point you've raised."

"But perhaps the law ..."

"To hell with the law! I want to get even with Sethji, we'll have a nikah even if I have to go to jail for it or be hanged. He made a fool of me for all the world to see, and I'm not going to ignore that."

"Why, what's the problem?" the mother interjected. "What's the hitch if both are Muslim?"

"My wife is right. She's a maulvi's daughter, after all."

"And she beats everyone at rummy, too," Samina piped in.

"Be quiet, you wretch! Stop interfering."

Maulvi saheb arrived. Giggling at first, Samina finally assumed a serious expression and covered her head. Tashar was offered a Karakuli cap the photographer had brought back from a recent visit to Pakistan. And seeing him handsomely decked out, Samina's eyes lit up provocatively.

Both received the honour of accepting Islam, and

both experienced difficulty reciting Arabic verses from the Quran; Tashar was visibly nervous. Maulvi saheb was a good-natured man, the atmosphere was just right, and Jawad Saheb agreed to act as the counsellor from the girl's side. One other person was needed to act as witness.

"Let Ammi be the witness," Samina suggested, speaking for her mother.

"Then we'll require one more woman."

"Why?"

"One man's testimony is equal to that of two women. But we can use the houseboy Shakura instead."

"Ammi is more important than ten Shakuras! This isn't fair," Samina stubbornly asserted.

"Be quiet, girl; don't keep butting in. There's the girl's father."

"Can I be a witness?" a startled Siddiqi Saheb inquired.

"Of course!" Maulvi saheb was a little disappointed. Residents of large and fancy bungalows were so unreliable; here was this man, a professor, and knew nothing about his own religion.

The nikah ceremony took place, sweets were distributed, the photographer was snapping away at every stage of the ceremony. The photographic sesion would have been a complete success if a shot of the couple affixing their signatures had also been included; such a shot would definitely succeed in scraping knives over Sethji's heart.

The photos were splashed across the morning papers along with the news that the couple was leaving for Bombay that morning, from where, it was said, husband and wife were to depart for England. The report indicated further that, God willing, they would perform Haj before they returned home.

Rooms had been reserved at the Ashoka Hotel for the wedding night. Family and guests accompanied the bride and groom to the hotel, and it was nearly two when the bride's family returned home. Everyone immediately fell into exhausted slumber. Siddiqi Saheb realized, for the first time, how difficult it was to marry off a daughter. All their lives parents wrestle with the fear of this one, special day. A sense of victory made him feel lighthearted the next morning — Jawad Saheb had indeed given a delicious twist to the whole matter. The paper must be in Sethji's hands by now; surely he stayed up for prayers after his ritual morning bath.

Siddiqi Saheb's heart danced with joy.

"I say, Sethji's newfound relative, are we going to get any breakfast today?" Jawad Saheb stood in the doorway. "Why, you appear six inches taller—how grand you look!"

"Not just six inches, a foot at least. By God, I've vanquished a pernicious rival — how riled up he must be! What do you think, shall we have breakfast at the Ashoka?"

"What a wonderful idea!"

"What do you say, my dear?"

"You know I never take long to get ready," his wife replied.

The three of them arrived at the hotel.

"Sir, they've checked out," the clerk at the front desk informed them.

"What? Where have they gone? When did they leave?"

"They sent for a taxi immediately after you left. I

told them again and again they could stay here until tomorrow night, but as soon as they had finished the phone conversation . . ."

"Phone conversation? What phone conversation?"

"It was a call to Allahabad; I connected them myself with Seth . . ."

"Seth!" The three of them were stunned into momentary silence. "So, they've run out on us, have they?"

"Did they say they were going to Allahabad?"

"No sir, they didn't mention anything like that . . ."

"He's going to raise a storm again . . . the rogue! Did Tashar make the call?"

"Yes, sir, I mean both did, sir, they were together in the booth for nearly twenty-five minutes. Oh, and they left a letter for you, sir." The envelope was heavy, or maybe Siddiqi Saheb's grasp was faltering.

The letter was in English, and contained two different kinds of handwriting: Samina and Tashar had taken equal space to express their ideas.

> Dear Papa, Mummy, Uncle Jawad:
> The best thing to do is to go away. No, not to Allahabad, for there, too, a stubborn father and a hysterical mother await us. Like decent people we spent four years getting to know each other well, then opted for a civil marriage after a great deal of serious thought. I'm not very brave, but Samina is a real coward. No, that's not true. I had suggested in the very beginning that we elope, run off somewhere far from here; that's why I called my father in Allahabad. Lovingly he beseeched us to come home: your mother is crying her heart out, come and calm her down, he said. And when we got there he made us go

around the holy fire. We thought, so what? This
ceremony isn't going to kill us. But he played
other tricks on us as well. We put up with
everything. And then, Papa, you arrived on the
scene; you're such a good actor — how genially
and amicably you convinced Papaji — I was so
touched. My father's so broad-minded, I told
myself. Papaji had managed to whisk us off to
Banaras with the help of his cronies. First it was
Papaji who waved the magic wand at us, but
when you warmly expressed forgiveness and
brought us to Delhi, you too exposed yourself
as someone really petty; you also made us
dance like a monkey and its mate. And we took
everything as a big joke, that comic drama too.
Don't worry, we're not going to give away your
secret — tomorrow morning when Papaji looks
at the newspaper there'll definitely be an explosion. No, we only said goodbye to them.
Goodbye to all of you too — no, you don't want
to know where we're going. If we've hurt you,
please forgive us. No, we haven't hurt you, it's
you who have caused us pain, you're the ones
who should apologize. You have made us a
laughing stock. What kind of parents are you,
who make your children dance like monkeys to
any tune you like?

I've told Papaji we don't subscribe to any religion, and now I'm telling you the same thing.
We have no religion. All religions are gifts from
the same Bhagwan, they're for all mankind;
He's also called God. You know Him only as
Allah, but we know of His thousand other
names,

He who takes many forms:
Who is within and without,
Who is above and below,
Who exists in darkness and in light,
Who exists and is not visible,
Who is in negation and in affirmation.

The letter ended with their signatures.

The girl's mother began to cry noisily. Siddiqi Saheb proceeded to make caustic remarks about women's tears.

Jawad Saheb scraped his pipe intently, almost as if he were trying to somehow disappear into it. After all, he was the formulator of this special prescription a la Galen. Who was to say which ingredient had proven ineffective, diminished the prescription's potency, and subsequently reduced the worlds of two sets of parents to desolation?

*Translated by Tahira Naqvi*

# The Eternal Vine

BARI Mumani's shroud was not yet soiled when the whole family began worrying about a new wife for Uncle Shujaat. A bride was now eagerly sought. Whenever the women sat down after a meal and started leisurely work on garments for a dowry or a son's bride-to-be, the talk invariably turned to the question of probable matches for Uncle Shujaat.

"How about our own Kaneez Fatima?"

"Good gracious! Have you gone mad? If Kaneez Fatima's mother- in-law gets wind of this she will cut off your nose and hand it to you. Since her son's demise she has jealously sat guard over her daughter-in-law. The poor girl isn't allowed to leave the house. If there were a death in her family, the unfortunate creature might just be allowed to visit her parents.

"My dear, there's no dearth of virgins for our brother," Asghar Khanum said, adding, "Why should he go running after used goods when people are ready to present their daughters to him? To be sure, he doesn't look forty at all."

"Good God, sister! You're leaving out ten whole years. Why, with God's grace he will be fifty in the month of Khali..."

Poor Aunt Imtiazi! She regretted opening her mouth. On the one side were Uncle Shujaat's five sisters and on the other, the unfortunate woman. With God's grace, all five possessed tongues that were capable of wagging vigorously; the minute a threat was perceived the sisters immediately formed a front and no one — neither Mughlani nor Pathani — could withstand their attack. Even the Sayyedani and the Sheikhani were reduced to helplessness; the boldest among them lost her cool.

But in opposition to these five Pandus, Aunt Imtiazi held the power of a hundred Kurus. Her most dangerous weapon was her screeching voice, thin and sharp like the point of a drill. When she opened her mouth it seemed as if bullets from a machine gun had whizzed into one ear and come out of the other. As soon as she tussled with someone, news of the altercation travelled like wild fire and soon, jumping over balconies and across rooftops, women from the neighbourhood came running towards the arena.

But the five sisters would spring on Aunt Imtiazi with such force that she was reduced to a state of helplessness. Her third daughter, Gori Begum, was still unwed. She was, unhappily, in her thirtieth year, and there were no signs of her luck changing soon. No bachelors were forthcoming and married men didn't become widowers often. In the old days nearly every man laid at least three or four wives to rest. However, since the advent of hospitals and doctors, wives were not dying as frequently. Aunt Imtiazi had made her calculations while Bari Mumani ailed; little did she know that obtaining even a widower's match would be like dipping bamboo rods in a well.

The question of Uncle Shujaat's age developed into a delicate one. As far as Aunt Qamar and Aunt Noor were concerned, he was still a young boy. Again and again they misrepresented his real age because if it were known, then the truth about their own ages would come to light, too. Consequently all five sisters directed their attack from different directions; they brought up the matter of her grand-daughter's husband, whose very name was a sore point with Aunt Imtiazi; he had married a second time while his first wife, namely Aunt Imtiazi's grand-daughter, was still living.

But our aunt was a tough customer, and a Mughlani to boot. She, whose father had been a musketeer in the King's army, was not about to admit defeat. Immediately she turned the tables on them and attacked Shehzadi Begum's grand-daughter, who had brought shame upon the family; every day she got into a sedan-chair and travelled to Dhankot to attend school there. In those days, going to school was considered as unseemly as singing or dancing in films today.

Uncle Shujaat was a handsome man. Of average height and lean build, he had sharply delineated features. Aunt Imtiazi had often broadcast that he dyed his hair, but no one had ever seen a single gray hair on his head so that there was no telling when he started using dye. He looked quite young, no more than forty. When inundated with proposals he became confused and handed the matter over to his sisters. All he said was that the bride should not be young enough to pass as his daughter nor should she be bedraggled or senile.

A frenzied search began. In the end Rukhsana's name was drawn.

"Oh God, what a name!" Unable to think of anything else, Aunt Imtiazi decided to criticize the name.

But the others formed a formidable front that prevented her from being heard.

"If the girl's a day older than sixteen you can hit me a hundred times in the morning, a hundred times in the evening, and give me tobacco water to drink." In vain she struggled to bring Goribi's boat ashore.

Once you laid eyes on Rukhsana Begum you could not tear your gaze away; coy like a new moon, it was a face you could look at forever. She was slender and fragile and her colouring shimmered like crystal. So supple you would think there wasn't a bone in it, her body was like kneaded dough smeared with butter. Her femininity gave the impression that she had been imbued with the essence of a dozen women; a warm glow emanated from her person. As Aunt Imtiazi had said, she was probably no more than sixteen, but she looked older, nineteen or twenty perhaps. The sisters informed Uncle that she was twenty-five, and although at first he expressed some reservations, he soon acquiesced; youth was no crime. She was the burden of a poverty-stricken home, and Uncle Shujaat had to bear the expenses for both parties. When she arrived in his house after the wedding ceremony, Uncle observed her closely and broke out in a cold sweat. "She's only a child," he exclaimed nervously to his sisters.

"Dear God, brother! Watch what you say. A middle-aged man and a young wife in her twenties — two or three children later all the silver coating wears off. When surrounded by wet diapers little will remain of this beauty, this colouring or the tiny waist. The arms won't stay as supple either. If she doesn't begin to look your age soon you can punish me as you see fit. I'm sure in another ten years she'll start looking like

Bari Apa."

"And then we'll get a twelve-and-a-half-year-old for our dear brother," sister Noor squealed in delight.

"Hush!" said Uncle blushing.

"A second wife doesn't live long, that's why we're already thinking about a third," Shama Begum spoke up.

"What nonsense is this?"

"Yes, dear brother. It is said the second wife's function is only to make way for the third. That is why people in the old days used to hold a ceremony with a doll the second time around so that when the next bride came, she would be the third."

The sisters offered explanations, and Uncle finally professed understanding. And soon Rukhsana Begum helped to carry that understanding further. In two or three years, a good diet, pretty clothes and a doting husband produced a magical effect on her; the new moon was transformed into a full moon whose brightness blinded all those who set eyes on her. Uncle Shujaat became drunk with the luminescence that radiated from her. It was fortunate he was going to retire soon, or his frequent absences from work would have caused problems.

He was the five sisters' only brother. He lost interest in Bari Mumani while she was still a new bride, and her star was never in the ascendant again. As long as he was alive she longed in vain for his companionship. God did not bless her with a child, so she had nothing with which to occupy her time and attention. Her husband was his sisters' beloved and only brother; if they didn't see him they couldn't rest. It was to them he went after work, staying at one or the other's house for supper. Still, Bari Mumani prepared his meals regularly and waited up for him every night. If, perchance he ate supper with her, she felt fulfilled. Nearly every day there was something special going on at one of the sisters' houses. In the beginning she was sometimes invited to these events, but the unfortunate woman was a misfit there and soon she was no longer asked to come. If Uncle Shujaat was to have a party for his friends, or qawalis and mujras, his wife never heard anything about them. Instead, all preparations were handled by the sisters and he simply handed them whatever money was needed for expenses.

Someone advised Bari Mumani that she ought to prepare delectable meals for her husband if she wanted him to stay at home. Well, she got hold of a number of exotic cookbooks, started making garlic pudding, almond balls, fattened chicken curries and fish kababs, and after having partaken of all of this Uncle came to the conclusion that she was trying to poison him.

Bari Mumani died spitting blood.

But the new bride's magic was undeniable. Uncle Shujaat no longer stayed out and didn't want any visitors either. Husband and wife were constantly alone with each other. What a wonderful brother he had been and how he was changed, like roughened twine now, cruel and uncaring. The world turned bleak for the sisters. They had brought this upon themselves; if they had chosen Gori Begum to be his wife instead, their brother would not have become a stranger to them.

They said to Rukhsana Begum, "My word, sister-in-law, how long can you tie him to your dupatta? He's a man, not a baby you can keep in your lap forever."

Husband and wife were ridiculed. But Rukhsana Begum giggled and her husband stammered like a fool. Completely overwhelmed by her, he stared at her as though she were someone from the neighbourhood and not his own wife.

Uncle was not the same Uncle anymore. Gone were the qawalis and the mujras; their place was taken by Uncle dancing to his wife's music.

"You'll see, it's just a matter of days now. She'll lose all her charm as soon as she's pregnant. One day brother will tire of her." Thus were hearts solaced.

After a prolonged wait Rukhsana Begum became pregnant. But, oh Lord! She experienced neither nausea nor vomiting; the gleam on her face intensified, and she exhibited greater energy than before. She lost neither her playfulness nor the loving manner characteristic of a new bride, so that uncle yearned to draw her into his eyes and present his heart to her on a platter. Instead of tiring of his wife, he daily grew more enchanted with her.

Her beauty did not wane even when she reached full term. Her body expanded, but the moon continued to shine. There was no swelling on her feet, no shadows appeared under her eyes, and no change could be seen in the way she carried herself.

After delivery she was up and about in no time. Not a hair's breadth had been added to her waist, and her body, still like that of a virgin, lost nothing of its pliancy and sprightliness. The best of women lose hair after delivery, but hers grew longer, so much so that she had difficulty washing it by herself.

Uncle, on the other hand, became slack, as if it were he and not his wife who had borne the child. His paunch slid forward somewhat, the long crevices along his cheeks deepened, and his hair became grayer; when he didn't shave the stubble appeared on his face like tiny white ant eggs.

When, two years later, a daughter was born to him, his paunch broadened and the skin under his eyes hung in loose folds. Then, the pain in one of his molars became unbearable and he was forced to have the tooth removed. The whole foundation became shaky with the shifting of a single brick.

That was the time when Aunt Rukhsana's wisdom tooth appeared.

Uncle Shujaat's dentures were more attractive than his real teeth. The workings of old age were attributed to an attack of flu.

According to Aunt Imtiazi's calculations, Aunt Rukhsana was now twenty-six years old, although when she romped with the children, she looked no more than sixteen. It was as if she had stopped growing older; like a stubborn mule her age seemed to resist moving further. Her sisters-in-law felt their hearts were being sawed. It's true that when you become weary yourself, the energy of young people disturbs you; you feel like you've been kicked by a headstrong horse, and Aunt Rukhsana was not being fair at all. In keeping with the tenets of decency and good behaviour, she should have stood by her husband in good times and bad. It wasn't at all proper that while he was hunched over with fatigue, she should run vigorously after the chickens in the courtyard.

"Now, sister-in-law, God give you sense — have you any idea what you're doing, running crazily after those hens?"

"What can I do, Aunt, the cursed cat . . ."

"Dear me! Just listen to her! Since when have I become your aunt? Brother Shajan is, by God's grace, older than me, and an older brother is like a father. So you, being his wife, are an elder too. Don't ever call me 'Aunt' again."

"Yes, of course ..." Before Aunt Rukhsana got married to Uncle Shujaat, her mother and her sister-in-law called each other 'sister'.

The beauty and youth which had once enslaved Uncle Shujaat now began to rankle in his eyes. When a crippled child is unable to keep up with his play-mates, he turns on them and accuses them of cheating. Aunt Rukhsana was betraying him; sometimes when he saw her laughing and frolicking in the company of young girls, he felt waves of pain take hold of him and it seemed to him that he was slowly burning to a cinder.

"You're sticking your chest out to attract young men, aren't you?" He started spitting poison. "Why don't you find someone young for yourself?"

At first she laughed off his sarcasm, then she blushed and reddened. This infuriated Uncle more, and he hurled even worse taunts and accusations at her.

She became silent. Tears flowed thickly from her eyes; dragging her dupatta from the line she covered her body with it and quietly withdrew into her room. Uncle felt terrible; the earth under him seemed to heave. He went to her and begged forgiveness, kissed the soles of her feet, rubbed his head on them, cried and apologized. "I'm a low-down person, a bastard, take your sandal and hit me as much as you want, my life, my Rukhi, my queen, my princess."

And, draping her silvery arms around his neck,

Aunt Rukhsana wept noisily. He said, "I love you too much, my life. I burn with envy and jealousy. My blood boils even when you take the baby in your lap. I feel like wringing his neck. Please forgive me, my love." And Aunt Rukhsana forgave him right away; indeed she continued to forgive him until the shadows under his eyes darkened, and for a long time afterward he huffed and puffed like an exhausted mule.

Soon a time came when he no longer begged forgiveness, and stayed away from her in anger many days at a stretch. The sisters became hopeful.

"Brother is destroying dear sister-in-law. It won't be long before all this ends in disaster."

Cloistered in her room, Aunt Rukhsana wept for hours. The redness in her tearful eyes only added to her loveliness, her pale skin reminded one of gold which a dishonest goldsmith had adulterated with silver, and her whitened lips, along with the stray strand of hair on her forehead, created a picture that drove onlookers to madness. This vision of melancholy beauty caused Uncle's shoulders to droop further; the desolation in his eyes grew.

There's a vine — *amar bel* — which has green serpentine tendrils. These tendrils entwine themselves around the healthy, broad trees trunk and the vine burgeons by drawing sap from the tree. As it grows and flourishes, the tree beings to shrivel and die.

As Rukhsana Begum's foliage flowered, Uncle became weaker. The sisters whispered among themselves. Their brother's speedily failing health troubled them deeply. He had weakened, and to add to the problems resulting from arthritis, was an oft- recurring cold. Doctors warned about the dangers of hair dye. Perforce he was compelled to begin using henna instead.

Poor Rukhsana! She went from person to person asking for a formula for turning hair gray. Someone suggested she use perfumed oil. When the fragrance of umber wafted into Uncle Shujaat's nostrils, he levelled the most filthy accusations against her. If she didn't have the children to think of, she would have killed herself by jumping into a well. Instead of graying, her hair grew softer and shinier, the tresses threatening Uncle like a snake.

To counteract Aunt Rukhsana's youth, Uncle began using Grecian drugs, aphrodisiacs and oils. For a few days his speeding youth paused and took a rest, his energy returned. Rukhsana, who had never been trained in the ways of the world, was like a flower growing wild; although twenty-eight now, she behaved like an inexperienced and uninhibited sixteen-year-old.

You can burn out the engine if you overwork a car; when the side effects of the drugs he had been taking manifested themselves, Uncle collapsed. Old age fell upon him in one stroke. If he had not taxed his mind and body to such an extent he would not be drowning at sixty-two. He looked much older than his years.

The sisters wept unceasingly. Doctors and hakims no longer offered much hope. There were many remedies for momentarily halting old age, but no one could come up with a drug which poor Rukhsana could take to hasten the process of aging. Without doubt, there was either a jinn or a saint who was in love with her and prevented her from growing older. Charms and amulets failed to work; all hopes were dashed.

The *amar bel* continued to flourish.

The banyan tree continued to dry up.

One can tear a picture into pieces and throw it away, a statue can be smashed to bits, but if it's a clay form shaped by God's hands, beautiful and alive, its every breath heavy with the spirit of youth, it can't be destroyed easily. There's only one way to bring down this rising sun: starve it. No more eggs, butter, meat or milk for her. Ever since Uncle Shujaat's digestive system suffered a breakdown, Rukhsana had cooked meat and the like only for the children, taking a small portion for herself from their food. Not anymore. Everyone was quite sure that the onset of middle age would now be hastened.

"Listen here, sister-in-law, why wear this shalwar-qamis? It's a young girl's dress," her sister-in-law remarked. "Why don't you put on something more in keeping with your age, something more elaborate."

Aunt Rukhsana donned an embroidered dupatta and gharara.

"Are you readying yourself to warm a lover's arms?" Uncle twisted a poisoned dart in her heart, and she became fearful of clothes as well.

"Look here, sister-in-law, why this occasional prayer? You should be saying your prayers five times a day ..."

Rukhsana started praying five times a day.

"Are you praying for my death?" Uncle asked.

She was already quite slim, but the day-to-day harassment made her thinner. Abstinence from butter and meat improved her colouring, her skin became clearer and transparent like crystal. Her face became radiant as if illuminated by some inner light. At first those who saw her had lusted after her; now they wanted a place at her feet. When, after morning prayers, she sat down to read the Quran, her face appeared to be suffused with the piety of the Virgin Mary and the purity of Fatima Zehra. And at that moment, her youth more marked than ever, she looked truly virginal.

Uncle's grave moved closer to him and he abused her cruelly, accusing her of having liaisons with nephews, of trying to seduce jinns and angels; he swore she was trying to ensnare jinns, and insisted she was receiving magical herbs from them to keep herself young.

He developed an allergy to henna, every application to his hair resulting in violent fits of sneezing followed by a cold. He had already come to dislike henna. When Aunt Rukhsana applied it on his hair, the tips of her fingers were stained with colour despite her attempts to be careful, and Uncle Shujaat felt that her fingers were stained with his blood. The very hands which he had once compared to unopened jasmine buds he now regarded as the claws of a dangerous red falcon threatening to gouge out his eyes. But the more he rubbed her nose in the dirt, the more she gave out a sandalwood-like fragrance.

The sisters, suspicious that their sister-in-law might be trying to poison their brother, brought him special foods which they proceeded to feed him under close personal supervision. But these foods only helped to worsen his condition. Chronic haemorrhoids flared up again and drained him of more blood. Lingering still were the effects of the ill-fated drug he had procured the previous winter from a well-known hakim in Muradabad, and for which he had paid many hundred rupees. It was a formula so potent that it could have breathed life into a corpse. But it only succeeded in causing Uncle's skin to erupt in sores like a tumescent gum tree.

Poor, sad Rukhsana strained butter a hundred times, blended sulphur with medicated powders and regularly applied the mixture to his sores. She boiled neem leaves in large pots of water and used the water to wash the pus day and night. Some of the sores had developed into chronic ulcers and had begun to consume Uncle.

And then one day something awful happened. Uncle had become extremely weak. His sisters were complaining about their sister-in-law as usual when, God knows from where, Najji, the old crone, walked in. First, mistaking Uncle Shujaat for Grandfather, she tried to flirt with him (a long time ago Grandfather had lavished undue attention on her). The old woman was mad. Grandfather had been dead for nearly twenty years, but she wanted to rekindle ancient dreams in her gummy eyes. Then, after much argumentation and when she finally recognized Uncle, she proceeded to lament Bari Mumani's passing away.

"Oh my, oh my! What a time to go, leaving you alone in old age like this." Suddenly she spotted Aunt Rukhsana who was feeding the pigeons in the courtyard. She made a pretty picture as she sat there with her head tilted to one side, as if posing for a photograph. The pigeons pecked at her glistening, crystal palm while she giggled involuntarily.

"O my God!" the old crone beat her flat chest and cracked her fingers over her ears to ward off ill-luck. "May God protect her from the evil eye! Your daughter's like the moon! If I'm not mistaken she has just started her eighteenth year. Listen, dear ..." She edged closer to Uncle and whispered secretively, "The merchant's boy has just returned from England. I swear by God, it will be the perfect match — sun and moon."

At one time the old hag was a successful match-maker but she had been out of business for a long time now. As the hair on her head turned gray and she became physically infirm, she began to support herself by begging.

For a while no one was able to make much sense of what she was trying to say. Everyone knew about the merchant's boy who had recently returned from England; no one guessed at first that the strumpet was attempting to arrange a match for Aunt Rukhsana.

"I swear by Imam Hussain, I'll take no less than a pair of bracelets. Shall I go ahead with it?"

When the truth came out it was as if a beehive had been disturbed; guns were directed at the old woman from all sides.

"Dear me, how was I to know? May I rot in hell . . ." The old crone grabbed her sandals and made for the door. As she left she cast a dubious eye at Uncle's dilapidated face and remarked, "Virginity is clearly written on her face."

That day Uncle swore on the Quran that the two children were not his and had been fathered by those others in the neighbourhood with whom Rukhsana Begum flirted.

He wept that night, groaned and tossed as if he were lying on a bed on live coals. Again and again he thought of Bari Mumani, whose hair had turned gray before her time, whose sprightliness and youth were washed away by tears. She had been the image of piety and loyalty, had gathered within herself his share of old age and departed to heaven. If she were alive today he could share with her his henna-covered hair, white at the roots, his blistering sores, his loneliness. Old age would not have troubled him then as much as it did now. They would have grown old together, understood each other's troubles, supported each other.

The *amar bel* grew and flourished; the trunk of the banyan tree was hollowed out; its branches became dry and limp, its leaves fell . . . the vine crawled away to a nearby tree which was alive and green.

What a heart-rending scene it was! Uncle Shujaat's adorned bier lay in the courtyard. His sisters wailed and swooned with grief. Uncle had left his entire property to his sisters.

Aunt Rukhsana leaned against a door, alone, apart from the others. Those who saw her that day proclaimed they had not seen a more beautiful or sadder widow. Her eyes were reddened and heavy-lidded from excessive weeping, her pale, drawn face shone like a topaz. People who came to offer condolences forgot everything and gazed upon her instead. They envied the dead man's fortune.

Rukhsana's face was clouded with helplessness and sorrow. An expression of fear and distress made her appear even more vulnerable. The two children huddled close to their mother who looked like their older sister.

She sat quietly, unmoving, as if she were a masterpiece painted with an unparalleled brush by one of nature's most skilled artists.

*Translated by Tahira Naqvi*

# Kallu

ALTHOUGH not quite seven, Kallu did the work of a grown man. He was shaken out of his sleep early in the morning and, dressed only in an old, tattered shirt in winter with Abba's old woollen cap pulled down over his ears, looking like a midget, dripping at the nose, he promptly set to work. Scared off by the cold water, he was always reluctant to wash his face, and just once in a while he would carelessly rub the tips of his fingers over his teeth which remained permanently coated with a thin film of mildew.

The first thing he did in the morning was to get the stove going. Then he put water on for tea, set the table for breakfast and made a hundred rounds to the door and back carrying butter, bread, then milk and, finally, the eggs — flapping his slippers noisily, he travelled to the kitchen innumerable times. And after the cook had prepared breakfast, Kallu made more trips to the table lugging hot toast and parathas. To ensure their good health, the children (nearly all of whom were Kallu's age), were forcibly fed porridge, milk, eggs, toast and jam while Kallu quietly looked on. When breakfast was over he sat alone in the kitchen and ate left-over burnt ends of toast and paratha, hurriedly downing them with some tea.

His next task involved taking care of small errands

around the house: he polished Maliha bi's pumps, scouted for Hamida bi's ribbons, located Akhtar Bhai's socks, recovered Salima bi's book-bag, fetched Mumani Jan's katha from the almirah, and retrieved Abba's cigarette case from beside his pillow. In short, he spun around like a top until everyone had left for either the office or school. Later, he washed Nanhi's dirty diapers, and then settled down to play with Safia bi; in between he made trips to the front door to receive mail from the mailman or to inquire the name of a visitor at the door. Around midday the cook handed him peas to shell or spinach to rinse. At lunch time he repeatedly dashed to the dining table with hot rotis, giving the baby's cradle a little push every now and then on the way. What more can I say? He came to this household at a very young age, did the work of a bearer and a sweeper, and all this for two rupees a month along with some old, ragged cast-offs. His mother lived in the village and had entrusted him to our care; he would at least have enough to eat, she thought. She herself worked as a cook for the village zamindar.

She visited him sometimes, usually at the Teej festival, and brought him molasses and parched wheat or fried corn. She too put him to work.

"Dear boy, come here and scratch my back."

"Son, bring me some water."

"Get some roti from the kitchen, son. And ask the cook for a little dal as well."

"Rub down my back, boy."

"Rub my shoulders."

"Massage my head."

The truth was, his little hands executed a great foot massage, and once he started you didn't want him to stop; often he would have to continue massaging the entire afternoon. Sometimes he dozed off and fell on your legs. A kick was generally enough to awaken him.

Kallu had no time to play. If, for some reason, he had a little respite between errands, he would be found slumped with exhaustion, silently staring into space like an idiot. Seeing him sitting like this, looking so foolish, someone or the other would stick a straw in his ear surreptitiously, and startled, he would bashfully turn to a task that required his attention.

Preparations for Maliha bi's wedding were under way. There was talk of weddings all day long—who's going to marry whom, how did so-and-so marry so-and-so, and who should marry whom. "Who're you going to marry, Nanhi?" Mumani would jokingly ask.

"Apa," lisped Nanhi, sending everyone into fits of laughter.

"Who're you going to marry, Kallu?" Amma asked in jest one day.

Kallu revealed his yellow teeth in a shy grin. When he was pressed for an answer he lowered his eyes and whispered, "Salima bi."

"May you rot in hell! You stupid fool! A curse on your face!" Peeved by the laughter around her, Mumani proceeded to box Kallu's ears.

Then one day, while he and Salima were playing, Kallu asked her, "Salima bi, will you marry me?"

"Ye . . . es," Salima nodded vigorously, her little head bobbing up and down.

Mumani, sitting in the sunny part of the courtyard, combing her hair, was privy to this exchange between Kallu and her daughter. Livid with anger, she removed her sandal from her foot and smacked him one with it. A blow landed in the wrong place, Kallu's nose began to bleed and soon blood was streaming down the side of his face. Kallu's mother, who was visiting at the time, saw the blood and screamed that her son had been murdered.

"Get out of my house, you hypocrite!" Mumani yelled and ordered both mother and son out. Kallu's mother wept and begged forgiveness, but her pleas went unheeded.

The years went by swiftly. As with other servants who came after him, Kallu too was forgotten. Maliha was now a mother. Hamida bi never married. Half the family had migrated to Pakistan, the other half remained here in India. Nanhi, Safia and Salima, having completed their education, were now waiting to get married. But husbands were difficult to come by.

Our uncle, Chacha Mian, was constantly on the lookout for eligible young men. He moved in official circles and had arranged a match for Maliha, but he too was helpless now. These were bad times; nice young men were nearly impossible to find, and those who were around demanded that a car and fare to England be included in the dowry. Such demands could be taken into consideration only if there was one girl in the family to be wed. But here there were many. Also, the loss of land had resulted in a lowering of status and income, and there were no parties any more, no fancy get-togethers; how were young girls to meet eligible young bachelors? Nonetheless, if a rare party did come around, Chacha Mian saw to it that the girls attended. And so, when a dinner was held in honour of Mr. Din, the new Deputy Collector, preparations in our house began several days in advance.

Mr. Din was a bachelor, and the eyes of all the mothers of unwed girls in the city were focused on him. We were stunned when we saw him. He was over six feet tall, had a wheatish complexion, very attractive features, and teeth which shone like real pearls. During introductions, he suddenly quietened at the mention of Salima's name and then quickly moved away from our group to chat with the other guests.

Chacha Mian approached us with an expression of bafflement on his face just as we were getting ready to leave.

"Do you know who this Mr. Din is?" he asked.

"The Deputy Collector, who else" Mumani answered gruffly.

"No, no. I mean, did you recognize him? My dear, he's our own Kallu."

"Kallu?" Mumani crinkled her nose.

"Yes, yes, Kallu. Kalimuddin. This is too much!"

"You mean that little midget who was our houseboy?"

"Yes, the very same, the one who suffered a beating at your hands." Chacha Mian guffawed.

"My God! What's wrong with the government? It seems just about anyone can land a job with it these days! But how did this happen?"

"Why not? He's a Qureshi, that's a good caste, and he even submitted to your beating when the need arose," my mother said in a mocking tone.

"Well, in that case why don't you give him your daughter in marriage?" Mumani spoke archly.

"I wish my daughters were so fortunate," Amma said. "I'd be only too happy to have him for a son-in-law. But why would he want to have anything to do with a family at whose hands he suffered such humiliation? Ayesha, his mother, left him with us so he could become somebody. But you turned him into a servant."

Chacha Mian said, "And the poor woman worked hard, sewed clothes, washed people's dirty dishes and finally succeeded in raising him to such heights. People are willing to present him their daughters on a silver platter."

"May they perish who do—I don't need him," said Mumani sullenly.

One day Chacha Mian arrived at our house in his usual state of nervous agitation.

"We were at the club, talking, and before I knew it, Kalimuddin walked out of there with me as I was leaving. Make some tea, anything!"

Amma ran towards the kitchen, but Mumani, a grimace firmly set on her face, didn't budge. The girls became pale; Salima was especially perturbed. We wondered whether 'Kalim Saheb' should be asked to come in or the ladies be sent to the lawn, or Chacha Mian be allowed to handle everything by himself.

"He's here for revenge," Maliha said with mock seriousness, and Mumani shivered. Salima's face was drained of colour.

"I don't care what happens," Amma said, he's here, which means he's a decent person, and we should respond with the same sort of generosity."

"No, I don't want to be humiliated," Mumani growled. "You are welcome to take your own girls — none of mine is going to stir from here. He's just here to show off his superiority."

"I won't go either. I'm already married," Maliha said with a laugh.

Finally it was decided that we would all go and, of Mumani's daughters, only Maliha would accompany us.

"What's he going to think, such uncivilized people!" Upset and bewildered, Chacha Mian started grumbling.

We arrived in the lawn to find 'Kalim Saheb' engaged in a lively conversation about the past with the old gardener, who smiled sheepishly, somewhat embarrassed, a little uncomfortable.

"Midu Chacha, remember how you used to holler, 'Wate . . . . er!' at the front door and immediately I used to pull a sheet in front of Dulhan bi (that's what he called Mumani) for purdah? Tell me truthfully, did you ever sneak a look through the sheet?" He burst into laughter, and then, seeing us approach, quickly turned to greet us.

While we were having tea he said, "Maliha bi, do you remember how you boxed my ears for not brushing my teeth regularly?"

Maliha blushed.

"No matter how unpleasant one's childhood has been, one always remembers it like a wonderful dream," he said. "All of you probably forgot about me, but I didn't forget you."

We talked for a long time afterwards, shared jokes and laughed. His carefree manner put us at ease in no time.

"Give my regards to Dulhan bi," he said before he left.

"She's not feeling well," Maliha lied.

He laughed, "Forgive me, but I have a very sharp

memory. I remember that when Dulhan bi was angry with someone she took ill. Well, I have to go, I have a dinner engagement tonight. I'll come again another time."

We talked about 'Kalim Saheb' late into the night.

"What if he proposes . . ." Chacha Mian spoke with some hesitation.

"He'd better stay away from my girls," Mumani retorted curtly.

"Why?" Amma was irritated.

"Because I say so!"

This was all artifice on her part; only God knew what was really going on in Mumani's heart.

Salima became tearful. Everyone had been teasing her.

A month passed. We had almost forgotten about 'Kalim Saheb' when suddenly he arrived at our house one day with Chacha Mian. This time Chacha Mian informed only Maliha and myself of his presence in the lawn.

"He wants to see his crochety Dulhan bi," Chacha Mian said.

"And she won't let him come near her."

We decided that since Mumani would never agree to a meeting voluntarily, the best course of action would be to just bring him in and surprise her.

"My dears, she's a witch! There'll be no place to hide my face if she insults him." Chacha Mian spoke fearfully.

"Don't worry," Maliha said, "She's not a child. I'll go and get her and you bring him in."

Our hearts beat uncontrollably. What if Mumani exploded like a bomb? Except for Maliha and me, all the other girls disappeared into the house.

'Kalim Saheb' walked into the room to find Mumani engrossed in cleaning her paan dan; her back was turned to him.

"Maliha, listen girl, get me the bowl of katha from the cupboard in the kitchen, will you," she called out.

He took the bowl of katha from Maliha and handed it to Mumani. She extended her hand towards it and said, "And some water, too."

Just then she lifted her eyes and found him standing by her side. "*Adab*." He whispered the salutation nervously and kept his eyes glued to the floor.

"God bless you," she responded in a deadened tone and started spooning out katha from the bowl. "Are you well?"

"I am fine, with your blessing."

"Why are you standing? Sit down," she ordered dryly.

He sat on the far side of the charpoy, on the *adwan*.

"Oh-ho! Not there, you will break the *adwan*!" she yelled. He jumped up hastily.

When 'Kalim Saheb' sent a message requesting Salima's hand in marriage, she was unrelenting. "Come hell or high water, I won't give him Salima," she said.

"But why?" Chacha Mian and the others pressed for a reason.

"Who're you to ask? I've decided I won't, and that's that!" she said obstinately.

'Kalim Saheb' said he hadn't taken no from life, and he wasn't going to take no from the old lady either. Determined to get his way, he boldly stationed himself on a chair next to Mumani's bed one day. All of us gathered around them with great interest, as if a fight between two wrestlers in a ring was about to commence. "I'm going to make myself very clear," he spoke firmly.

Mumani frowned.

"You're turning the tables on him, Dulhan bi — that's not fair," Chacha Mian interjected.

"Don't say anything, Chacha Mian, I'll take care of this myself."

'Kalim Saheb' brushed Chacha Mian aside and turned to Mumani. "At least tell me what my crime is, Dulhan bi?" he complained."

"Dulhan bi! Hunh! As long as you call me Dulhan bi . . ." Mumani muttered indignantly.

"Amma bi . . ." he began in a tearful voice.

Mumani's eyes also filled with tears. She began scolding us.

"Is this a circus? Why are you standing around watching like idiots? I know these girls won't be any help with the wedding arrangements. I'll have to take care of everything myself, as usual. Useless, these girls are, good-for-nothing!"

Mumani's cantankerous chastisement fell upon our ears like the sound of wedding trumpets.

*Translated by Tahira Naqvi*

# Chhoti Apa

EVERYBODY knows it's wicked, but how delicious it is to sometimes steal a little something when no one's looking. Secret letters, old scraps of paper, notebooks, precious possessions that people stash away in the folds of old clothing. How delectable if one could lay one's hands on these goodies!

The weather was unusually warm and oppressive. Fed up of Chhoti Apa's lectures, I began browsing through her old books. What superb inscriptions. What an impression she had left on her teachers! Enviable. Last month when the Principal wrote an ambiguous remark on my card, Chhoti Apa burst into a lecture- tirade, "Wild, ill-mannered, insensitive. This trash you read has turned your head! Weak-willed fool, tossed around by the tide." I wanted to hit right back: "What the hell? Who are you? I will do exactly . . . " Suddenly my eye was caught by a few musty sheets thrust inside a crevice. Useful discovery. Ha! Chhoti Apa's diary. A few missing pages were not enough to spoil the anticipation of romance. Just a little effort on my part and wham! My wonderful sibling's myth had exploded!

Written on the first page:

*1. Today, why do I long to pour my heart out to someone? There is Apajan. Talks in breathless whispers to her friends. I wonder what the hell she talks about? Does she get the same sensations as me in her heart, mind and body? Hell, who will hear my story? Shammo, the bitch, will laugh her head off, and pour the entire tale into Apajan's ear. Next, Amma will find out. Then in a moment of amorousness she will tell Abba. Then I'll be torn to shreds. God forbid. Today I feel compelled to blurt it all out. Vomit it into my pillow. How quickly these pleasant reveries will soak into the old moth-eaten stuffing. Amma . . . she has a passion for taking apart old stuffing. My story will scatter into wisps of old cotton . . .*

*So, today I was putting a leash around the neck of the black puppy when he appeared out of nowhere.*

*"Why strangle this poor wretch?"*

*My grip slackened, the pup ran off.*

*"What if anyone strangled you?" A hand at my neck. I ran.*

Chhoti Apa's romances were most amusing. I read on.

*2. Now what am I to do? Was taking a glass of milk for Bhaiya . . . "Now where will you run?" Materialising out of thin air he stood, arms outstretched, blocking my path.*

*Lathering his face, he put a great quantity of shaving foam on mine!*

*3. Amma says Shaukat is very shy! Shy my . . . ! His eyes. How they rove and pierce, pierce and rove. Scared the daylights out of me in the upstairs gallery.*

*"Some people are bloody scared. As if I would swallow you whole." Heart pounding, I ran like a thief. Wanted to cry, but no outlet. Sat concealed behind the lamp during dinner. No — I am not bloody scared. Of the mouse, yes, because it suddenly leaps out at me. But seeing him, well . . . makes my whole body a playground for leaping mice.*

*Gave him a glass of water, and yes . . . promised to knit him a sweater. Midnight, and I was still knitting to keep my word. Amma complains that I keep the lights on until very very late. Electricity bill has gone up to Rs. 13! If her favourite daughter reads her trashy novels all night, the bill does not add up!*

4. *Wherever I go he sneaks up behind me. How quietly and expertly he pinches. Amma says that I am shameless. . . Talking back whenever they discuss my marriage. If I am shameless why do I find the stairs leading to his room so insurmountable? No matter how hard I try, I cannot climb up. Once, having made the heroic ascent, I started rummaging through the cupboards. Looking for . . . my lost senses! He did not speak one single word. I ran.*

"Listen."

"Just coming." *Snatching a few useless items I stumbled out, panting.*

*At the foot of the stairs I caught my breath,* "How can I go upstairs again? Eye of the needle. Damn! *Hovered around the stair-well. No guts, no guts. Put one foot forward, and the sweeper arrived to mop the stairs. End of effort. Took a deep breath . . . the parrot spoke,* "Mith-thu!" *Almost fell over. Blast the bastard. Cat should swallow him up. Seeing Amma appear, started ripping out the neckline of a perfectly good shirt.* "Why is this neckline being ripped open?" *Her tone was acid. Heart sank.*

"Tight," *I mumbled. My fingers clawed at the stitches, as if the shirt was strangling me.*

"It was perfectly alright. Now rip it apart so that half your bosom can show. Such plunging necklines are poison." *Wrinkling her nose in disapproval she sat down right there at the foot of the stairs. How could Abba ever have endured Amma, I thought? He should have married Aunt Rahat. Oh God! He will be gone for three years. Wonder when he'll come back?*

6. At the time of his departure, Amma embraced, Apa kissed. Apa really gets away with murder. She finds every excuse to closet herself with Rasheed Bhai. The moment you enter the room they spring apart. What the hell are they up to, these two? No one thinks of asking her, "Sweetheart, are your molars out yet?"

7. Flipping a few blank pages of life. I cannot remember such a long lesson — history, geography and seventeen questions.

8. Went to a movie with Mahmood. Was reminded of the last time. His hat on my lap, for which his fingers searched time and again. Cigarette and petrol, what a strange mixture in my nostrils. God knows what Mahmood smokes. Smells like burnt cowdung cakes.

9. Mahmood, what a strange guy!

10. During dinner, Mahmood's feet dance under the table. Creeping snakes! Looking intently at his plate he devours his food, the picture of innocence. . . . not responsible for the footwork going on under the table! Like nooses, his legs get hooked here and there.

11. Delightful trip to Delhi. A thousand stairs, almost broke my ankles. Why can't they instal a lift? So bloody dark in here.

12. His Eid gift was a stud for my nose! Was this the only thing he could find for me? And that too with my pierce having closed a while back. Mahmood found a god-given excuse to get even with me. All day he went around suggesting that my nose be pierced with a screw-driver, paper-cutter or industrial needle. I wrote, "This is useless." He also wrote, "This is indeed useless because this girl needs a stronger noose. Send her a massive stud!" What a mar-vellous gift to look forward to!

13. Shaukat's letter is so engrossing, like a bloody

*confusing crossword puzzle. Makes me sick!*

14. Mahmood says, "In one week I will teach you swimming." The waves at night are like fire-spitting dragons rising from the ocean; my body heats up. Mahmood always threatens to drown me. New bathing suit; all torn. Must buy blue knitting wool.

15. Shaukat writes that life is a vehicle. I think of that fat female who covets the winding stair. The vehicle runs on two wheels, Shaukat says. Him and me. What a horrible thought. I am not a beast; how will I pull my share of the cart?

16. Went for a game of cricket. What a stupid game. Why does the bowler always aim at my nose? I had to lump it, thanks to Askari. What rough hands he has. Feels like he'll break all my fingers.

17. Went for a ride behind Askari on his motor-cycle. Mahmood got wildly jealous. Who cares!

18. Askari burnt my arm with his cigarette. Then wanted to heal the burn. I said to him, hands off. He said, "Honestly ... in two seconds. Tell Mahmood he is an expert." I slapped his face. Talks such nonsense. Will come for dinner tomorrow.

19. Riding behind Askari, a long way from home. Sometimes life is so wonderful, I want to ride forever on its cresting wave. The entire universe should stand still. Ears blocked, eyes closed. Sightless, soundless. Each leaf should become motionless. Only one sound should be heard — the beating of our two hearts, all the rest should drown. Where is that blue handkerchief? Askari had it tied around his neck. This hair, always in my face!

20. Again, Askari forgot the handkerchief. I fought twice with Mahmood. If he failed his exam. . . . Hell! did I ask him to teach me Algebra instead of cramming?

21. Shaukat is to be engaged to Razia. Felt slightly

*heartbroken.* Tauba! Tauba! *A real dog in the manger!*

22. *When he throws the ball, Askari appears ruthless. Teeth clenched, eyebrows knitted, silk shirt plastered to his body with sweat. Mahmood's nose is covered with sweat. Makes me puke.*

23. *Tara, the bitch! Started drooling over Askari. As if Askari had not heard everything about her. Is there any fellow she has not lusted after?*

24. *No news of Askari for two days. Heard he's gone to Delhi.*

*We consider ourselves alive by virtue of living in this world. But one shock and we realise what it's all about! Life begets life. Stone strikes against stone and a flame is born. Flame which first burns, turns to ash, then fertilizes. Along the mountain slopes the rain-forests start swaying in the wind. Askari is the rock. The volcanic rock.*

25. *Fickle. How fickle these men are! A parrot's roving eye momentarily focuses on one object. But their eyes, blue, black, brown, flecked, are like a spinning top on an endless spin. Directionless, the spinning top. The* kibla *is in all directions.*

26. *Why is there nothing visible in the world? The only visible objects are Askari's blue eyes. Gone for six months. What a long tour!*

27. *Both letters were returned. Askari has probably gone on a tour of Europe. Throws the ball as if he will first grind it between his teeth. Squeeze, bounce and a long throw! Instantly another ball appears between his fingers.*

28. *Shaukat has had a son. Why do I care? Wasn't snatched from me. Lovely child.*

Pae mera lung neest
Mulk-e-Khuda tung neest.
My leg is not maimed
This Kingdom of God is not narrow!

*29. Love should not be left to rot in the grave and
become a feast for worms. Love is a restless flame. Once it
begins its magnificent dance, the entire universe is sub-
sumed in its embrace. A massive river, once its rises, slices
gigantic rocks, uproots trees and drowns deserts. People say
that true love occurs only once in a life-time. But define
this word "once". Man is a spinning top. Kibla is
everywhere. Love has eyes at the back of its head.*

*In my small world of love, how many Shaukats, Mah-
moods, Abbases, Askaris, Yunuses and others have been
shuffled together in a pack of cards and spread out. Which
one is the knave? Shaukat's hungry eyes, filled with tales?
Mahmood's snake-like creeping limbs? Askari's ruthless
hands? Is it the mole beneath Yunus' lower lip? Or is it
Abbas' vague smile? A thousand broad chests, high
foreheads, thick hair, smooth ankles, strong arms. All are
jumbled together like freshly spun threads. Helplessly, I
look at that entangled mess. Which end shall I pull so that
it disentangles into a long skein upon which I can ride and
reach out to the horizon?*

Crumpled scraps of paper adding up to a beautiful
life were gathered before me. Amazed, I started feeling its contours. Chhoti Apa ... !

Chhoti Apa was cleaning the baby's bottles.
Ahmed Bhai was calling her into the drawing room
to meet his friends.

She sat quietly in one corner of the sofa, the end
of her sari drawn modestly over her hair. "Why are
you so shy? Modern girls leave the men light years
behind." His sarcastic reference to me did not go
unnoticed. But I was busy looking at Chhoti Apa. Like
the motionless illusion of a madly spinning top, she
was staring vacantly into space. Piled up before her
still was that mess of entangled threads and she was

looking carefully for a secure end upon which she could fasten herself.

To divert attention, I passed a cup of tea to Ahmed Bhai's most debonair friend.

*Translated by Syeda Hameed*

# The Rock

WHEN Bhabhi came to our house as a bride, she was no more than fifteen. She still had some growing-up to do; in Bhaiya's presence she trembled like a cow about to be butchered. But within a year she was transformed from a tight-lipped bud to a flower. Her body filled out, her hair became more lustrous, and the hunted look in her eyes was replaced by a look of confidence and mischief.

Bhabhi came from a liberal family and had been schooled at a convent. The previous year her sister had eloped with a Christian, so her parents, worried that she might do something similar, took her out of school and quickly married her off.

Having been raised in a modern household, she was as playful as a doe. But her parents and her in-laws were keeping a close eye on her now. Bhaiya was anxious to set her up as a housewife without delay because he was afraid that even though she was married, she might still follow in her sister's footsteps. As a result, he earnestly embarked on the task of moulding her into a homemaker.

In four or five years, with everyone's help, she turned into a complete housewife. As the mother of three children she became overweight and ungainly. Amma fed her chicken soup and sweets and Bhaiya furnished tonics; with each child Bhabhi gained ten or fifteen pounds.

Gradually she stopped using make-up. Bhaiya hated lipstick, and the sight of mascara or kohl on a woman's eyes infuriated him. But he liked pink and red. So Bhabhi generally wore pink or red clothes; red sari with a light-pink blouse, or a pink sari with a red blouse.

She had short hair when she got married. But now it was plastered down and tied at the back so that no one could tell that the bride was a short-haired *mem*. Her hair had grown since then but had become thin because of frequent pregnancies. She usually kept it tied in a pony tail with a dirty old rag. Her husband found her pleasing just the way she was, untidy and bedraggled. And her parents and in-laws also praised her simplicity. She was pretty, no doubt. Fine features, a butter-white complexion and small, dainty hands and feet. But she had let herself go and her body slackened like dough left out overnight.

Bhaiya was nine years her senior, but compared to her he looked really young. Still quite slim, with a well-kept figure, he exercised daily, carefully monitored his diet, smoked only on occasion, and once in a while took a sip of whisky or beer. He was still boyish in appearance. Although he was thirty-one, he didn't look a day older than twenty-five.

Oh, how Bhaiya hated jeans and skirts! He was also repelled by the sight of tight shirts hugging the body and particularly despised shalwars that were tight at the ankles. Anyway Bhabhi, poor thing, couldn't get into shalwar and qamis anymore, and generally went around the house dressed in a blouse and petticoat with a dressing-gown thrown over them. If an informal guest arrived, she stayed as she was, and if someone special came to the house unexpectedly, she chose to stay in her room with the children. When forced to make an appearance, she would come out wearing a rumpled, mousy-coloured sari. She was a housewife, a daughter-in-law, and she was everyone's darling; why should she dress up and deck herself out like a prostitute to please people?

And it's quite possible that Bhabhi would have continued in this bedraggled and untidy state until she became middle-aged and then old; she would have brought home daughters-in-law who would come to her every morning, respectfully offer salutations and then deposit her grandson into her lap to hold and play with. But God had other plans.

It was evening. We were all having tea in the lawn. Bhabhi had gone to the kitchen to fry papads. The cook had over-fried them and Bhaiya liked them lightly browned. He glanced lovingly at Bhabhi and she immediately got up to go to the kitchen to fry some more for him. We calmly continued drinking tea. Ah, what was Bhabhi but an angel! I could never be persuaded to go to the kitchen after I returned from college, and my evening clothes were especially unsuited for cooking. In addition, I didn't know how to fry papads. My sisters were also in the same boat as I. Farida was entertaining her fiance who had come for a visit; Razia and Shameem were busy chatting with their friends and certainly they couldn't be expected to fry papads. Anyway, we were all little birds in our parents' home, testing our wings for flight.

"Boom!" The football landed right over Bhaiya's cup. We all jumped. Bhaiya snapped angrily: "Who is this idiot?" He was looking in the direction from where the ball had come.

A round curly-haired head and a pair of large eyes appeared over the hedge. In one leap Bhaiya was over the hedge and the culprit's hair was in his grasp.

"Ohhh!" the sound of a scream filled the air and in the next instant Bhaiya reared as if stung by a scorpion, or as if he had taken hold of a live coal.

"Sorry . . . I'm very sorry . . ." he was stuttering. All of us ran to see what was going on. Standing on the other side of the hedge was a slight, fair-complexioned girl dressed in white drain-pipes and a lemon-coloured blouse; she was running her slender fingers through short hair cut Marilyn Monroe style, and laughing sheepishly. We started laughing, too.

Bhabhi returned with the plate of papads and, presuming there was something funny going on, joined in our laughter without really knowing what had happened. Her loose stomach bounced as she laughed. And when she discovered Bhaiya had mistaken Shabnam for a boy and had caught her by the hair, she laughed even louder and pieces of papad went flying from the plate in her hand and landed on the grass. Shabnam informed us she had arrived at her Uncle, Shahid Jamil's house that very morning and when she got bored doing nothing, came out to play with a football which, as luck would have it, landed on Bhaiya's cup.

Shabnam was staring at Bhaiya with her sharp, mascara-laden eyes. Stunned into magical silence, Bhaiya was gazing at her. There was a current darting between them. Cut off from this current, Bhabhi seemed to be miles away from them; her bouncing stomach became fearful and was stilled. Laughter stumbled on her lips and died. Her hands became limp, the plate tilted to one side, and the papads slid and fell on the grass. All of a sudden Bhaiya and Shabnam awakened and returned from the world of dreams.

"Come and have some tea," I said, giving the still atmosphere a little nudge.

In one graceful leap Shabnam swung over the hedge to our side. Tiny moccasins began prancing on the green grass like a pair of doves. Her complexion glowed like molten gold. Her hair was jet black, but her eyes reminded one of small black goblets filled with honey. The neckline of her lemon blouse was very low. Her lips were pink, a model for an American ad. Although she appeared to be much taller than Bhabhi, the difference in their heights couldn't have been more than two inches. She had a delicate bone structure, which is why her waist looked like it could fit into a ring.

Bhaiya sat lost in silence. Bhabhi was watching him the way a cat watches a bird getting ready to take off, waiting to pounce as soon as it flaps its wings. Her face was red, her lips were pressed together, her nostrils flared.

Without warning Munna came and jumped on her back just then. He always jumped on his mother's back like this, as if he were a soft little pillow, and she always laughed at his antics. "*Tarakh! Tarakh!*" Today she slapped him hard twice.

Shabnam became agitated.

"Oh, stop her, please," she touched Bhaiya's hand. Then she turned to me. "Your mother's easily angered," she said. Introductions are rare in our society. And it seemed strange to introduce Bhabhi. Her appearance was unmistakably that of the daughter-in-law of the house. We all burst out laughing at

Shabnam's remark. Dragging Munna by the hand, Bhabhi went into the house.

"No, no, she's our sister-in-law," I said, watching Bhabhi trudge away.

"Your sister-in-law?" Shabnam looked astounded.

"Bhaiya's wife."

"Oh." She lowered her eyes. "I see, I ..." she continued in a serious tone and then stopped, mid-sentence.

"Bhabhi is twenty-three," I explained.

"But ... don't be silly!" She laughed. At this point Bhaiya got up and left.

"I swear."

"Oh, lack of education ..."

"No. Bhabhi graduated at fifteen from St. Mary's."

"You mean she's three years younger than me? I'm twenty-six."

"In that case, certainly."

"Oh God! And I thought she was your mother. Actually my eyesight is quite bad and I hate wearing glasses. Do you think she's upset?"

"No. Bhabhi's never upset."

"Oh, poor thing."

"Who? Bhabhi?" I don't know why I said that.

"Bhaiya dotes on his wife," Shameem said, coming to Bhabhi's defence.

"The poor man must've been married when he was really young."

"He was twenty-six."

"But I didn't know people in the twentieth century got married without seeing each other first," Shabnam said derisively.

"All your conjectures are incorrect. Bhaiya saw Bhabhi, liked her immensely, and then they were married. But at that time she was as delicate and beautiful as a lily."

"So what happened to her after she got married?"

"What could have happened? Bhabhi is the mistress of her house, queen among her children, not a film actress. At any rate, Bhaiya despises thin, skinny girls." I deliberately took a jab at her. She wasn't stupid.

"Well, I don't care if somebody loves me or not, I'm not about to turn into a baby elephant . . . excuse me, your sister-in-law must have been beautiful once, but now . . ."

"Your viewpoint is entirely different from Bhaiya's," I said evasively.

And when she walked toward the hedge, taking small steps, her lean body swinging, Bhaiya was standing in the verandah. His face was ashen white and again and again he rubbed the back of his neck with his hands as if someone had placed burning cinders on it. She skipped over the hedge like a bird. Turning for a moment, she gave Bhaiya a honeyed look and then disappeared into the bungalow in a flash.

Bhabhi was bent over in the lawn picking up the tea things, but she was the invisible strand that had sprung up between Bhaiya and Shabnam.

One day I saw Shabnam from the window. Dressed in a fluffy red skirt and a white blouse open at the neck, she was dancing the samba with Pappu, her cousin. Her little Pekinese bounded between her legs. She was laughing loudly. Her well-shaped, voluptuous legs pirouetted on the green grass, and her black, silken hair flew in the air. Five year-old Pappu was kicking around like a monkey, but she

swayed like an intoxicated female serpent. Once she
made a face at me and I showed her my fist. But soon
I realized her gesture was not meant for me. Bhaiya
was standing in the verandah, massaging the back of
his neck, and she was tormenting him with her teasing. Her waist was gyrating, her hips moved from side
to side, her arms fluttered, her mouth was open and
her lips quivered. She thrust her tongue out like a
snake and licked her lips with it. Bhaiya's eyes were
gleaming, he revealed his teeth in a grin. My heart
convulsed. Bhabhi was in the pantry doling out the
daily portion of grain to the cook.

Shabnam, you wretch! I said to myself. But I was
also angry with Bhaiya. Why was he grinning? He
hated *chrantis* like Shabnam, he was repelled by
English dances. Why then did he stand there staring
at her? And why was he so overcome that his body
moved to the rhythm of the samba without his knowing it?

About this time the houseboy came out to the lawn
with tea. Bhaiya summoned all of us and instructed
the houseboy to get Bhabhi. A sense of formality compelled us to ask Shabnam to join us. I wanted to turn
my face away from her, but when she climbed over
the hedge with Munna perched on her shoulders, for
some reason she seemed perfectly innocent to me.
Munna hung on to her scarf as if it were reins, and
she cantered like a horse across the lawn. Bhaiya tried
to get Munna off her back, but he clung to her stubbornly.

"Let the horse run some more, Auntie!"

"No, my dear. Auntie's exhausted!" Shabnam
yelled.

With great difficulty Bhaiya got Munna off and

smacked his face. Distressed by his action, Shabnam immediately picked up the child and slapped Bhaiya's hand.

"Aren't you ashamed? You as big as a camel, and striking a small child?" Seeing Bhabhi approach she handed Munna over to her. Bhaiya smiled at the slap he had received from Shabnam.

"Look how hard he hit the poor thing. If someone tried to hit my child, I'd break his hand." The honey in her eyes was shot with poison as she glared at Bhaiya. "And on top of everything he's laughing shamelessly!"

"Hunh! Do you have the strength to break someone's hand?" Bhaiya twisted her wrist. She turned and let out such a scream that Bhaiya was alarmed and quickly let go of her. She fell on the grass, gasping with laughter.

Shabnam's antics continued during tea; she behaved like a young, mischievous girl. Bhabhi sat in stunned silence. You would think that threatened with Shabnam's presence, she would start taking care of herself. Not at all. She became more shabby in appearance and ate with added vigour. We were all busy laughing, but she kept her head down and proceeded to devour the cake with intense concentration; she ravenously swallowed fried potatoes dipped in chutney, and rapidly gulped down pieces of toast laden with butter and jam. Bhaiya and Shabnam had become a source of apprehension for us, and Bhabhi must have been worried too, but she was burying her dread in rich foods. Constantly suffering from gastric distress, she nevertheless managed to successfully digest pulao and qorma with the aid of churan. Her gaze fell restlessly upon Shabnam and Bhaiya as they chuckled and talked.

Bhaiya looked younger than before. Every morning and evening he went with Shabnam to swim in the ocean. Bhabhi could also swim quite well, but Bhaiya hated women in bathing suits. One day we were all swimming. Wearing only two tiny strips, Shabnam was executing serpentine moves in the water. Just then Bhabhi, who had been looking for Munna, made an appearance. Bhaiya was in a playful mood. He caught hold of her and together we all pushed her into the water. Since Shabnam's arrival Bhaiya had become quite roguish. He would lovingly grind his teeth and squeeze Bhabhi in front of us, or sometimes he would try to pick her up in his arms, but she slipped from his hands like a large fish, leaving him feeling a little foolish. Perhaps in his imagination it was Shabnam he was lifting in his arms. And, rueful like a butchered cow, Bhabhi would immediately leave the room to start planning the pudding or some other delectable dessert. When she was pushed into the water that day, she slid from our hands like a heavy bundle. Her wet clothes clung to her body and revealed her unshapely figure, a frightening sight; it seemed as though someone had wrapped a comforter around her waist. She didn't look that horrible when dressed in normal clothes.

"Oh God, how fat you are!" Bhaiya exclaimed, squeezing a lump of fat on her buttock. "Oh my goodness! Look at your tummy! You look just like Gama the wrestler."

"Hunh! After four children my waist . . ."

"But I also have four children and my waist hasn't been transformed into a Dunlop tyre." He patted his lean, solid body with his hands. Bhabhi made a sour face and walked away looking like a wet chicken, pulling Munna with her as she dragged her feet heavily in the sand. Ignoring her, Bhaiya proceeded to plonk Shabnam in the water. But Shabnam wasn't going to let him get the better of her; she gave him such a push that he turned upside down with a splash.

When they returned from their swim, they saw Bhabhi arranging a layer of cream over apricot jam. Her head was lowered, her eyes were red, her lips were white, and her doll-like plump cheeks were puffier than usual.

At lunch Bhabhi looked extremely unhappy. She proceeded to consume the apricot jam and cream with ardour. Shabnam looked at the dish and shuddered as though it contained not apricots, but snakes and scorpions.

"It's poison, just poison," she said, nibbling on a slice of cucumber. Bhaiya glared at Bhabhi, but she continued to gobble up the jam noisily.

"This is enough!" he muttered, his nostrils flaring.

Bhabhi paid no attention to him and emptied nearly the entire dish of apricots into her stomach. Seeing her devour the jam in this manner, you felt as if she were building a dam to halt the storm of envy and jealousy. The cream would be converted to granite and make the castle that was her body invincible. And perhaps then her heart would ache no more, and the flames that darted every time Bhaiya's eyes met Shabnam's would lose the power to melt those granite walls.

"Stop, for God's sake! The doctor said you shouldn't — what kind of toothsomeness is this!", Bhaiya finally said. Bhabhi melted like a wall of wax. Bhaiya's remark cut through the layers of fat and plunged right into her heart. Thick tears trickled down her puffy cheeks; sobs wracked the pile that was her body and caused a tremor like an earthquake. Slim, delicate-looking girls look so attractive when they cry. But seeing Bhabhi cry one was amused rather than saddened. She looked like a heap of cotton-wool that was being thrashed with sticks.

Wiping her nose, she started to get up, but we scolded Bhaiya and cajoled her into staying. The poor thing sniffled and sat down again. But as soon as she had deposited three spoonfuls of sugar in her coffee and extended a hand towards the cream, she became inert. With a fearful expression in her eyes she looked at Bhaiya and Shabnam. Shabnam curbed a twitter with great difficulty, and Bhaiya fumed.

Things just got worse after this. Bhabhi openly declared war.

There was a time when her Pathan blood boiled easily and she would come to blows at the slightest provocation. Instead of sulking, often she would attack Bhaiya like a ferocious cat when she was angry with him, and scratch his face and rip his shirt-front with her teeth. Bhaiya would crush her in his arms. Reduced to helplessness, she placed her head on his chest and sobbed like a frightened, thirsty little bird. Then they would make up. Feeling sheepish, she'd lovingly apply tincture to the scratch marks on his face, mend the rips in his shirt and continue looking at him with gratitude.

This was when Bhabhi was as delicate as a butterfly, and when she quarrelled with Bhaiya she reminded one of a little Persian cat. Instead of showing anger, he would express great affection for her. But the attack of blubber had left her blood cold. She rarely lost her temper anymore, and if she did, she'd quickly occupy herself with something or the other and soon forget all about it.

That day, ignoring her heavy, thick-set body, she attacked Bhaiya with full force. Her weight was enough to crush him against the wall. He was repelled by the bouncing heap of flab. He didn't get angry, nor did he raise a clamour. Embarrassed and sad, he lowered his head and bolted from the room. Bhabhi collapsed right there and started weeping.

Matters deteriorated further and one day Bhaiya's brother-in-law came to fetch Bhabhi. Tufail Bhai was Bhabhi's cousin. No sooner did she set eyes on him than she put her arms around him and began crying. He had seen Bhabhi after five years. The sight of the domed figure startled him momentarily, but then he clasped Bhabhi to his chest as if she were a little girl. Bhaiya was at a cricket match with Shabnam that day. Tufail Bhai waited until it was dark. When Bhaiya didn't show up, he instructed Bhabhi to pack her things and get the children ready.

Bhaiya made an appearance for a few moments just as they were leaving.

"I'm handing over the houses in Delhi to her as *mehr*," he addressed Tufail Bhai gruffly.

"*Mehr*?" Bhabhi trembled.

"Yes. And the divorce papers will be forwarded through the lawyer."

"Divorce — who said anything about divorce?"

"That's best for all concerned."

"But . . . the children?"

"If she wants she can have them. Otherwise I'll send them to boarding school. I've made arrangements."

With a loud scream Bhabhi lunged toward Bhaiya. But she didn't have the courage to scratch him. Terrified, she stood transfixed. Then she relinquished the last shred of her womanly dignity. She fell at his feet. She begged.

"You can marry her ... I won't say a word. But for God's sake don't give me a divorce. I'll spend the rest of my life like this, I'll never complain."

But Bhaiya glanced hatefully at Bhabhi's quivering obesity and turned away.

"I've already given the divorce. Nothing can be done now."

But who could mollify Bhabhi? She continued to lament.

"You fool!" Tufail Bhai pulled her up in one jerk. "You idiot, get up!" Dragging her, he took her away.

What a tragic scene it was! The children howled along with Bhabhi. Amma stared vacantly at everyone. After Abba's death she had no authority in the house anymore. Bhaiya was his own master and our guardian too, as a matter of fact. Amma had tried everything in her power to make him reconsider; she had been expecting something like this to happen. But what could she do?

Bhabhi left. The atmosphere in the house was so depressing that Bhaiya and Shabnam also left for the hill-station after their wedding.

Seven or eight years went by. By now we had all set up housekeeping. Amma passed away. Abba's death had left her in a state of torpor. She had wept and wailed at the time of Bhabhi's divorce, but she knew Bhaiya well; he had never paid attention to anything Abba said either. A son who starts earning his living becomes his own master.

The nest was destroyed. The house that lived and breathed once was now desolate. Everyone was scattered. The years seemed to slip away in the twinkling of an eye. Every two years or so we'd get some news of Bhaiya. He travelled a lot, usually outside India, but when a letter arrived from him saying he was coming to Bombay, childhood's forgotten memories were revived. As soon as Bhaiya got off the train, I ran to him and we clung to each other like children. I couln't see Shabnam anywhere. No sooner had I finished asking Bhaiya about her than a heavy hand fell upon my shoulders with a thud, and a mountain of warm flesh engulfed me.

"Bhabhi!" I said, holding on to the train window in order to prevent myself from falling over.

I had never called Shabnam "Bhabhi". She always looked like Shabnam. But today the word "Bhabhi" suddenly escaped from my lips. How could a sprinkle of dew become a dome of flesh? I looked at Bhaiya. He was the same. Lean and slim, not an ounce out of place. Hair still thick like a boy's. Just two or three shiny strands peeped out from his temples, giving him a rather distinguished look. He was as solid as a rock. Waves leap toward the rock, crash at its feet, shatter and disintegrate, and weak and exhausted, return to the sea. Some die at the feet of the rock, while new waves, nourishing a desire for self-sacrifice, find themselves irresistibly drawn to it.

And the rock? Distanced from this worship, it continues to smile cynically. Unmoving, careless and pitiless! When Bhaiya married Shabnam, we all said that because Bhabhi, Shehnaz (I always called her Bhabhi), was too young and naive at the time of her marriage, she was easily suppressed by Bhaiya. But

Shabnam, who was mature and wordly-wise, would poison Bhaiya with her bite like a female serpent and leave him flagging. She would definitely make him suffer.

But only the rock can make the waves suffer.

"The kids are in boarding school. They didn't have any holidays." Shabnam blew her smelly, hyper-acidic breath in my face.

And I was searching in this heap of flesh for the sprinkle of dew, for the Shabnam who had doused the fire of Shehnaz's love and ignited a new flame in Bhaiya's heart. But what was this? Instead of burning to a cinder in the fire of her love, Bhaiya had come out more burnished than ever, like gold. The fire had consumed itself and turned to ashes. Bhabhi was like a mound of butter. But Shabnam was singed, muddy-looking ash; her dark, gleaming complexion had turned yellow like a lizard's stomach; those liquid eyes had become murky and lifeless; the thin, serpentine waist was nowhere in sight — Shabnam looked permanently pregnant; the well-rounded arms that had glowed like the delicate, shiny limbs of a tree were now thick and ungraceful and looked like a pair of dumb-bells. Her face was plastered with make-up, her eyes were smeared with mascara, and she had probably plucked her eyebrows too much so that she had to use a darker pencil on them.

Bhaiya was staying at the Ritz. We arrived there for dinner.

The cabaret was at its climax. The Egyptian beauty was contorting her flat stomach, her hips gyrated in circles, her voluptuous arms fluttered in the air, her golden legs could be seen quivering like pillars of ivory behind a thin veil of chiffon. Bhaiya's hungry eyes crawled over her body like scorpions. Again and again, he rubbed a secret wound at the back of his neck.

Bhabhi, who used to be Shabnam, who, like the Egyptian dancer, was once an electric current that burned Bhaiya, sat immobilized like a hill of sand. Bad diet and anaemia had given her plump cheeks the yellowed-green look of a mummy. Viewed under the neon lights, her complexion made one think of someone bitten by a cobra. The Egyptian dancer's hips were creating a storm and Bhaiya's heart bobbed up and down like a boat in the maelstrom. Shabnam, Bhabhi now, and the mother of five children, fearfully watched them both. She rapidly downed large morsels of roast chicken in order to distract herself.

The orchestra took a deep breath; the instruments groaned; the drum's heartbeat vibrated; the Egyptian dancer's waist spun for the last time and she slid to the marble floor in exhaustion.

The entire hall echoed with the sound of applause. Shabnam's eyes sought Bhaiya. The bearer arrived with fresh raspberries and a jug of cream. Without thinking, Shabnam filled her plate with raspberries. Her hands were trembling. Restless like a pair of wounded deer, her eyes darted in all directions.

Away from the crowds, on a darkened balcony, Bhaiya was lighting the Egyptian dancer's cigarette. His impassioned gaze tangled with the dancer's rapture-filled eyes. Shabnam's face was colourless, and she sat listlessly like a ponderous mass. Finding her glance directed toward them, Bhaiya led the dancer by the elbow to where we were sitting and introduced us.

"This is my sister," he said, pointing to me. The

dancer swayed in acknowledgement of my presence.

"My wife," he said in a dramatic tone, as if he were showing the dancer an injury received on the battlefield. The dancer was stunned. It seemed that it wasn't Bhaiya's wife she was looking at, but his own body drenched in blood. She stared at Shabnam with horror. Then she filled her eyes with every ounce of maternal affection she could muster and gave Bhaiya a special look in which a thousand stories were concealed. "Oh, this Hindustan! Where such beautiful people are sacrificed on the altar of custom and practice. These people, who submit to such punishment, are to be pitied, are worthy of worship."

Shabnam, my Bhabhi, read all this in the dancer's eyes. Her hands shook. To hide her anguish she quickly picked up the jug of cream and emptying it over the raspberries in her plate, she began eating with great fervour.

Poor Bhaiya! Handsome and pitiable! Beautiful like the sun god, romantic, honey-eyed Bhaiya, unmoving like a rock — he sat smiling in the role of an immortalized martyr.

An old wave, tired and broken, lay dying at his feet.

A new wave, bright and undulating, was waiting breathlessly to be clasped in his arms.

*Translated by Tahira Naqvi*

# The
# Wedding Shroud

ONCE again a freshly-laundered floor-covering was laid at the entrance of the room with the three doors, the *seh-dari*. Sunshine filtered through the chinks in the broken tiling on the roof and fell over the courtyard below in odd geometrical patterns. The women from the neighbourhood sat silently, apprehensively, as if waiting for some major catastrophe to occur. Mothers gathered their babies to their breasts. Occasionally a feeble, cranky infant would let out a yell protesting an impediment in the flow of sustenance.

"No, no, my love," the thin, scrawny mother crooned, shaking the infant on her knees as if she were separating rice husks in a winnowing basket. How many hopeful glances were rivetted on to Kubra's mother's face today. One side each of two narrow pieces of cloth had been placed together, but no one had the nerve to measure and cut at this point. Kubra's mother held an exalted position as far as measuring and cutting were concerned; no one really knew how many dowries had been adorned by her small, shrunken hands, how many suits of clothing for new mothers had been stitched, nor how many shrouds had been measured and torn. Whenever someone in the neighbourhood ran short of fabric and every effort to correctly mark off and snip had failed, the case was brought before Kubra's mother. She would straighten the warp in the fabric, soften the starch in it, sometimes rearranging the cloth in the form of a triangle, sometimes a square. Then, the scissors in her imagination would go to work, she would measure and cut, and break into a smile.

"You will get the front, back and sleeves from this. Take some snippets from my sewing box for the neck." And so the problem would be solved; proper measuring and cutting having been dealt with, she would hand over everything along with a neatly-tied bundle of snippets.

But today the piece of fabric at hand was really insufficient. Everyone was quite sure Kubra's mother would fail to accurately measure and cut this time, which was why all the women were looking apprehensively at her. But on Kubra's mother's face, which bore a resolute look, there was not even a shadow of anxiety. She was surveying and patterning a four-finger length of coarse cotton. The reflection from the red twill lit up her bluish-yellow face like sunrise. The heavy folds on her face rose like darkening clouds, as if a fire had broken out in a dense forest. Smiling, she picked up the scissors.

A heavy sigh of relief rose up from the ranks of the women.

Infants were allowed to whimper, eagle-eyed virgins leapt up to thread their needles, newly-wed brides put on their thimbles. Kubra's mother's scissors had begun their work.

At the far end of the *seh-dari*, Hameeda sat pensively on a couch, her feet dangling, her chin resting on one hand, her mind somewhere else.

Every afternoon after lunch, Amabi settles down on the couch in the *seh-dari*, opens her sewing box and scatters about her a colourful array of snippets. Seated next to the stone mortar, washing dishes, Kubra observes these colourful pieces of cloth and a red band of colour surges across her pale, muddy complexion.

When Amabi lifts tiny gilded flowerets from the sewing box with her small, soft-skinned hands, her drooping face suddenly lights up with a strange, hope-filled luminescence; the glow of the golden flowerets is reflected on the deep, craggy folds of her face, glimmering there like the flames of tiny candles. With every stitch the gold sparkles and the candles flutter.

No one knows when the net of gold flowerets was first made for the fine muslin dupatta, and when the head-covering was lowered into the grave-like depths of the heavy trunk. The edges of the flowerets had faded, the patterned gilt border had become pale, the coils of gold thread wore a forlorn look, but there was no sign of Kubra's wedding procession yet. When a suit of clothing made especially for *chauthi*, the fourth day of the wedding, lost its lustre with the passage of time, it was discarded on one pretext or another and new hope was kindled by starting work on a new suit. After a thorough search a new bride was selected for the first snip, a freshly-laundered floor covering was laid at the entrance to the *seh-dari*, and the women from the neighbourhood, carrying their babies and paan-containers, their anklets tinkling, arrived on the scene.

"You will get the border from the smaller piece without any difficulty, but you won't have enough left for the bodice."

"What do you mean? We're not going to use the twill for the bodice, are we?" And with that everyone's face took on a troubled look. Quietly, like a silent alchemist, Amabi used her eyes to calculate width and length while the women whispered amongst themselves about the sparseness of the fabrics. A few laughed, one of them broke into a wedding song and before long, someone else, impelled by new-found boldness, launched into a song about unpopular in-laws. All this was followed by a spattering of dirty jokes, teasing and giggling. At this point the young unmarried girls were asked to leave; they were told to cover their heads and find a place to sit somewhere near the tiling. On hearing the sound of laughter the young girls sighed: Oh God, when would they be able to laugh like this?

Overcome by shyness, her head hung low, Kubra sat in the mosquito-infested ante-chamber, far from all this hustle and bustle. Without any warning the measuring and cutting process would arrive at a delicate stage; a gusset had been cut against the grain and one would think the women's good sense had also been snipped in the process. Kubra would watch fearfully from a chink in the door. That was the problem: not one suit had been stitched without trouble. If a gusset was cut the wrong way you could be sure the matchmaker's gossip would create a hitch — somewhere a mistress would be discovered, or the groom's mother would cause a problem by making demands for a pair of solid gold bracelets. A warp in the area of the hem meant there would be a falling out on the matter of *mehr*, or over the question of copper logs for the wooden bed. The omen associated with the dress for *chauthi* was indeed a critical one. But all of Amabi's expertise and capability came to nought; who knows why, at the last minute, something as minute as a coriander seed suddenly assumed undue importance.

With God's grace, Amabi had started preparing Kubra's dowry early. The smallest remnant was immediately stitched into a cover for a decorative glass bottle, adorned with fretted lace of gold thread, and stored. There's no telling with a girl: she grows so fast, like a cucumber. If a wedding procession does appear at the door, this very foresight and astuteness will prove invaluable.

However, this special astuteness lost its edge after Abba's death. All at once Hameeda remembered her father. Abba was as slight as a pole; if he lowered his body he had difficulty straightening up again. Early in the morning he would break off a twig from the neem tree and, with Hameeda in his lap, lose himself in thought. Then, as soon as he started brushing, a small fragment from the twig would go down the wrong way and he would begin to cough violently. Upset, Hameeda would slip off his knees; she did not like being shaken like that. Amused at her childish anger he would laugh, thus causing the choking cough to flutter in his throat like the flapping wings of a slaughtered pigeon. Finally Amabi would come along and slap him on the back.

"Good grief! What kind of laughter is this?"

Raising eyes reddened from the coughing fit, Abba would look at her and smile helplessly. The coughing eased, but he sat huffing and puffing in the same place for a long time afterwards.

"Why don't you find a cure for this cough? I've told you so many times you should do something about it."

"The doctor at the big hospital says I will need injections. He also said I should have a quart of milk and one ounce of butter every day."

"Dust upon the doctors' faces! There's a bad cough and then all that fat on top of it — why, if that does not create more phlegm what will? Go to an allopath, I say."

"I will." Abba would gurgle his tobacco-pipe and start coughing again.

"May this hukkah burn! This is the root of your coughing. Have you ever taken the trouble of looking at your grown daughter?"

And Abba glanced at Kubra's youth with a wistful look in his eyes. Kubra a grown woman — who said she was a grown woman? One would think that soon after the *bismillah* ceremony marking the beginning of lessons, she learned of her impending womanhood, staggered, and came to a standstill. What kind of womanhood was this that never put a sparkle in her eyes, nor allowed her tresses to caress her cheeks; no storm ever raged in her breast, nor did she ever sing playfully to the dark, swirling monsoon clouds for a beloved. Her shrinking, timorous womanhood which stole up on her without warning, left as furtively as it had come. The intoxicating drug first became salty, then bitter.

One day Abba stumbled over the threshold and fell on his face. Neither a doctor's prescription nor an allopath's remedy could lift him up again. And that was when Hameeda ceased to make demands for sweet roti.

That was also when proposals intended for Kubra somehow lost their way. It was as if no one knew that behind the sackcloth curtain at the door there was someone whose youth was drawing its last breath, and someone else whose youth was lifting its head like a cobra's hood.

But Amabi's routine remained unchanged; everyday, in the afternoon, as if she were playing with dolls, she scattered about her in the *seh-dari* all the colourful remnants and snippets from her sewing box.

Scrounging and saving from here and there, Amabi finally succeeded in buying a crepe dupatta for seven rupees and eight annas. Circumstances demanded that the dupatta be purchased immediately. A telegram from Hameeda's uncle had arrived: his oldest son, Rahat, was going to be in town for police training. Amabi was beside herself with anxiety. One would think that the wedding party was at the door and she hadn't even chipped up the gold for the bride as yet. Panicking, she lost her cool altogether and sent for her friend, Bundu's mother, who was also her adopted sister. "You'll never see my face again if you do not come this very moment."

Putting their heads together the two women whispered conspiratorially. Every once in a while they would glance at Kubra who was winnowing rice in the verandah. She knew perfectly well what this hushed conversation implied.

Right then Amabi removed her tiny clove-shaped earrings and handed them to Bundu's mother with the request that no matter what, she was to get her one tola of fettered gold lace, six *masas* of gold leaf and stars, and a quarter yard of twill. The room at the outer end of the house was swept and dusted; using a small amount of slaked lime, Kubra whitewashed the interior of the room herself. The walls became white, but the lime flaked the skin on her palms. That evening when she sat down to grind spices she fell back in pain. In bed she tossed and turned all night, first because of her palms, and then because Rahat was arriving by the morning train.

"Oh God, dear God!" Hameeda entreated after morning prayers. "Please let my sister have good luck this time. I promise I will say a hundred *rakats* at prayer."

Kubra was already ensconced in the mosquito-ridden chamber when Rahat arrived the next morning. After he had partaken of a breakfast consisting of parathas and vermicelli cooked in milk he went to the sitting room. Kubra came out stealthily, taking small steps like a new bride, and started picking up the dirty dishes.

"Apa, here, let me wash these," Hameeda teased.

"No," replied Kubra, hunched over shyly.

Hameeda continued to tease her, Amabi continued to smile and stitch gold lace on the crepe dupatta.

The gold flowerets and cockades and the silver anklets went the way of the clove-shaped earrings. In no time they were followed by the four bangles Amabi's brother had given her at the ceremony marking the end of her mourning period after Abba died. Eating humble fare themselves, the women cooked sumptuous parathas, fried meatballs and biriyani for Rahat; while Amabi herself subsisted on bread and water, she fed the best cuts of meat to her son-in-law-to-be.

"These are hard times, my child," she would tell Hameeda when the girl complained. And Hameeda thought: we remain hungry so that we can nourish the son-in-law. Kubra Apa gets up early in the morning, drinks a glass of water and starts working like a machine. She prepares parathas for Rahat and keeps the milk on boil for a long time so that a heavy layer of cream forms on it; if she could, she would take some of the fat from her own body and knead it into the dough she used to make parathas for Rahat. And why shouldn't she do all this? After all, one day he will be hers, and whatever he earns he will entrust to her care. Don't we all water and nourish a fruit-bearing plant? And then, when the flowers bloom and the bough bends with their weight people who now gossip will be silenced forever. It was this very thought that made my Kubra Apa's face glow with bride-like luminescence. The sound of wedding trumpets echoed in her ears and she rushed to sweep up the dirt in Rahat's room with her lashes; lovingly, as if they talked to her, she folded his dirty clothes, washed his soiled, foul-smelling socks, laundered his stinking undershirts and handkerchiefs filled with mucus, and on his pillow-case she carefully embroidered the words, "Sweet dreams." But things were not falling into place. Rahat ate a hearty breakfast consisting of eggs and parathas every morning, returned at night to eat meatballs, and then went to bed. Amabi's adopted sister whispered complaints.

"Yes, but the poor fellow is very shy," Amabi offered excuses.

"That's all very well, but we should get a hint or a clue from his actions or the way he looks at her."

"Heaven forbid that my daughter should exchange looks with anyone! No outsider has even glimpsed her head-covering." Amabi spoke with pride.

"My dear, no one is suggesting that she come

before Rahat."

Observing Kubra's well-developed acne, Bundu's mother secretly lauded Amabi's foresight. "You are so naive, my dear sister. When is this young thing going to be of use?" She looked at me and twittered. "You, good-for-nothing girl, you must jest with your brother-in-law and clown around with him, you silly child."

"But Auntie, what do you want me to do?"

"Why don't you talk to him?"

"I feel embarrassed talking to him."

"Why? He is not going to tear you to pieces, is he?" Amabi spoke angrily.

"No, but . . ." I was speechless. Then everyone conferred. After prolonged deliberation special kababs, using dried mustard seeds, were readied; Kubra Apa smiled a lot through all this. Then she whispered to me.

"Now don't start laughing or else you'll ruin the game."

"No, I won't," I promised.

"I've brought your dinner," I said, placing the tray of food on the stool before Rahat. But when he glanced up and down at me while washing his hands, I ran from the room. My heart was beating uncontrollably; what a fierce expression he had in his eyes!

"You fool, go and see how he reacts to the kababs. You're going to spoil the fun."

Kubra Apa looked at me. There was pleading in her eyes, the dust of departing wedding processions, a sadness reminiscent of old wedding clothes. I lowered my head and returned to where Rahat sat eating.

He ate silently without a glance in my direction.

While he was eating I should have joked and laughed with him. I should have said, "Are you enjoying these special kababs, dear brother-in-law?" But I felt as if someone had clutched at my throat.

Angered, Amabi called me back and scolded me under her breath. How could I tell her that the wretch seemed to be enjoying his food.

"Rahat Bhai, do you like the kababs?" I asked, as I had been instructed by Amabi.

There was no answer.

"Do you like the kababs?"

"Go and ask him properly," Amabi nudged me.

"You brought them to me and I ate them. They must be good."

"What an ignoramus!" Amabi was forced to exclaim.

"Why, you ate kababs made with dried mustard seeds, Rahat Bhai, and you couldn't tell the difference?"

"Mustard seeds? But I eat the same thing every day, don't I? I'm used to eating mustard seeds and chaff."

Amabi's face fell. Kubra Apa couldn't lift her eyes. The next day Kubra Apa spent twice the usual amount of time sewing and when I took Rahat his food in the evening, he said:

"And what did you bring me today? It must be sawdust this time."

"Don't you like our food?" I snapped at him.

"That's not what I mean. It's just a little strange. Sometimes you give me kababs made with mustard seeds, sometimes curry made with chaff."

I was infuriated: we eat dry bread so that we can provide him with enormous rations, stuff him with parathas dripping with butter, and my poor sister, who can't afford medicine for herself, lavishes him with milk and cream. Fuming, I came away.

Amabi's adopted sister's advice worked and Rahat began to spend the better part of his day at home. Kubra Apa stayed at the stove most of the time, Amabi was always busy stitching the *jora* for *chauthi*, and Rahat's filthy looks plunged into my heart like arrows. He teased me without any provocation while he was eating or making a request for water or salt, and made insinuating remarks; embarrassed, I would go and sit next to Kubra Apa. I wanted to say to her, "Whose goat is this anyway, and who's giving it fodder? Dear sister, I won't be able to put a ring in your bull's nose." But Kubra Apa's tangled hair was covered with ashes from the stove ... No! My heart sank. Quickly I lifted the gray lock of hair from the side of her face and tucked it into her plait. A curse on this recurring cold! The poor girl's hair is turning gray from it.

Using another excuse this time, Rahat called me again.

"Hunh!" I was furious. But when Kubra Apa turned around with the look of a slaughtered animal, I had to go.

"Are you angry with me?" Rahat took the glass of water from me and grabbed my wrist. My heart leapt into my mouth, and pulling my hand from his grasp, I fled.

"What was he saying?" Kubra Apa asked in a voice stifled by shyness. Silent, I just stared at her.

Then I began hurriedly, "He was saying, 'Who cooked the food? How delicious it is! I can't stop eating ... I want to devour the hand ... oh, no, kiss the hand of the person who cooked all this'." Taking Kubra Apa's roughened hand which smelt of turmeric and coriander, I clasped it in mine; my eyes filled with tears. These "hands", which grind spices from morning to night, draw water, chop onions, make beds, polish shoes — hapless, these hands are at work from morning to night like slaves. When will their subservience end? Will they ever find a buyer? Will no one ever kiss them lovingly, will they never be adorned with henna, will they ever be drenched in bridal attar? I wanted to scream at the top of my voice.

"What else did he say?" Kubra Apa's hands were rough, but her voice was so melodious and sweet-sounding that if Rahat had ears . . . but he had neither ears nor a nose, just an infernal stomach.

"Well, he said tell your sister she shouldn't work so hard and she should take something for her cough."

"Liar!"

"No, I'm not lying. It's he who's a liar, your . . ."

"Hush, you silly girl! Here, I've completed the sweater . . . why don't you take it to him. But promise you won't tell him I knitted it."

I wanted to say, "Apa, don't give him this sweater. This body of yours which is just a handful of bones needs it more than he does." But I couldn't bring myself to say it. "Apa, what will *you* wear?" I asked instead.

"I don't really need it. I feel scorched from sitting next to the stove."

Upon seeing the sweater Rahat raised one eyebrow mischievously and asked: "Did you make this yourself?"

"No."

"In that case I'm not going to wear it."

I felt like scarring his face. You wretch! Mountain of clay! This sweater has been knitted by hands which are living, breathing slaves; caught in its every stitch are the hopes of an ill-fated woman; the hands that made it are meant to rock a cradle. Grasp these hands, you idiot, they will be like life-saving oars when your boat is threatened by overpowering waves in a storm. They may not play a melody on the sitar, they won't twist and turn in the poses of Manipuri or Bharata Natyam, they haven't been taught to dance over the keys of a piano, they haven't had the good fortune to play with flowers, but these are the hands that toil endlessly to provide sustenance to your body, they sew for you day and night, suffer the heat from the stove, wash your filth so that you can maintain your image of unblemished wholesomeness. Wounded by hard work, they have never been adorned with tinkling bangles, and no one has ever clasped them lovingly. But I remained silent. Amabi says my thinking has been poisoned by my new friends who tell me new things, frightening things about hunger and starvation, about hearts suddenly ceasing to beat.

"Why don't you wear this sweater," Rahat said, "your shirt is so flimsy."

I scratched his face, nose, shirt-front and hair like a crazed cat and, running to my room, fell on my bed. Kubra Apa quickly put the last roti on the pan, washed her hands and, wiping them with a corner of her dupatta, came and sat on the edge of my bed. "Did he say anything?" Unable to stop herself, she asked me, her heart beating fast.

"Apa, Rahat is not a nice person." I decided I would tell her everything today.

"Why?" she smiled.

"I don't like him ... look, he broke all my bangles." I was trembling.

"He's so mischievous," Apa said coyly.

"Apa, listen Apa, he's not a nice person at all," I said angrily. "I'm going to tell Amabi today."

"What happened?" asked Amabi, unrolling the prayer mat.

"Look Amabi, my bangles."

"Did Rahat break them?" she asked gleefully.

"Yes."

"And why shouldn't he? Aren't you always pestering him? Why are you so upset anyway? You're not going to melt with the first touch." Then she spoke in a pacifying tone. "When the time comes you can make up for all this — Rahat will not be able to forget your revenge!" And saying this she began her prayers.

There was another conference with her adopted sister and, satisfied that matters were moving in the desired direction, they both smiled happily. Bundu's mother said to me, "My word, girl, you *are* a good-for-nothing! When we were young we made life miserable for our brothers-in-law."

She then proceeded to describe how brothers-in-law should be harassed, giving her own example to illustrate her point. She explained how just teasing and mischief had resulted in the marriage of her uncle's two daughters for whom there had seemed to be no hope at all.

One of the men was Hakim ji; whenever the young girls played pranks on him or joked with him, he would suffer one attack of bashfulness after another until he became quite distraught. Finally a day came when he informed Uncle that he wanted to be his son-in-law.

The other was a clerk in the Viceroy's office. No sooner did the girls hear he had arrived in the house than the teasing and pranks commenced; sometimes they sent him paan filled with hot chillies, sometimes vermicelli in which they had put salt instead of sugar. What do you know, he started coming every day, regardless of whether it rained or stormed. And one day he requested an acquaintance to arrange a match for him in that family. When asked, "With which girl?" he answered, "It doesn't really matter." And by God, looking at the older girl you would think a banshee was coming your way. And the younger one, well, she too was something else: one eye faced west, the other east. Her father gave her fifteen tolas of gold in her dowry and also arranged a job for her husband in the Barre Saheb's office.

"Well, how can someone with fifteen tolas of gold and the influence to provide a job in Barre Saheb's office have any difficulty finding a boy," said Amabi with a sigh.

"No, my dear, that's not it. These days men's hearts are just like brinjals on a tray — you can make them roll whichever way you like."

But Rahat isn't a brinjal; he's a mountain. I hope I'm not the one who gets crushed while trying to make him roll, I thought.

Then I looked at Kubra Apa. Seated at the threshold of the room, silently kneading dough, she was listening to everything that was being said. If she could, she would have rent the bosom of the earth and vanished within it, taking the curse of her virginity with her.

Was my sister hungry for a man? No, she had shrivelled up before she had even an inkling of that hunger. The idea of a man has come to her mind not as desire, but as a question of food and clothing. She is a widow's burden and the burden has to be removed.

However, no amount of insinuation or innuendo elicited a word from either Rahat or his family. Despondent, Amabi finally pawned her heavy anklets and arranged a *niaz* in the name of Pir Mushkil Kusha. All afternoon young girls from the neighbourhood created a racket in the verandah, Kubra Apa retreated to her mosquito-ridden room so that the last drops of her blood could be sucked, and feeling spent, Amabi sat on her couch putting the last stitches on the wedding suit. Today the expression on her face spoke of destinations; her ordeal would soon be over. Once again the wrinkles on her face lit up like candles.

Apa's friends were teasing her, they were trying to invigorate the few drops of blood that remained. Her fever had not recurred for many days; her face shone brightly for a moment and then languished like a dying candle. She signalled me to come to her, then quietly handed me a plate containing *malida*, a sweet, buttery cake.

"Maulvi saheb said a special incantation over this." Her hot, feverish breath swept across my ear.

Taking the plate from her I thought, Maulvi saheb has said a special incantation, this *malida* will now be dropped into Rahat's furnace, the furnace that has been kept warm for six months with our blood. This special *malida* will make the dream come true. I heard the sound of wedding trumpets: I run to the roof to see the wedding procession approach, there's a long *sehra* over the bridegroom's face, it is touching the horse's mane . . .

Wearing the wedding dress, laden with flowers, Kubra Apa advances shyly, taking slow steps . . . the dress glimmers, Amabi's face has blossomed like a flower . . . Apa's eyes, heavy with modesty, are raised once, a tear of gratitude slips, becomes entangled in the chipped gold and sparkles like a diamond.

"This is all due to your hard work," Apa's silence seems to be saying. Hameeda's eyes filled with tears.

"Go, my dear sister," Apa awoke her from her reverie and startled, Hameeda advanced towards the sitting room wiping her tears with a corner of her dupatta.

"Here's some *malida*," she said nervously, trying to control the pounding of her heart. Her steps wavered; she felt as if she had entered a snake's hole. The mountain shifted and gaped open. She moved back. But somewhere in the distance wedding trumpets screeched as if they had been strangled; with trembling hands she rolled some *malida* between her fingers and moved it towards his mouth.

With a snatch her hand was drawn into the depths of the mountain, into putrescence and darkness, and a large rock stifled her scream. The plate with the sacred *malida* slipped from her hands and fell over the lantern, the lantern tipped, sobbed for a few seconds and was extinguished.

The next day Rahat took the morning train, thanking them for their hospitality as he left. The date for his wedding had been fixed and he was in a hurry.

After this no eggs were ever fried again in this house, no parathas were warmed and no sweaters knitted. Tuberculosis, which had been pursuing Kubra Apa for a long time, seized her with one pounce and she quietly deposited her weary existence into its lap.

Once again a freshly-laundered floor covering was laid in the *seh-dari*. The women from the neighbourhood gathered. The white cotton of the shroud stretched before Amabi like the mantle of death. Her lineaments were quivering from the burden of constraint, her left eyebrow was twitching, the lines on her face appeared frightening, as if there were thousands of serpents hissing in them.

After straightening the warp in the cotton, she folded the fabric to form a square, and innumerable scissors snipped through her heart. Today there was a look of terrifying peace on her countenance; a flowering calm reigned there, as if she were absolutely certain that like the other suits for *chauthi* which had always remained incomplete, this one too, would be discarded.

All at once the young girls in the *seh-dari* began chirping like starlings. Pushing the past aside, Hameeda joined them. The coarse white cotton . . . the red of the floor-covering! Who knows how many innocent brides have mingled their blood with its redness and how many unfortunate virgins have sunk the despair of their lost hopes in its whiteness. Suddenly everyone was silent. Amabi put in the last stitch and broke off the thread. Two thick teardrops slid slowly down her soft, cushiony cheeks, rays of light burst forth from the wrinkles on her face, and she smiled. It seemed that today, at last, she was convinced that her Kubra's dress for *chauthi* was ready and that the trumpets would sound any time now.

*Translated by Tahira Naqvi*

# The Mole

"CHAUDHRY, O Chaudhry . . ."

Garishchand Chaudhry remained silent.

"Shush."

"Why are you making noises like a cricket?"

"I'm tired."

"Sit still or else . . ."

"I cannot sit still anymore! My back is as stiff as a board. Hey Ram!"

"Hnnk, hnnk . . ."

"Brrr . . . . I'm so cold."

Chaudhry was quiet.

"It feels as though there are ants crawling under my thigh."

"Look here, Rani, it's only been ten minutes and already you're tired."

"So? I'm not made of clay. Hunh!" Stretching her thick lips, Rani grunted and slid off the stool she was sitting on.

"Witch! I'm telling you, sit still. Slattern!" Chaudhry flung the palette on the stool and catching hold of her shoulders, shook her hard.

"Well, all right then . . . here." She slipped to the floor. Chaudhry was livid. He wanted to mark her smooth, dark cheeks with a whip but he knew that would only make her lose control altogether and give her an excuse to start weeping. And the painting for which he was killing himself would remain incomplete.

"Look, just sit quietly for a little while longer, that's all." He spoke in a subdued tone.

"But I'm tired." She rolled over and stretched.

"Tired! And don't you get tired when you're out collecting cow-dung on the roads all day long? You bitch!" Chaudhry's anger returned.

"Who is collecting cow-dung? You? What a mean one you are, taunting me like a quarrelsome mother-in-law!" Annoyed, she sat up and began to sulk. Chaudhry was certain another day was about to go down the drain.

"All right. Keep still for just another half hour. Understand?"

"Not half-an-hour. Six minutes only," she said, climbing back onto the stool.

The truth of the matter was, she could only count up to six or seven. Chaudhry was sure he could keep her sitting for half-an-hour. Rani straightened her waist, adjusted the heavy, flowered pitcher on her shoulder and sat down. But for how long?

"Is this right?"

"Yes." Chaudhry quickly bent over his canvas.

"Look at me . . ."

"Yes, yes, it's all right."

"Look at me . . ."

"Yes, yes, it's all right."

For some time his brush moved with urgent haste and colours rapidly coalesced into one another, but no sooner had a minute or so gone by than Rani breathed a heavy sigh.

"Ahhh . . . That is all, Chaudhry. Your six minutes

are over."

"Hmm . . ." His glance bolted from his incomplete, dappled painting to her and back again.

"I'm cold. Can I wear my shawl?'

"No."

"Ohhh . . . ahh . . ..It is so cold." She started whining like a dog. Chaudhry was quiet.

"My back, oh my back, Chaudhry ji!" Actually she was in a mischievous mood today. "Shawl, my shawl, my shawl. . . ."

Chaudhry said nothing.

"Hunhi! Didn't you hear me say I'm tired? I will throw down the pitcher if you don't listen to me."

Chaudhry quickly turned to look at her. He had borrowed the pitcher from the museum for his painting. He would crack Rani's skull if she broke it.

"Can I help it if I'm tired? I think there are lice crawling in my hair." Resting the pitcher on the floor, she lifted her hand to her head and began untangling a thick, knotted lock of hair with her fingers.

His feet set apart, the muscles in his face quivering with anger, Chaudhry glared at her. His grizzly beard fluttered like a sailboat flapping wildly in the storm, and tiny beads of perspiration appeared on the surface of his bald, smooth head.

"My back hurts from sitting for such a long time." Scared, Rani quickly eased back into position. Then she burst into tears.

"Boohoo . . ." Her lips flapped as she blubbered.

"Boohoo . . . Nobody cares if I live or die," she said between sobs.

Chaudhry widened his eyes and glared at her again. Whenever she started crying, the muscles in Chaudhry's jaws quivered violently, the bridge on his nose went askew, the brushes in his hand danced like fire-crackers, and the colours on his palette flowed into a muddle and lost their glow. Thought was impossible while this condition lasted, reason returning to him only when the thorn in his brain had been dislodged. And at this very moment, Rani's behaviour was not so much a thorn as a spear that threatened to carve through his very soul.

There wasn't a person alive who could ward off the effects of Chaudhry's histrionics, and Rani was no exception. She quickly sucked in her stomach and making whining noises, sat down again.

For a while the world continued to revolve on its axis, Chaudhry's brush moved rapidly, and his palette began to take on an untidy look.

But, "Chaudhry," Rani spoke lovingly this time. Chaudhry felt something jump in his chest. The foundation of the world's axis swayed just a mite. To be sure, something did happen.

"Chaudhry, have you seen this?"

Chaudhry's shoulders convulsed, beads of sweat broke out on his smooth-surfaced skull. Rani spoke again.

"Look, do you see this black mole, just below my neck, see, to the left here?" Holding the pitcher with one hand, her mouth hanging open as she lowered her face to examine the mole, she looked down at her neck.

"Did you see this mole? So, you are looking, Chaudhry." She pretended to be coy. "Oh, I'm so embarrassed."

"Sit still," Chaudhry growled.

"Hunh! What airs you put on! Why would anyone want to sneak a look at somebody's mole, especially when it is in such a bad place?" She chuckled shame-lessly.

"I'm not interested in any mole. I didn't see it and I'm not going to either." Chaudhry's irritation grew.

"Hunh! Liar! You saw it, you looked at it from the corner of your eye. And . . ." she continued to snicker immodestly.

"Rani!"

Rani stuck her nose up at him. Defeated, Chaudhry sat down on a wooden box next to his easel. "Do you know how old I am?" he asked her.

"Hey Ram! How old?" Lowering the pitcher, she leaned towards him.

"I'm older than your father, actually even older than your grandfather. And you? Tell me, how old are you? No more than fifteen, I'm sure. And who taught you all this vulgar talk?"

Chaudhry wasn't even as old as her father. He only said that to shut her up.

"You are the one who talks vulgar. Peeping at my mole! And it is in such a bad place too." She slowly groped for the mole. "And who says I'm a little girl? If I had been that young, why . . ."

"Well, what then?"

"Ratan says whoever has a mole on the breast is . . ." she stuttered.

"Ratan? How does Ratan know where your mole is?"

"I showed it to him." She slowly massaged the mole.

"You . . . you . . . you showed Ratan your mole?"

Chaudhry's blood began to boil again; there was a tremor in his armpits, the flesh in his cheeks began to flutter once more, and his brushes danced.

"Uh ... well, Oh! he saw it, so what could I do?"

"How ... how did he manage to set eyes on it when you, you ..." Chaudhry's jaw shook like a door loose on its hinges.

"I was bathing and he ..." she began. Picking up the pitcher she climbed on the stool again. "Yes, I was bathing. I was scared to go alone so I took him with me to the pond. I had to wash my blouse and what if someone came just then? I took him along because I was scared, yes." She spoke artlessly.

"Rani ..." Chaudhry edged forward.

"I told him to keep looking the other way, but ..."

"But?"

"He sat some distance away. Then I said, 'Ratan, I have a mole in a very bad place.' He didn't say anything. Then I said, 'All right, don't look if you don't want to, I don't care.' Right Chaudhry?"

"But you said he saw it."

"Yes, because I started to drown — the water was this deep, you know," she said, placing a finger just below the mole.

"Slut!" Flinging the brush aside, Chaudhry leapt towards a wooden stick lying nearby.

"Hey Ram! But, but ... listen, Chaudhry. Would you have liked me to drown?"

"Don't you know how to swim, you bitch? You've been in and out of that pond all your life. Why is it you never drowned before?"

"Why, I wasn't really going to drown. I just wanted to show him my mole."

"So you pretended to be drowning just so you could show him your mole, eh?" Chaudhry waved the thin stick in the air. He was smiling now.

"Hey Ram! Let me put on my dhoti first,

Chaudhry ji." Monkey-like, she jumped from the stool and landed on the mat. "I will run out on the road if you hit me. I will be so humiliated I'll have to tell everyone that Chaudhry, Chaudhry . . ."

The old man stopped in his tracks. "What will you tell them?"

"I will say, 'Chaudhry says that my mole . . . '" she twittered.

"Slattern!" Chaudhry danced like a mad fox. Rani knew the arrow had hit its mark.

"I will tell everybody, Chaudhry. Do you understand? Come on, hit me if you want to. Why are you staring at me like that? I'm so young, just a little girl . . . you are really very naughty!" She gradually edged toward the door.

Chaudhry sat down with his head in his hands. For a moment he was overcome with the temptation to burn the painting and beat Rani to a pulp, but in the next instant he remembered the exhibition at which he was to receive an award of five thousand rupees for his painting.

His mind had been in a swirl to beging with. For years he had been painting pictures of roses blooming timorously, of undulating verdure, of leaping, swirling torrents; he had even successfully endowed pain and fragrance with colour. And women from faraway places, both naked and clothed, felt honoured to pose for him. But this sprightly, illiterate chit of a girl he had picked up from the filthy gutters to sit for his masterpiece, was completely unmanageable. His greatest problem was that despite all his experimentation with hundreds of tints, he was unable to duplicate the exact shade of her skin. He mixed gold with black and then added blue, but the gloss on her skin appeared to come from a mixture of gold, black and blue, along with a wave of ochre. It wasn't just one thing either. One day her complexion was inky, the next he could see early-morning vermilion bursting from it, and then suddenly her body would resemble lilac clouds at night, while at other times he could definitely see the blue of a viper's skin shining through. Her eyes, too, appeared to change colour constantly. On the first day he calmly prepared a coal-black tint. But suddenly he saw fine red circles around her pupils, and then in the area around them he thought he caught a glimpse of blue which reminded him of clouds. He became flustered. So much paint had been wasted. But his vexation knew no bounds when, within minutes, the coal-black pupils changed colour, became green and danced like two emeralds. The surface around the pupils was transformed to a milky-white and the red circles grew redder. "Oh God!" He clasped his head with both hands and shuddered. And to make matters worse, this:

"I got biten by a mosquito," she was saying, whimpering like a child.

Chaudhry had decided today he would remain unruffled and not say a word.

"They are biting me to death, you know."

No word from Chaudhry.

"Ohh . . . they bite so hard, these mosquitoes . . ." Rani blurted out a filthy invective, not something that you heard often. Chaudhry jumped. He didn't know that many obscenities, and the ones he did know were mild compared to what he had just heard. As a matter of fact, his knowledge of vulgar language was extremely limited.

"Where did you learn to swear like this?" he turned around to ask her.

"Which one? You mean this?" She repeated the obscenity without artifice.

"Rani!" he growled.

"Chunan was cursing once. There are lots of mosquitoes in his *kholi*." She tried to be evasive. "In his *kholi*? You were in his kholi?"

"Yes. He told me he had some *gurdhani* there he was going to give me."

"Did you eat the *gurdhani*?"

"Of course not. There was no *gurdhani* there. He was lying. But he brings it for me now."

"Chunan gives you *gurdhani*?"

"And *kheel* too." She traced the pattern on the pitcher with her finger.

"*Kheel* too?" Chaudhry knew that his surprise was unwarranted. Rani was crazy about *gurdhani*. Not only would she go to Chunan's room for the cane sugar sweet, she would snatch some from the jaws of a dog in the gutter and devour it.

"I've been giving you money and you're still going to Chunan for the sweet?"

"I'm not a beggar, why should I go to him for it? He brings it to me and then he says, 'Come with me to my *kholi*.' I don't like him at all. Such a big moustache he has — it makes me sneeze. Achoo!" She sniffled as if someone had pushed a wick up her nose.

"Chaudhry, can I scratch my back? Can I?"

Once again Chaudhry began to feel the effects of the old madness. He thought he could hear clapping noises in his head, his cheeks fluttered, and five thousand jingling rupees took the shape of tiny stars and danced away from him. Brown, black, gray and yellow

— all the shades coalesced and he felt there were mushrooms sprouting from his skull.

The question he was now faced with was: Should he continue painting or go mad? If this went on any longer he would soon be seen rolling in the dust in the streets like a crazed dog, his clothes tattered, his thin body scratched, or he would be found with his burning head submerged in the waters of the small pond.

His steps led him to the pond. It was not far. He went there frequently to sit on the banks and gaze at the swaying and flickering reflections of sunlight on the water's surface. He was a poet. A poet from birth. He lived in the world, but was distanced from it. He was not an old man, but one couldn't think of him as young either. He had let his beard grow because he was too careless to trim it, and now it was also speckled with gray.

"Ohh . . ." Something fluttered in his armpits again. Rani's voice fell into his ears. It sounded like the croaking of a frog. Was it a frog? But the rainy season was still to come. Perhaps it was the sound of a cat growling. It had to be something. When his pious eyes glimpsed Rani and Ratan romping in the water, he thought for a moment he had imagined them there. His imagination tormented him harshly and often. And today it had gone too far.

But the torrent of laughter ceased when he advanced, and the two images, transfixed as if in marble, stared wide-eyed at him. How clear the illusion was! How translucent each feature! The bulge of Ratan's thighs, his wet hair, his small eyes set together. And Rani's tousled, wet plait, the colour of her skin a mixture of charcoal-black, pink, brown, camphor-

white and blue. And the mole. That fleshy, protu-
berant mole. To Chaudhry it seemed that the mole had
struck his chest with a thud, like a flying bullet.

Ratan grabbed his dhoti about him and made his
escape from the side, but Rani stood undaunted, noisily slapping the water with her hands. Chaudhry felt
as if he were on a swing, swaying, swaying rhythmi-
cally.

"You are looking at my mole, aren't you? That is
so naughty of you." She spoke coquettishly in an
attempt to pacify him.

Chaudhry held himself back at the brink of the
precipice.

"Come out of there," he said, pushing aside the
new Chaudhry who was slowly sinking.

"Unhuh . . . you will hit me." She lifted her torso
above the water.

"If I don't skin you alive today I'll change my
name!" Chaudhry realized he was talking to a girl who
had been raised like a frog in the gutter.

"Won't you feel ashamed, lifting your hand to hit
a woman?"

Chaudhry smouldered.

"Do you hit naked women? What a thing to do!"
She lifted herself higher.

"You are not ashamed?" She gazed into his eyes
and smiled, the water up to her knees now. Her fear
had made her bold.

"Go away, you . . ." she said coyly.

The stick fell from Chaudhry's hands and his
height increased by inches; the muscles in his arms
bulged and grew taut, and he felt ants crawling inside
his brain; a strong gust of cool, black wind blew over
the pile of embers, the spark was ignited and soon

there were flames leaping in all directions. His eyes plunged at the black, fleshy mole like hungry vultures and . . . Ohhh . . . As if transformed into a black stone by his revulsion, the mole crashed against his forehead. He turned and ran. Ran like a defeated dog. Where? To his bed.

That same day Chaudhry fired Ratan. Ratan pleaded that he had his loincloth on the whole time, but Chaudhry was like a man possessed. All night he battled with his thoughts. He felt as if someone was trying unsuccessfully to drill a hole through his body, hindered, it seemed to him, by a rock that stood in the way. Tonight he had a myriad tints at his disposal: ochre with a little blue was transformed into a shade that was alive and deep like the bottom of the ocean, and for the eyes a little green mixed with black, no just a hint of purple, edged with a pink border. He wanted to get up and examine his own eyes in the mirror. But he hadn't seen his face in the mirror in ages. What need does an artist have to look at his own face? What is there to see in the mirror? His innumerable paintings constituted the mirror in which he could not only see his face, but also view every nook and cranny in his soul. His heart and his mind, both clothed in paint, appeared before him in his paintings.

Nevertheless, he still wanted to see his face in the mirror. Taking a tin box which had once carried the paints that came for him from all over the world, he turned it upside down and shook it. A couple of crickets jumped out and, brushing against his nose, flew off. With his elbow he rubbed off a spider's web from the bottom of the box and proceeded to examine his face. At first he could not see much. Whatever was visible looked like circles of foam on sea water, or something that one views through blurry, watery vision. Then he saw a hideous beard and eyes burning with hunger. Oh! This was his own face. His face? But he was never like this. Was he? He turned the box upside down and looked for his reflection again. A part of his beard was still visible and if he squinted one eye he could see his smudged nose and some of his moustache. The moustache. If he had scissors he would trim the moustache so it looked like . . . Rani had said Chunan's moustache made her sneeze. Achoo! He made sniffling noises with his nose. He knew Ratan was wearing his loincloth. Or maybe he did have the dhoti on, or was about to don it when he appeared on the scene. But what about Chunan and his *gurdhani*? Chaudhry suddenly had a feeling that the walls of his room were made of *gurdhani* and they were caving in on him, squeezing him, making him stick to the sweet like a half-crushed fly barely able to move.

When he got tired of walking and his legs grew heavy, he sat down on the stool, lifted the cover from his painting and gazed at his unfinished endeavour. Within minutes the spots and dabs began to fly around and then became stationary; the shoulders gleamed like polished leather, the eyes shimmered with blue, black and green lights, and the mole! Where did the mole come from? The mole that protruded like a coiled snake? Tick! Tick! Tick! His heart beat like a clock.

Quickly he rose and his feet carried him in the direction of Rani's hut. A dirty, squalid confining hut with a small door! He would have it enlarged tomorrow. No, the unused room where he stored empty boxes would be right. He advanced in the darkness.

His heart still beat like a clock. The darkness in the hut clung to him like wet charcoal. His hands collided with the charpoy, then plunged into the curve of the charpoy's roped bottom. He groped feverishly, but . . . Rani wasn't there!

Mosquitoes attacked his entire body. Large, cackling mosquitoes. Soon after that great slabs of *gurdhani* fell over him. The next morning he wanted to ask Rani, "Bitch, where were you last night?" But someone might want to know why he was in her hut, poking around in her bed.

He continued working quietly and Rani was silent too. He wished she would speak so he could find out where she had been the night before. But, angry with him, she remained silent and sulked.

"Are you tired?" he asked gently when he saw her putting the pitcher down. He didn't want to fight with her today.

"What do you think? I'm not made of clay, you know." She started massaging her waist with both hands.

Chaudhry wanted to say something nice to her, but he felt awkward changing his manner.

"All right, that's enough rest for now." He thought she would respond with belligerence, but instead she lifted the pitcher and straightened her waist again.

Today his colours were mutinous; whatever he dabbed on seemed to ridicule him. He had planned to paint on the mole this morning. Just like that. Could one not have moles in pictures? But when he saw how rebellious his colours were, he postponed the idea.

As Rani got up to leave, a piece of *gurdhani* fell from her dhoti. She was unaware of what had happened, but Chaudhry felt as if the roof had collapsed over his head.

"This *gurdhani!*" he roared, foaming at the mouth with anger.

At first she paused with the intention of picking up the sweet, but changed her mind when she saw Chaudhry's expression of anger.

"You eat it," she said, arrogantly throwing back her head as she walked away.

Chaudhry was numbed into a death-like stillness. He watched her leave. Then he ground the *gurdhani* into the dirt with the heel of his shoe.

The next day Rani disappeared. God knows where she went; she didn't even bother to take her clothes with her, leaving as she had come. The miserable creature had gone back to wallow in the dirt again, no doubt.

Chaudhry's painting remained imcomplete. Five thousand rupees congealed in his mind like a black stain. A stain that looked like a fleshy black mole. But what a bad place for a black, singed mark. Right over Chaudhry's heart!

In the days that followed, Chaudhry's anguish grew. Terrified that people might want to know what his interest in her was, he didn't tell anyone that Rani had run away. And so time passed. He tried to continue painting. But no one wanted to pay even six annas for his work. The reason for this was that now he was filling his flowers and sunsets with such grotesque and frightening shades of black and brown that people thought he had lost his mind. All his colours became jumbled and were reduced to nothing.

Some time later several interesting developments took place. People started asking Chaudhry about Rani. He said he didn't know where she had gone. But people are not satisfied with such simple answers.

"Chaudhry sold Rani."

"He sold her to a businessman for several thousand rupees."

"He had illicit relations with her . . . must have got rid of her."

The gossip about him was unending. Chaudhry's life was reduced to a darkened hole. It seemed that the world wanted to roast and devour him. And that's not all. What excitement, when Rani was caught by the police in the act of depositing a bloody bundle by the side of a road. Immediately people rushed to the village and Chaudhry's remaining sanity was threatened with extinction. The riddle of Rani's disappearance was solved in seconds. Chaudhry was thunderstruck. His mouth fell open in shock and surprise. A life of piety and honour trampled upon so easily! But he knew God was not his enemy. He would be saved just as all other innocent individuals are saved. Truth is without fear. But if only he had remained guilty!

Yes, if only he had remained guilty. Imprisonment, grief and pain, vile disgrace at the world's hands. If he had known, he would have willingly and happily taken it all upon himself. If he had known he would be freed in this fashion, he would not have offered evidence of his innocence to God and begged for help. True, there was that mole. But was God not aware of the weaknesses of His creatures? He is the one who has burdened man with all these weaknesses. But how could Chaudhry know that when Rani was questioned and caught in a net of logic by the lawyer, she would use this special strategy to free or, more appropriately, destroy him completely?

"The baby was not Chaudhry's," she swore before a full court.

"Chaudhry's not a man," she added carelessly. "But ask Chunan or Ratan. I can't tell you which one it is, I don't know.

Hunh!" She assumed her usual coquettish manner.

Accompanied by lightning and a quiet peal of thunder, a black mountain shattered over Chaudhry's being, and far away, in the darkness, a circular, protruding dot gyrated like a top.

To this day Chaudhry traces lines with a piece of charcoal on the side of the road. Long, triangular, round lines, like a singed mark.

*Translated by Tahira Naqvi*

# A Morsel

PANDEMONIUM reigned in the *chal*.
Either a snake had been spotted in one
of the rooms, or someone was in the throes of labour
pains. Women dashed wildly from one room to another, and then, lugging jars, boxes and glass phials,
they hastened toward Sarlaben's room as if she were
about to take her last breath and could only be saved
by her neighbours.

Actually, Sarlaben was indeed nearing the end;
her train was about to depart.

She would have been exactly thirty-four if her
far-sighted parents had not tampered with her birth
certificate and deducted five whole years from her
age. But what is officially recorded on paper doesn't
always prove helpful. Coming from some nameless
village in U.P., she had lived in Bombay long enough
to pass off as a true native of that city. As a matter of
fact, she did not carry the stamp of any particular
region; sometimes she was mistaken for a Gujarati,
sometimes a Marwari or a Sindhan. But, once Jagat,
now she was only Sarlaben.

Sarlaben was a nurse at E.M. Hospital. Her salary,
including the inflation allowance, came to two-hun-
dred-and-forty rupees a month and after paying, the
rent for her room, which was twelve rupees, she had
enough money left over to lead a very comfortable

life. She brought First Aid supplies, APC tablets, Mercurochrome, pure glycerine, and samples of other patent medicines from the hospital and distributed them free of charge among the inhabitants of the *chal*. Her room was something of an infirmary for her neighbours.

Sarlaben was a very useful person. Again, her character (in keeping with her appearance), was such that it never posed a threat to any of the families in the *chal*. For this reason she was extremely popular and well-loved. Wherever she went she was waylaid by whimpering, bawling children she had delivered; people welcomed her at every step, and shopkeepers and vendors gave her discounts. During her shopping rounds she stopped regularly to inquire about the welfare of her patients.

"Hey, Tulsi, how is your wife's backache now? I say, Shakir mian, has the swelling on Amina bi's feet subsided yet? Bring her to me in the evening, I'll give her an injection. Hey, Rajni, how is the pain in your knees? Is your man coming home drunk again?"

She enquired after everyone's well-being as she slowly made her way to the corner bus-stop, leaving in her wake patients who praised and blessed her.

There was just one thing that saddened everybody: Sarlaben was still unmarried. It might have been different if she had been widowed, or if, after marriage, her husband had abandoned her, but oh, woe! her train was about to depart and there was no sign of a life-partner yet. This was Bombay, here life races ahead at top speed. The go-between and the matchmaker have become extinct. In Bombay, your eyes meet and you are wed, and although Sarlaben was no film actress, she was not so plain either that a man could never fall in love with her; as a matter of fact, she was not bad-looking at all.

She lost her father when she was a child and was raised by an ailing mother who provided for her by sewing clothes for people on a Singer machine. When Sarlaben grew up and finally got a job, her mother's health failed altogether. Once or twice the thought of finding a husband for her daughter crossed the old woman's mind, but she passed away before the idea could take any real shape. Sarlaben worked diligently after her mother's death, never really giving any thought to marriage, and even if she did dwell on the subject, she certainly never told anyone about it.

It is said that an unmarried woman is a burden for all creation, the ensuing sorrow leaving its mark on each individual, making everyone accountable. At least that's what Sarlaben's friends and well-wishers maintained. Her unblemished character and virtue were indeed admirable, but there is a limit to how virtuous one should be. Of course, her friends did not want her to throw her arms around the first vagabond who came along, but there was no harm in using (properly, of course), those special womanly wiles. Snaring a husband was a job that parents could no longer tackle on their own; even the most genteel girls tried to capture the prize themselves and then, bashful, with their heads bowed, they handed over the catch to their parents. If an indiscretion occurred, no one came to know about it; parents beamed with the pride of accomplishment, the bride and groom were radiant — and that was how weddings happened. But for the likes of poor, unfortunate Sarlaben, all of this was not possible. No one came along to administer a balm on the wounds of those quietly suffering women who were engaged in providing comfort and solace to others, with no time for themselves. They shared the burdens of others, spent sleepless nights, tended new-born infants, and returned to the half-darkness of their rooms to gulp down whatever there was before stretching out on a lonely bed. No one provided comfort or solace to these women, or offered to heal their bruised, lonely selves.

Was there no man alone and hungering for the love of a woman in the enormous, noisy, tumultuous city of Bombay? Did nobody here yearn for a woman's touch? Sarlaben depended on no one, she took care of herself, and owned a room in the *chal* which was a little jewel — the only one of its kind, no less than a flat: there was a sofa here and a chair, also her own private toilet — what more could one ask for in this life?

What helplessness! If you weren't married you were like an open wound; people tormented you with talk about possible cures, and then once you had found a husband there was talk of having children: such a bother, a baby, even just one, and before long there would be another. Anyway, Sarlaben firmly believed she was not going to remain single forever. There had to be a man somewhere in this vast universe whom God had fated to be her partner in life. That she might never find him, was another matter. With all this chit-chat going on around her, she found herself becoming increasingly preoccupied with thoughts of marriage. But no sooner had she eyed a man from the standpoint of marriage than he turned out to be forbidden fruit; he usually ended up asking her for advice about his wife's secret ailments. Many were willing to spend a little time with her, but she hadn't come across one who was anxious to clasp her hand forever, who wanted to bring a wedding party to her house. Even in the hospital she had never been the recipient of darkly-mysterious glances, and no one ever felt the need to treat her with special consideration; always, people brushed past her rudely as she stood awkwardly flattened against a wall, trying to keep out of their way.

She took the eight o'clock bus every morning at the corner of Gam Devi. Most of the people who travelled with her were old acquaintances, and everyone usually sat in the same seat each time. This morning she absently advanced towards her usual place but on coming closer, saw that it was occupied by a stranger. With a fleeting glance about her, she grasped the nearest strap with one hand and remained standing. The stranger looked up and down at her, then got up.

"Please sit down," he said, motioning towards the seat and, taking hold of a strap, commenced reading his paper.

Baffled, she clutched her purse for fear that he might be a pick-pocket. Then it occurred to her that he might be the husband of one of her patients. She waited for him to embark on an account of his wife's backache or the swelling on her feet, but he continued to sway back and forth silently, his hand still around the strap. She was stunned when she realized he was not suffering from some deadly disease. Things like this just did not happen!

When he relinquished his seat for her the moment she boarded the bus the next morning, she felt quite uneasy and didn't know how to react. Her first impulse was to offer him a handful of sulpha pills, to seek a bruise somewhere on his person, apply a balm of mercurochrome on it and tie it up in a foamy-white bandage. The fact that he was so completely healthy dashed her hopes; she couldn't see even a tiny scratch anywhere. Swaying nonchalantly, he continued to peruse his paper.

Sarlaben broke out in a cold sweat when he offered her his seat again, for the third time.

*You bastard, why do you give me your seat every day — don't you have a mother or a sister at home?* She cast about for a reason to shout at him angrily, but watching him swaying unconcernedly made her feel exceedingly foolish for having entertained such thoughts.

A week passed and nothing changed. Sarlaben was stupefied. She was accustomed to helping others, not to receiving favours. Her heart felt burdened; again and again, at work and at home, she asked herself what the right thing to do would be. She knew it would be impossible to get to work on time if she took another bus.

Sarlaben was baffled. She turned inward, as if hurting from some sort of mistreatment; she became irritable and cried often, and when she returned from work she lay on her bed with her eyes shut, oblivious of the need to eat or do anything else. Her friends were afraid to approach her.

"Sarlaben's in love," Satu Pickpocket informed Ramwai.

"You idiot, may you rot in hell! Sarlaben is a saint, a saint!" Ramwai blasted Satu with invectives.

"I'm telling you the truth."

"What are you saying? May ashes fill your mouth!"

But Satu Pickpocket explained that his business

took him to the corner of Gam Devi where making assessments about people and relieving them of the burden in their pockets was his daily job, and he had seen a man regularly offer his seat on the bus to Sarlaben. The man remained standing the entire time, added Satu, and this had been going on for some days; it was obvious something extraordinary was going to happen soon.

"O my God!" Ramwai beat her chest and rushed to tell Shabo.

Shabo was dumbfounded. Then the two went to Saadat Bahu's house. She was in the courtyard with her baby straddled across her hands; he was urinating.

"Wonder of wonders!" The boy nearly fell into the drain.

The news spread like fire throughout the entire *chal*.

"So this is how it happens," Lakshmi Ghai said. She sewed buttonholes on ready-made garments and knew the ways of the world. Her husband's whereabouts were unknown, and her only daughter was in a convent. Her friends constantly admonished her for giving up her daughter to Christians, but Lakshmi allowed their talk to go in from one ear and come out of the other. Was it possible to make a decent living by sewing buttonholes? People also knew she went out every night, and that she didn't bring her clients to the *chal* only because she was scared of Lala, the owner. But what did people care? She never ran amok when she was drunk, unlike Entree (whose real name was Edith and who was just Entree now), who openly carried on the business of selling liquor; Lala was well-paid, and the police also received their weekly payoff. The others didn't bother with Entree because she became rowdy and foul-mouthed when drunk, and swore profusely in English — at least that was what the inhabitants of the *chal* thought it was. Pregnant often, she was grateful to Sarlaben for rescuing her each time. Although there were several respectable and decent women in the *chal*, no one dared to scold or criticize Entree; all of them had something to conceal.

"So, will the wedding be here in the *chal*?"

"Of course. We can hitch up a tent in the maidan in front — some of the best weddings in Bombay are held under tents." Shabo expressed her opinion with an air of confidence.

"Oh, it's going to be such fun, our Sarlaben will be a bride!" Ramwai loved weddings. Every year she celebrated a new one for herself, and after a few days had passed, her husband beat her up or stole her things and disappeared. Her last wedding had been quite authentic; tents etc., would have been expensive, so the pandit brought along a *havan* (which looked like a steel brazier) to her room, and she walked around the sacred fire with her groom right there. She adorned herself prettily as a bride, and it wasn't long before the spirit of celebration overtook the entire *chal*. Henna was prepared in large quantities and all the women applied it generously on their palms; tin canisters were used instead of drums to provide accompaniment to the singing of film songs, and when the ceremonies were over, Ramwai hugged all those who came her way and wept noisily: "Ah, my father, my protector, don't let me leave your courtyard," she wailed in imitation of a scene from a film. The paan-wala immediately started up the gramophone and raised the volume: "Why are you being given away to a stranger from a strange land?" Although the women sang with screeching voices, completely out of tune, this damn song cast a pall of gloom on everyone's spirits. A daughter's departure from home is always a disquieting experience, and so it was here, even though Ramwai was not leaving home and her new, cross-eyed husband was going to live with her in her room in the *chal*.

For many days Ramwai went about shyly with her anklets jingling noisily. Then her husband began beating her. Every night he came home drunk and pummelled her until her bones rattled, and in less than a month he was gone, making off with her silver bracelets and nose-ring. Ramwai sulked for a few days, cursing him as she walked around with a limp. But, despite her bitter experiences, the thought of a wedding never failed to excite her'. What did it matter that the wedding was not hers — the occasion would be a happy one nonetheless.

Cautiously the women started teasing Sarlaben.

At the first sign of bashfulness on her part they assailed her with advice.

"You must get married now . . ."

"Yes, this is just the time to enjoy life . . ."

"Your parents' souls will finally be at peace . . ."

"O Ram! We're going to have so much fun!"

"We'll set up a tent at the crossing . . ."

"The bridegroom will arrive on horseback."

"Sarlaben, will you wear a long veil?"

"Why not? Have you ever seen a bride without a long veil?" Ramwai interjected. She was considered an expert in these matters.

"Ahhh . . . the *chal* will be so lonely without you."

"Who is going to deliver Saadat's daughter-in-law's baby?"

(Saadat's daughter-in-law sought Sarlaben's assistance practically every year.)

"What a hullabaloo about nothing!" Sarlaben sounded upset. "Who told you there is going to be a wedding?"

"Well, why does he give you his seat on the bus every morning?" Shabo asked tartly.

"He's just polite, that's all," Sarlaben said, breaking into a soft smile.

"Good gracious! Haven't you noticed the signs? Today he's offering his seat, tomorrow he will offer his heart," Saadat's daughter-in-law declared as she pushed the baby up on her hip. The women twittered in agreement.

All this pleasing talk made Sarlaben dreamy-eyed; overcome by affection for these ignoble, chatty women, she felt her heart swell with gratitude.

"You're not having any problems with breast-feeding this time, are you?" Anxious to change the subject, she became a nurse again.

"Not yet," Saadat's daughter-in-law murmured.

"And Edith, you had better watch out. If you get into trouble this time I'm going to hand you over to the police. Anyway, why don't you get an IUD?"

"It's not my fault. Every time I go there they want my husband's name." Edith exclaimed in exasperation.

"Entree, why don't you give them Sadik Babu's name?" Ramwai suggested.

"But I am Catholic and that son-of-a-bitch is . . ."

"Well, how about Sarmaji then?"

"Be quiet, you witches!" Sarlaben scolded them all, and taking the boy from Saadat's lap she proceeded to give him a teaspoonful of syrup to quieten him. "Get out of here now."

"First you have to tell us when the wedding is going to be," Shabo said stubbornly.

"Yes, we have to pick a date," declared Lakshmi.

"Whose wedding, what date? No one has said anything yet!" Sarlaben shouted angrily.

"No one has said anything? The groom is mute, is he?" The women giggled in unison.

And then everyone explained to a confused and bewildered Sarlaben that it was because of her own laxity and indecisiveness, that she, despite her many qualities, was not married yet. Men, by their very natures, are slow; until they are fed morsels forcibly, they are capable of nothing. The women were all her friends, they were not her enemies, and if she only gave the word, they would sacrifice their lives for her; the bird should not be allowed to escape.

"I can talk to him if you like," Saadat's daughter-in-law said.

"Hey, I'm ready to talk to him! I'll say, 'If you like the girl, come right out and say so.'" But Ramwai's offer met with resistance; no one trusted her. True she had had great practice in ensnaring men, but the woman had acquired a taste for marriage. What if temptation waylaid her? No, no, may God save us all from Ramwai.

"Perhaps men just don't have the nerve to approach her. She dresses so soberly, looks so prim, and those glasses are no help either — the unfortunate creatures are probably afraid to look at her lovingly because they think she'll scold them." Shabo offered her own analysis of the situation.

"Of course, clothes and appearance do make a

difference."

"It's one thing to be dressed like this when you're on duty, but to look like a doctor all the time, well . . ."

"A woman has to wear some make-up. I tell you, a little colour on her face — the gentleman will lose his cool altogether!"

"And pretty clothes, colourful and bright . . ."

"Also some oil and perfume . . ."

"Bangles on her wrists . . ."

"Earrings too — and then we'll see how the gentleman stays mute."

At the time Sarlaben scolded everyone, but later she began to ponder: This is the way of the world; when women dressed in flashy clothes, with heavy make-up, are milling around Bombay, why would anyone want to pay attention to someone drab and colourless? One's mode of dress must suit the occasion, after all.

But all she had were a few simple bordered saris, and perhaps one or two others that were dull-coloured Khatau. And her only jewellery was the flattened chain around her neck which had belonged to her mother and could not really be called jewellery.

In the still of the night her mind came alive with images of brightly coloured clothes and jewellery.

"Maybe he is already married," Shabo said in a worried tone the next morning.

"No, he's not", replied Satu.

"How do you know?"

"On the bus a friend of his asked him if he had found a room yet, and he said, 'Yes, I have.' And then his friend said, 'You should get married now.'"

"And what did he say to that?" Ramwai edged closer.

"He laughed."

"Well, we don't have to worry about that, then. What about his caste? Is it okay?"

"Yes; the name-tag on his bag said, 'Ram Sarup Bhatnagar.' I checked the very first day."

"Then why is she dilly-dallying ?"

"He hasn't said anything yet."

"But he must have said something with his eyes?"

"No, and even if he did, Sarlaben would never notice. If it were Ramwai or Edith, or even Shabo, she'd get the message in a second and in two days the gentleman would be in her clutches."

"Did he sigh?"

"No."

"God! What is he made of, the wretch!" Saadat's daughter-in-law was losing her temper.

After much debate it was decided that Sarlaben should use some foresight. Properly armed, she should place a morsel in this man's mouth — only then would her boat come ashore.

And that was why all the women had brought out their armour and were rushing to Sarlaben's aid. Shabo had once been an extra in films and had accumulated all kinds of things; Saadat's daughter-in-law found some Hazeline Snow which had been lying around for nearly a year; and Edith was in possession of all the smuggled cosmetics imaginable. Not only did she personally know a hairdresser, she could also fashion a stylish, balloon-like, elevated hairdo herself. In addition, she had special sparse items of clothing which were guaranteed to convert an idol.

Now began a concentrated effort to repair Sarlaben. She resisted, but to no avail. Shabo wrapped her in her pink nylon-georgette sari which had been embroidered with sequins. The selection of the right blouse was preceded by much debate; Shabo insisted that the latest fashion dictated that the petticoat and blouse should be red so that one could see flashes of colour from under the sari. And, only red sandals would do. Poor Sarlaben, what did she know of fashion or the secrets of matching colours? She was like a pliant toy in their hands.

First a lot of cream was applied to her face, including Saadat's daughter-in-law's Hazeline Snow which was now dry but had to be used so as not to hurt her feelings. Next came a plastering of rouge and powder, followed by the creation of a huge dome-like hairdo which necessitated the use of large amounts of black cotton yarn. Finally the jewellery. About this time a battle among the women was averted with some difficulty: each wished her contribution to be the greatest.

When Sarlaben arrived at the bus stop wearing high-heeled gold sandals, swaying and tottering, she found stars dancing before eyes that were now bereft of glasses. Her whole body was drenched in sweat.

Is it not enough to be a woman? Why should one need to stuff in so many condiments and chutney in just one morsel? Tears floated in her eyes. And then, a lifetime of punishment to preserve this one little morsel.

Not too long afterwards people saw a dishevelled Sarlaben scurrying back to the *chal*. They were shocked. Trembling and unsteady on her feet, she was walking home alone, without the groom by her side. Her face was heavily streaked with kajal, and she nearly fell as she stumbled towards her room.

The morsel had been spat out!

How did this happen? Why did it happen? Felled by the onslaught of questions, exhausted and numb, Sarlaben fell on her bed.

He did not rise from his seat when she boarded the bus; he continued reading his paper as always and never once did he look in her direction. She stood nearby, swaying as she gripped the strap. Frequently he lifted his face to glance expectantly at the entrance to the bus, as if he were waiting for someone. She aimed her every glance at him but, face averted, he continued to watch the door.

She allowed her scarf, which was drenched in perfume, to slip down, but he did not look up from his paper even once.

She stretched languidly, but failed to see sensuousness floating in his gaze. He glanced stonily at her, and then, ignoring her splendour, bent over his paper once more.

She dropped into a vacant seat before her. All the carefully aimed strikes made with her arrows had missed their mark and the empty quiver now shook and trembled forlornly.

Cautiously, with trepidation, she turned to look at him again. He was getting off the bus. As he alighted, he asked Satu Pickpocket, engaged in his usual business at the bus-stop, "Hey, you scoundrel, where is Sarlaben today? Why didn't she come?"

Satu Pickpocket could only stand there stammering while the stranger, taking large strides, walked off in the direction of a galli and disappeared from view.

*Translated by Tahira Naqvi*

# By the
# Grace of God

"O GOD! You tell me, what should I do?" Sakina asked with tears in her eyes.

"I still believe that Farhat should ask for talaq."

"Talaq! O God no!" She was trembling. "No one in our family has ever asked for talaq. What with Razia still a millstone around my neck ... who will marry her? Where are the suitors for my sweet little daughters?"

"Suitors" need not necessarily mean healthy, handsome young men. It means bulging wallets and well-to-do parents. Something to fall back on.

"We had to beat the bushes to find a boy for the older one. (The 'boy' is no more than 60 or 65, one wife, four daughters, but no son.). Married Farhat for a male issue. But let alone a son, she has not even managed to produce a daughter fox six years! Her dried up tree has seen neither flower nor fruit, nor even the light of day. What all didn't I try? Amulets, charms, chants — nothing worked. Even Khwaja Sahib of Ajmer Sharif has turned a deaf ear to poor Sakina."

"Now don't get into this charm-chant rubbish. Take her to a proper doctor."

"The best of doctors have looked inside her womb. They say there's nothing wrong with the girl. It is the will of God. If she produces, well and good; if not, who's to blame?"

"Problem with Imdad Mian?"

"*Tauba! Tauba!* God forbid that menfolk should start having problems. Damn! People are beginning to hint at a third try! No scarcity of girls. The best of families will offer their daughters to him on a silver platter."

One day I met Farhat at the cinema. Buxom, fair, with laughing eyes — seemed ready for the kill. It was the mother whose juices were sapped, worrying continuously about her daughter's blighted kismat.

Farhat herself was not the least bit concerned. She was barely twenty-two or three. My friendship with this family was of recent vintage. They lived in a beautifully furnished four-room flat. Imdad Mian's first wife had been banished to Khar to live with her father. This flat was especially set up for Farhat, but the property deed had not been transferred in her name. To hell with Imdad Mian! Farhat can get thousands of suitors. I thought of Anwar who was staying with me those days. Gets Rs.550 now, and is destined for better things!

That day, at the movie theatre, Farhat was stealing glances at Anwar. Sakina Behan, too, was bestowing kind looks on him. When I spoke to her, she beamed.

"What can be better? They are made for each other. Sun and moon, they'll dazzle the world!"

"You arrange the talaq, I'll take care of the rest," I promised.

Anwar got a bit of a shock. "I don't want to get into this mess," he protested.

"Silly boy! She's such a nice girl."

"After the divorce . . . .?"

"The old lady's a witch."

"For shame! Such a sweet old lady!"

Anwar was outnumbered and outwitted. Trapped between Sakina and me, he found himself entangled in the Farhat web. We found every excuse to throw them together. Eyes brimming with tears, Sakina Begum never tired of telling me how grateful she was.

From a reluctant dragon, Anwar was transformed into an eager beaver! Farhat was now the focus of his attention. Although married, Farhat had never known love. Anwar gave her life a new dimension. At first he was openly hostile towards Sakina, but before long he started adoring her. And she openly doted on him. Her very breathing seemed somehow connected to him! My presence was no longer required. Even before the formal announcement, Anwar had become a part of their family. He often stayed over till two in the morning. Sometimes Farhat would drop by and, behind closed doors, I could hear them romping around. I had to leave for Poona, but when I returned I learnt that Farhat had spent most of her time at her mother's place. Her visits to her own flat were a rare occurrence. Their romance, undoubtedly, had reached its peak.

"So . . . what are your plans?" I asked Sakina.

First she tried to side-step the issue. Then, "Swamiji from Ahmedabad has given us a special herb . . ."

"To hell with Swamis! Damned fakes! I'm asking about the talaq."

"I hate the word, talaq."

"Then what?"

"By the grace of God it will be all right."

"Don't count on God's grace. You will live to regret this — a young boy and girl meeting like this every day . . ."

"Why? Has Farhat said anything?"

"No. But I have eyes in my head." For a long time I sat down and explained the pros and cons to her. She sat with downcast eyes thinking God alone knows what.

"Swamiji has given seven packets. Every Tuesday, one packet with paan or hot milk."

"For Farhat?"

"No, for Imdad Mian."

"Imdad Mian!" I fumed. "If he were to swallow seven bombshells instead of seven packets, the result would still be zero. Does he visit?"

"Every Tuesday. After a bath and two *rakat* prayers he swallows the stuff with hot milk."

"And then? What the hell are you up to?"

"He is her husband, after all!"

"But Anwar . . . ? Damn Imdad Mian!"

I didn't know how to shake her out of her complacency. Was the idiot blind as well as deaf? I couldn't make myself give her the turn of the screw that she deserved.

"Next Tuesday it will be packet number four."

What was on her mind? "Swamiji says, God willing, packet number five . . . ."

"Sakina, this is no joke. Now smarten up and do something about the talaq. Get her *mehr* out of the old fool."

I had thought that Anwar and Farhat would be able to set up a separate flat and live happily together for the rest of their lives.

"*Mehr*!" She looked at me aghast.

"How much is it?"

"A pittance! Why should I hide anything from you? Of the total 55,000, Sarfaraz Mian borrowed 10,000 for a ticket to England. Now he doesn't talk of returning home. Married a honky and produced a brat."

Farhat's marriage had been arranged through a friend of Sarfaraz's. Although Imdad Mian was quite aged, Sakina did not allow that to come in the way since her son's future was at stake. After all, chances were that Sarfaraz would do well and get them out of a tight spot. As it turned out, despite borrowing another 6,000 for his return fare, Sarfaraz never came back. Every paisa thus advanced was entered by Imdad Mian into the ledger of Farhat's *mehr*.

"So that makes 16,000. What about the rest?"

"Flat at Worli. But that too is in Razia's name. Thought there should be something for her, too. These days all eligible boys have perpetually growling stomachs!"

I felt sorry for Farhat. A sacrificial lamb for her siblings' futures. Striking similarities between Sakina Begum and the *naikas* of the brothels. No wonder she was so petrified of talaq.

"If Imdad Mian remarries we will be ruined. You would be surprised how many *mannats*, *wazifas* and *chillas* I have promised to prevent him from contemplating another marriage. But you know these busy-bodies, always provoking a childless man."

This really got my goat. What a blockhead this woman was. Didn't she understand? What if something happened between the young couple?

"Look, behan, stop worrying. You will make your home with Anwar and Farhat. Razia will be married off, inshallah, even without a flat. You just arrange the talaq."

As usual, the answer I got was evasive. What happened next was exactly what I had predicted. One day Anwar looked more disoriented than usual. Farhat was equally distraught. I asked, "Have you two fought?" They looked at me, startled.

At night there was a commotion behind closed doors in Anwar's room. I could hear Farhat sobbing. I knocked.

"Come in." He took me by the hand. "Now try to reason with this fool."

"What . . . .?"

"Aunty!" She fell at my feet.

"She was climbing over the window sill . . ." Anwar was trembling from head to toe.

"Have you taken leave of your senses?" I lifted her tear-stained face. "Stop crying. Everything will work out after the talaq . . . ."

"Never! She'll never agree. I could die," she howled.

"You would rather die than stand up for your rights?"

"Can't see her in that state. Yesterday she almost had a stroke. Clenched jaw, cold sweat. All I said was that she should stop him from this business of Tuesday visits. Ugh! I don't even want to look at him — repulsive animal!" She dissolved into more tears.

"Did you say this to your mother?"

"No!"

"When she finds out she will definitely see reason. I will talk to her tomorrow morning. And, within eight days, talaq . . ." My consoling seemed to work. She started to smile through her tears. She looked beautiful. Anwar's blue eyes rained love all over her radiant face.

I returned to my room and tried to sleep. Tossing and turning, I thought that if Imdad Mian found out he would raise hell; and Anwar in the military! The wretch would be court-martialled. Imdad's first wife was already on the warpath and would tear strips off Sakina Begum and Farhat.

With great kindness I spoke to Sakina about Farhat's condition. I swore to her that Anwar would never betray her daughter. Sakina seemed to have gone into a trance. Her reactions were dazed. Then it seemed as if she had been shot through with a machine gun. She started laughing madly, then wept like a baby. Trembling like a leaf, she fell in a heap. Razia was in college. Farhat sat terrified in her room. Sakina neither cursed anyone nor spat in my face for having been the cause of her daughter's betrayal.

"*Now*. Come at once to the lawyer's. I will immediately despatch Farhat to my sister in Bombay. Every type of pressure will be applied to make Imdad pay. Just stop this hysteria."

Completely broken, she sat down with her head bowed. "Lawyer . . . lawyer," she repeated incoherently. "Now, at this time . . . .Go home now, I'll phone you later. May God give you every joy in this world." Closed her eyes.

All day I waited anxiously for the phone to ring. What if the mother and daughter committed a double suicide? I would be stuck with the guilt of it for the rest of my life. How was I to know that things would take this drastic turn?

Anwar was in a frenzy. It is normally believed that men are fickle. After getting women into trouble, they usually take off. But Anwar was on the verge of a breakdown. By the evening I had had enough. The phone rang and rang. Where was everyone? In desperation I sent Anwar. When I saw his face I almost died.

"What's happened?"

"No one was home. I knocked. Lock on the door. The Gurkha said they've gone."

"Gone where?"

"Didn't know."

All night I felt I was being raked over the coals. Anwar dialled every corner of the country but the only answers he got were: "Gone somewhere, no one knows where. Maybe Versova." Anwar dashed to Versova. I tried to stop him but he was like a demon. A servant informed him, "Maybe Khar, maybe Churchgate, possibly Peddar Road." No trace of them in any of these places. A few days later we heard that they had gone overseas. Called the office. The wretch had three or four offices. No one could help us.

On the sixth day we got a soggy, dirty envelope. "Help me, for God's sake. I am under continuous surveillance. Can't breathe. O, God."

It was as if a bombshell had exploded in our faces. With great difficulty we read the seal: Begumpeth. So she was in Hyderabad.

Save her? How the hell? Anwar dashed to Hyderabad but, after knocking around, returned empty-handed.

Acutely depressed, I tried to pull myself together. When I think back, I choke at the memory of those oppressive days. What an uphill task it was to bring Anwar round. I felt like an accomplice in this crime. My hands were stained with the blood of innocents!

That year Anwar was transferred to Delhi, thank God. Several years went by. A beautiful wife and a clutch of kids helped him get over this unfortunate incident. I was stepping out of Marks and Spencers when I almost collided into her. For a few seconds we gaped at each other.

"You!" Wrapped in a sable fur she threw herself into my arms. "It's been such a long time."

"Sakina!" I was barely able to croak.

"Staying a Sarfaraz's. He never returned. So I thought, what the hell! I better swallow my pride. In any case it's a good excuse for travelling. What a beautiful place these *feringhis* have built for themselves!" And she rambled on about her travels in France, Italy and Switzerland.

She was utterly changed. This youthful looking woman with pleasantly distributed flesh around her formerly emaciated body, seemed to have stepped out of a beauty parlour. The barren heath had become a resplendant garden.

"Farhat — how is she?" I asked, almost dreading the answer.

"Both husband and wife are very well, by the grace of God. Nadir Mian, *mashallah*, goes to school. Nadir is such a beautiful child. Ditto his father."

"Father?" By now I was thoroughly confused.

"The same fair complexion . . . the same blue eyes."

"Imdad Mian's blue eyes!"

"Now don't *you* start pretending." Laughing shamelessly, she started piling up her shopping cart.

"Those seven packets?" I was groping my way down memory lane.

"I swear, you don't forget a single detail. Swami,

the old goat, took four thousand rupees!"

"For the packets or the knack?"

"The wretch did mutter some such gibberish."

"Was offering his services, no doubt."

"And asked for another 10,000! But he was sickening."

"Was Imdad Mian suspicious?"

"Suspicious! If all men started becoming suspicious about their children . . . ! If he had any brains he would never have blamed my innocent child, but taken a close look at his own shrivelled self. Oh, let's forget all this, it makes me sick."

"Anwar was inconsolable. And you people . . . you never showed your faces again."

"Don't give me that tragic line! When they litter the streets with their bastard offspring, don't their hearts break with remorse? May he live long and produce a dozen brats." Started on a string of blessings for Anwar.

I took one long look at her expensive furs and China-silk scarf. Then I visualized the sprawling mansion at Nazimabad, glanced at the packets of currency notes at the bottom of her handbag. Started feeling a wave of nausea coming over me. Why had I felt so guilty? My sympathies had played a major role in Farhat's motherhood. And how stupid Anwar was! Living with guilt all these years. What his innocent mind regarded as the greatest sin, turned out to be the greatest blessing, by the grace of God.

*Translated by Syeda Hameed*

# Poison

WHAT a strange death it was! People who had attended her lecture and had tea with her the previous evening simply couldn't believe that Mrs. Nu'maan was dead. Because of her chronic insomnia she had to rely heavily on sleeping pills — surely there could be no suspicion that she had mistaken that little bottle for something else?

As usual, she returned home at midnight. Mr. Nu'maan's door was closed. He was used to going to bed at 10 p.m. When the Ayah asked if she wanted dinner, she refused, but accepted a glass of milk. That glass however, remained untouched. Late to bed and late to rise was Mrs. Nu'maan's usual routine. Her husband faithfully went off to the office at his normal time. When, at 11 a.m., she had still not asked for her tea, the Ayah got worried. No sooner did she touch her feet to wake her up, than she screamed as if she had touched a naked wire. The doctor's report stated that the death had occurred between 2 and 3 a.m., a clear case of an overdose of sleeping pills.

Mrs. Nu'maan's death created pandemonium in the entire city. She had quite a following, a large circle of friends and acquaintances, plus the labouring classes whom she visited as part of her social work routine. A great believer in education for women, a torchbearer of women's rights, her sudden and untimely death led to the closure of many schools. For months afterwards, condolence meetings were held all over the city.

The gods had been overly generous to Mrs. Nu'maan. The only daughter of a wealthy father, she was beautiful and educated. As soon as she graduated from Rohini College, her admirers started lining up at her doorstep. Ever since she was a little girl, Mrs. Nu'maan had been extremely bright. A superb tennis player and an ace rider, she had also won innumerable swimming trophies. Her skill in handling the sitar reminded people of Vilayat Khan. Her excellent repartee and wit made people adore her wherever she went. It was as if she had ensnared their innocent hearts in her magical fingers.

When the Muslim League came into prominence she detached herself from the Congress Party and became a rostrum-thumping supporter of the League. Her days and nights were dedicated to the movement. People were moved to tears by her commitment. Prominent among the women who protested against purdah, Mrs. Nu'maan was one of the first to cast aside the veil and stride into the political arena.

The best thing that could happen to any town was Mr. Nu'maan's posting there as Deputy Commissioner. The moment she stepped into her husband's territory, Mrs. Nu'maan took charge of its various clubs and committees. Heart and soul, she dedicated herself to reforming local conditions. You could safely call her Mr. Nu'maan's right hand. A born hostess, she was at her best while arranging social events. Mr. Nu'maan was meek and mild-mannered; had his better half not been excessively capable, he would never have progressed so rapidly on the social and career ladder. Mr. Nu'maan's plush job was a fringe benefit of his marriage, a gift from his influential father-in-law; were it not for this, he may never have left his childhood fiancee, Ayesha Begum. When Mr. Nu'maan got married Ayesha Begum resolved to stay single. A school-teacher by profession, she moved into the school quarters after her parents passed away. There she started leading the life of a reclusive spinster.

In matters pertaining to the heart, Mrs. Nu'maan was extraordinarily lucky. Within her circle of friends, there existed an inner core of admirers. During her college days she was considered a ravishing beauty. A few young students, smitten by her, had gone to the extent of committing suicide. Inspired by her beauty, progressive writers of the day had written sublime poetry and prose. Several short stories owed their success to the liveliness of Mrs. Nu'maan's personality sparkling through the narrative. An anthology of anonymous love letters addressed to her had become an instant bestseller. Some envious wags had spread the rumour that the letters had been written by none other than Mrs. Nu'maan herself. Still no one could deny that the letters were literary gems. It therefore followed that in addition to all her other talents, Mrs. Nu'maan was a first-rate letter-writer as well!

Mrs. Nu'maan was a staunch believer in birth control. She often said that it was these innumerable children who were responsible for the deplorable condition of our country. They were born of poverty and poverty is born because of them. Only illiterate peasant women have a limitless capacity for littering babies all over the place.

I recall my mother, who was always a little scared

of Mrs. Nu'maan, seeing that she had nine other children in addition to me. The ten of us, robust little urchins, were living proof of Ammi's boorishness. Poor Mrs. Nu'maan used to have a fit whenever she saw the dirt plastered on our knees and the sores on our feet. Our noisy games made her head ache, and our greedy gestures at mealtimes made her throw up. She had a habit of taking us by surprise. And while we stood around her with our mouths open, Ammi felt like drowning herself and all of us in the nearest pond. Some foul mouths had floated the rumour that Mrs. Nu'maan was barren.

Her visits always led to the commencement of a massive hygiene programme that lasted for several days. Ammi became obsessed with cleaning her whole brood. Our snot-filled noses were threatened with a pair of iron tongs; shoes, like the curse of hell, were strapped around our chubby feet. My mother's innate slovenliness, however, came to our rescue, and before long, we were allowed to romp around the backyard like wild animals again.

Mrs. Nu'maan gave Ammi innumerable recipes to keep her womb from succumbing to the onslaughts of pregnancy. But thanks to Abba's sabotage, Mrs. Nu'maan's prescriptions never worked. He was a strange man, our father. If he had had his way he would have ordered us in pairs! It was thanks to him that we had the pleasure of growing up like free-wheeling cave-children!

Great people often have a great number of enemies. Mrs. Nu'maan's popularity led to many raised eyebrows and unkind comments, but no one dared to speak a single word to her face.

"Did you hear the small-minded comments of

these people?" she said, laughing, to Ammi. "You know Nu'maan Sahib. Can you believe such disgusting behaviour being attributed to him?"

"Senseless gossip!" agreed Ammi readily. "He is crazy about you, and why not? Is there a single quality you lack? If there were more ladies like you, I swear our country would not remain as backward as it is today." Ammi repeated a few well-rehearsed lines.

"No, my dear, not me. I am a rough stone, not worth anything at all." This generous display of self-effacement was most touching.

"You're much too modest," protested my mother. "The city has taken on a new personality since you came on the scene. Take the growing literacy among the common people as an example . . ." Ammi borrowed sentence after sentence from the local newspaper. "Women's education was in the garbage bin before you arrived." Ammi made desperate attempts to divert her attention so that she would not catch a glimpse of the ten of us running wildly behind the chickens. She mentally cursed and despatched us to hell for causing her severe embarrassment. She knew that if Mrs. Nu'maan's gaze came to rest on us, she would abandon all other reforms and concentrate on the uplift of our snot-filled noses.

"Honestly, sometimes I tire of the love he showers on me! Can you believe that if I am not at the dinner table he goes to bed hungry?" My mother knew this wasn't true, but she wouldn't dream of contradicting Mrs. Nu'maan. Quite inadvertently she said, "Perhaps he eats elsewhere." (She could have swallowed her words or bitten her tongue, but it was too late.) "People spin such stories, you know," she said in a desperate bid to cover up her faux pas.

"Oh, they love splattering dirt on snowhite linen! This is precisely why we are backward and illiterate. Mr. Nu'maan's spotless reputation is an undeniable fact. And on top of that, can anyone hide anything from one's own wife? If something were brewing, would I not know?" Looking quickly at my mother she added, "You are an innocent, my dear," (meaning you are a blockhead, a simpleton and a fool). "But as for me . . . Mr. Nu'maan can't hide anything from me!"

"How can anyone hide anything from you?" said Ammi hastily.

"And who is the subject of their insinuations? Ayesha Begum! Have you seen Ayesha Begum?"

"A shrivelled sourpuss, may God forgive me."

"Oh no, please, she's human too. Who am I to talk? Who can be plainer than me? But Ayesha . . . she looks like . . . like . . ."

"The soul of tragedy."

"Precisely! A cursed barrenness."

"Without a man's love a woman's face becomes the index of her damned desolation."

"Lifelong spinsterhood devastates the countenance."

For a long time Ammi and Mrs. Nu'maan would sit and talk, using medical and social arguments to prove that Ayesha Begum was destined to look like a dried up bean for the rest of her life. *Tauba, tauba*, they kept repeating, while Mrs. Nu'maan's florid prose reached its peak.

Even Ammi became eloquent: "Time hasn't been kind to Ayesha Begum. But to tell you the truth, even at her best, she couldn't have touched the hem of your skirt. Otherwise why would Nu'maan Sahib have left his childhood fiancee and become enamoured of you?

Although some people say that Nu'maan left her because, more than anything else, he wanted the position of Deputy Collector." Ammi could say the oddest, almost cruellest, things with complete ingenuity.

"Bloody lies!" said Mrs. Nu'maan angrily. "Nu'maan would never have taken such a big obligation. All these rumours have been started by her relatives. After all, it isn't easy to bring up half a dozen brothers and sisters. Ayesha was one of them, naturally the family was disappointed. Let's face it, if a woman cannot defend her basic rights, who else can protect her? If she were all that attractive why would Mr. Nu'maan have rejected her?"

"Her looks are what God gave her, poor thing," sighed my mother.

"Of course they are, but what about brains? Nature's deficiencies can be corrected if only one tries. With a little care, the most homely face can look attractive. Poor Ayesha Bi! She cannot conduct even an ordinary conversation. Tell me, is there any liveliness at all in her? The slightest trace of animation?"

"Good heavens, no! I dread her company. She seems to have taken a vow of silence."

"In Europe there are schools that train women to become attractive to their men. And our women ... no wonder we're so backward." Mrs. Nu'maan was off on her hobby horse again.

One day when she had soundly lectured Ammi on women's rights, my mother asked Abba, "Why do you flirt with English women?"

"Come along with me one day. You too can flirt with their men!" said Abba mischievously.

"God help me!" exclaimed Ammi, but from that day on she didn't dare assert her conjugal rights!

Mrs. Nu'maan was given to teasing her husband. "You have ruined her life, poor thing." But he usually laughed off such remarks.

"She must curse me with every sip of water she drinks." Mr. Nu'maan began to look embarrassed.

"Tell me, did you dislike Ayesha Begum from your very childhood?"

"Something like that." He tried to evade the issue.

"Then did your family force the engagement?"

"A helpless man can be forced into doing anything," he sighed, playing with Mrs. Nu'maan's hair.

"Men are such frauds!" said she reeling with the intoxication of Mr. Nu'maan's love. Nu'maan puffed nervously at his cigar and turned away.

Mrs. Nu'maan's heart was a boundless ocean which overflowed with sympathy for the plight of humanity. She felt a surge of pity for Ayesha Begum. Had she been married to the Deputy Collector, a grand life would have been hers! Parties, at-homes . . . alas! She shuddered at the thought of Ayesha's mismanagement of it all! More likely, the house would have been full of squealing brats. At least Mrs. Nu'maan had kept her environment free from this epidemic. One of her favourite sayings was that a woman who refrains from producing kids renders a great service to her country. There was just one fallacy with this line of thinking. Had Mr. Nu'maan married Ayesha Begum, he would have remained a school-teacher all his life.

During school inspections Mrs. Nu'maan sometimes ran into Ayesha Begum. Naturally, Ayesha Begum was jealous, although, she reasoned, it was no one's fault, not hers nor Mr. Nu'maan's. How could he have turned from the shimmering moon to a piece of dried tamarind?

People said that after presiding over the school function Mrs. Nu'maan walked across the compound towards Ayesha Begum's quarters.

"Won't you give us a cup of tea?" she said with her usual grace. Ayesha invited everyone, and served tea with her own hands. As usual, Mrs. Nu'maan began to tease her.

"Sorry, I snatched your fiance, but you can hardly blame me."

Ayesha smiled with embarrassment. "Begum, why should it be your fault?"

"How angry you must have been with me!" Mrs. Nu'maan laughed even louder.

Ayesha Begum turned pale but spoke with the utmost dignity.

"Nothing to be angry about, Begum. These are the vagaries of kismat."

"Kismat! Stuff and nonsense! These outdated notions make life a living hell for our women. Man gets up and goes, leaving the woman in an abject state of despair. And the woman, her lips sealed, spends all her life in jahannam." Mrs. Nu'maan's lecture had begun. That day Ayesha Begum was in a surprisingly bad mood. She seemed to have lost her cool. Trembling, she spoke in a clipped voice. "Snatching is a fine concept, Begum. Is a human being no more than a clay toy that anyone can grab? Physically, you can smash and grab, Begum, but who can seize the heart?"

"You are almost a philosopher, Ayesha Begum. But your concept of empty love . . ."

"Love is never empty, Begum. It is life's greatest bargain." Ayesha Begum was beginning to lose control. "Oh, Begum, you poor simpleton."

Mrs. Nu'maan and her coterie went into peals of

laughter. Mrs. Nu'maan a simpleton! What an absurd idea!

"Irfan," Ayesha Begum called out to someone on the other side of the screen. "Son, come here."

A sixteen or seventeen year old boy appeared from the other side, racket in hand. "Come, son, say *adab* to your aunt."

The cup fell from Mrs. Nu'maan's hand. Standing before her was Mr. Nu'maan, as he must have been twenty years earlier. Ayesha Begum, affectionately stroking his thick mane of hair, was heard saying, "This is the only memory I have of my late sister. Greet your aunt, my boy."

People still whisper that Ayesha Begum must have administered poison in Mrs. Nu'maan's tea.

*Translated by Syeda Hameed*

# A Pair of Hands

RAM AUTAR was returning from the war. The old sweepress came to Abba Mian with a letter. Ram Autar had been granted leave — the war was over, was it not? That was why he was finally coming home after three years. Tears glimmered in the old woman's eyes as she ran from person to person, bending to touch everyone's feet in sheer gratitude, as if these were the very people responsible for her only son's safe return from the battlefield.

She could not have been more than fifty, but looked at least seventy years old. Of ten or twelve pregnancies, some full-term, others not, only one had resulted in the birth of a child who survived, and that too after many prayers and offerings. Nearly a year after his wedding, Ram Autar was summoned to the front. The sweepress wailed and lamented, but to no avail. And when Ram Autar donned his military uniform and came to touch her feet, she was vastly impressed, as if he had been promoted to the rank of colonel.

There was sniggering among members of the servant class. All of them eagerly awaited the drama they expected would unfold at Ram Autar's return. Although he had not gone to the front to fight, nevertheless, the three years he spent in the company of soldiers cleaning their excrement must have imbued him with a certain degree of soldierly pride and dignity. Surely he would not be the same Ram Autar now that he wore a military uniform; there could be no doubt that when he heard of Gori's misdeeds, his young blood would boil with the fury of insult.

How meek she had been when she first came here after her wedding, and as long as Ram Autar was around, her veil hung low and no one saw even a glimpse of her glorious face. And how she cried when her husband left, as if the sindhur were about to be permanently removed from her hair. For a few days afterwards she quietly minded her business, the basket of refuse set on her hip, her head cast down, her eyes reddened. Then, gradually, the length of her veil began to diminish.

Some people blamed it all on the season of basant. Others bluntly asserted that Gori was a woman of loose morals to begin with and as soon as Ram Autar disappeared from the scene, she immediately reverted to type and began to exhibit bold and bawdy behaviour. The fool, she giggled constantly, provocatively swung her hips, and whenever she walked by with the basket of refuse on her hip, her brass anklets jangling noisily, men lost their cool. The cake of soap slipped from the hands of the washerman and fell into the fountain, the cook's gaze wandered away from the roti which soon burned on the pan, the water-carrier's bucket descended deeper and deeper into the well, and the turbans of the watchmen came loose and fell about their necks. When this disastrous vision of delight had retreated from view, the entire servant class stood transfixed, as if drained of life. Then, startled, they would begin to taunt each other. In anger the washerman's wife threw down the pot of starch, the watchman's wife, for no apparent reason, began scolding her infant son who had quietly clung to her breast all this time, and the cook's third wife swooned in a fit of hysteria.

Gori was her name, the feckless one, and she was dark, dark like a glistening pan on which a roti had been fried but which a careless cook had neglected to clean. She had a bulbous nose, a wide jaw, and it seemed she came from a family in which brushing one's teeth was a habit long forgotten. The squint in her left eye was noticeable despite the fact that her eyes were always heavily kohled; it was difficult to imagine how, with a squinted eye, she was able to throw darts that never failed to hit their mark. Her waist was not slim; it had thickened, rapidly increasing in diameter from all those handouts she consumed. There was also nothing delicate about her feet which reminded one of a cow's hoofs, and she left a coarse smell of mustard oil in her wake. Her voice, however, was sweet. When she sang folk songs at the festival of Teej, her lyrical voice rose and fell mellifluously above all others'.

The old sweepress, Gori's mother-in-law, became distrustul of her as soon as her son left. To be on the safe side, she verbally abused her every now and then, often for no good reason. Sometimes the old woman followed Gori just to keep an eye on her, but she was getting on in years and her back was bent to one side from forty years of lugging baskets of refuse. She had been our sweepress for a long time and had been present to tie off our umbilical cords. As soon as Amma went into labour, the sweepress stationed herself in the doorway, often giving the lady doctor valuable advice, and occasionally she would tie an amulet to our mother's bedpost to ward off evil spirits. She held a position of considerable respect in our household.

And it was this very sweepress' daughter-in-law who had, quite suddenly, become a thorn in everyone's side. The behaviour of the cook's wife or that of the watchman's wife was understandable, but lamentably, our own proper sisters-in-law had also begun to view Gori's swaying hips with displeasure. If Gori happened to be sweeping the floor in the bedroom while one of our brothers was present, our sister-in-law would immediately snatch her breast from the baby in her lap, and run to the room in alarm in order to prevent Gori from casting a spell on our brother.

What was Gori but a loose-limbed, long-horned animal? People clung to their fragile china if she chanced to be coming their way. When things got completely out of hand, a delegation consisting of the female members of the servant class approached Amma. The danger and its possible repercussions were hotly debated and discussed; a committee for the preservation of husbands was formed, our sisters-in-law voted in its favour, and the honour of being the leader of the committee fell to Amma. The women occupied places according to their status, some squatting on the floor, some sitting on stools, while others settled on charpais. Paan was distributed among them and the old woman was summoned. Infants were calmly given their mother's breasts to maintain quiet in the assembly, and the proceedings began.

"You witch! Why have you given your daughter-in-law absolute freedom to disrupt our lives? What are you thinking of? Are you getting ready to have your face blackened?"

Already quite upset, the sweepress became tearful and exclaimed, "What can I do, Begum saheb? I have beaten her, the good-for- nothing wretch, and starved her, but she is out of control."

"My, why should she want for food?" the cook's wife cried out sarcastically She was from Saharanpur and belonged to a family of cooks of long standing, and to top that, she was the third wife. What airs she put on! Following this, the watchman's wife, the gardener's woman, and the wife of the washerman further qualified the case against Gori. The poor sweepress simply sat on the floor scratching her dirty ankles as she meekly listened to the women's complaints.

"Begum saheb," she finally pleaded, "I'm ready to do whatever you ask — but what can I do? Shall I wring her neck?"

The thought of wringing Gori's neck proved to be a happy one and, pleased, the women immediately expressed sympathy for the old woman.

"Why don't you send her back to her parents?" Amma suggested.

"Oh no, Begum saheb, that is impossible." The old sweepress proceeded to explain that the daughter-in-law had cost money. An entire lifetime's savings, all of two hundred rupees, had been used to obtain this strumpet. With the same money two cows could have been bought instead, and easily there would have been a bucketful of milk every day. But this strumpet knew only how to kick. If she were sent back to her parents, her father would sell her right away to another sweeper. A daughter-in-law not only warms a son's bed, she also does the work of four people. In Ram Autar's absence the old woman could not have managed by herself; in her old age she was being tended by her daughter-in-law's two hands.

The women were not fools. The matter had shifted from a question of morals to a question of economics. There was no doubt in anyone's mind that the daughter-in-law's presence was essential to the old woman's existence; who can throw away two hundred rupees? Besides, what of the money spent on clothes for the wedding, and the amount borrowed from the merchant? Guests were entertained, other family members had been put up during the wedding — how were all these expenses to be met with all over again? Ram Autar's entire salary went into repaying old debts. A well-built, stalwart daughter-in-law like this one could not be had for less than four hundred now. After cleaning one bungalow she was able to tackle four other houses; at least the strumpet was hard-working.

Nevertheless, Amma delivered her ultimatum: "If something is not done about the slattern very soon, she will not be allowed to set foot in this house."

The old woman protested noisily, then went home and, dragging the daughter-in-law by the hair, beat her soundly. The daughter-in-law had been bought. She quietly submitted to the old woman's anger without a single word of reproach. But the next day, as an act of revenge, she openly aired the servants' dirty linen. Exasperated, the cook, the water-carrier, washerman and watchman, all came home and beat their wives. That was not all; my civilized brothers and their repectable wives also began having disagreements, and soon telegrams from my respectable sisters-in- law were dispatched to their parents. In short, Gori was like a spike in a wire chain for this once happy family.

But not too long afterwards, the old sweeper's brother-in-law's son, Ram Rati, came to visit his aunt and stayed on. There was additional work in one or two houses which he took charge of. Back in his village there was nothing for him to do, and his bride, who was a minor, still lived with her parents.

Following Ram Rati's arrival in the village, a sudden change came about. It was as though thick clouds had suddenly been dissipated by gusty winds. The daughter-in-law's laughter became muffled, her copper bracelets were silent, like a deflated balloon slowly coming down to earth, her veil gradually dropped lower, and instead of acting like an unruly bull, she started behaving like a shy, retiring bride. All the women heaved sighs of relief. Now when one of the men teased her, she cast a sidelong glance at Ram Rati with her squinted eye, and coming forward quickly, scratching his arm, he stationed himself before her. The old crone quietly sat on her doorstep, gurgled her tobacco pipe and through half-shut eyes, watched this comedy unfold. A soothing calm settled all around, as though an abscess had been completely drained of purulence.

However, a new front now came into existence, comprised this time of the male members of the servant class. The same cook who used to fry parathas for the daughter-in-law now repeatedly scolded her for not cleaning the pots carefully; the washerman complained that whenever he starched laundry and hung it out to dry, the strumpet came along and swept up dust; the watchman made her sweep the men's sitting room ten times over and still complained that she had done a sloppy job; and the water-carrier, who in the past had always readily given her water to wash her hands with, now avoided sprinkling the courtyard before she swept it, so that the dust rose in the air and descended on the clothes the washerman had hung on the line, thus giving him reason to reprimand her.

But the daughter-in-law mutely submitted to all the abuse and ignored whatever was being said. No one knows what she told her mother-in-law afterwards, but the old woman came out screaming angrily at people; as far as she was concerned, her daughter-in-law was now pure and chaste and beyond all blame.

And then, one day, Daroghaji, who was the head of all the servants and was regarded as Abbaji's special messenger, appeared before Abbaji and embarked on a long tirade about the gross and abhorrent vileness resulting from the illicit relationship between Ram Rati and the daughter-in-law, which threatened to infiltrate and contaminate the entire fabric of the servant class. Abba referred the matter to the sessions court, namely Amma. Once again, the women congregated and the old woman was summoned.

"Listen, you foolish woman, do you know what your daughter-in-law is up to?"

The old woman stared at them dumbfounded, as if she didn't know what they were talking about. When she was told that her daughter-in-law and Ram Rati were guilty of improper behaviour and had been caught, several times, in compromising situations, she didn't thank the women, who had only her best interests at heart. Instead she started to rant and rave, violently protesting that if Ram Autar had been here he would have been greatly disturbed by the unjust accusations levelled at his innocent wife. The daughter-in-law mourns the absence of her husband, works hard so that no one need complain, and does not indulge in any kind of unseemly behaviour; people have become her enemies for nothing. Everyone tried to explain the matter to her, but the old sweepress beat her breast in a frenzy and lamented that the whole world was out to destroy her daughter-in-law. After all, what had they done, the two of them? She herself had nothing to do with anyone's business, she was everyone's confidante, never had she betrayed a secret; what reason could she have for interfering in someone else's affairs? What was there that didn't take place in the outer courtyards of the houses she cleaned? No one's dirt was hidden from the sweepress; her old hands had buried the crimes of many a respectable person. If she wanted to, she could overthrow the thrones of many a queen with these very hands. But she bore no ill will towards anyone. It would be a mistake to threaten her with a knife at her throat. But she was not about to let any secrets slip out of her heart.

The old woman's outspoken remarks caused the hands on the knife to slacken; the women rallied to her viewpoint. Regardless of what the daughter-in-law had done, at least their own castles were secure. So why complain? For some time after this episode, talk about the daughter-in-law's misconduct waned and people ceased to make a fuss about what was going on. However, the discerning guessed that something was terribly amiss. The daughter-in-law's heavy body could no longer conceal her secret and, once again, people made an effort to explain the situation to the old woman. But talk of this new subject seemed to fall on deaf ears; she pretended she couldn't hear properly and ignored what the people were saying. These days she spent most of her time reclining on her sleeping mat from where she issued orders to her daughter-in- law and Ram Rati. Sometimes, coughing and sneezing, she came out of the house and sat in the sun while the two waited on her as if she were a queen.

The respectable wives did their best to make her see the truth. Throw out Ram Rati and find a cure for the daughter-in-law before Ram Autar returns. She was an expert herself, in two days she could have the mess cleaned up. But the old woman was impervious to all talk about the girl. She complained of this and that instead; her knees hurt more than they had ever done before, the inmates of the big houses were eating too much of something they could not properly digest because everyone had diarrhoea all the time, etc. This very obvious attempt by her to turn a deaf ear to the good advice being showered on her angered her well-wishers. It was true the daughter-in-law was a woman, simple-minded and foolish — the best of women in the most respectable of families make mistakes. But mothers-in-law from such families do not assume attitudes of total negligence. Why had this old woman become so senile? The monster she could easily bury under the pile of excrement from one of the houses she cleaned was being allowed to grow unhindered, while she pretended to shut her eyes to it, refusing to accept its existence.

Ram Autar's return was anxiously awaited. The old woman continually threatened: "Wait until Ram Autar comes back, he'll break your bones ..." And Ram Autar was coming home, returning from the war alive. People waited for a dreadful catastrophe.

But they were disappointed when the daughter-in-law gave birth to a son. Instead of poisoning it, the old woman beamed with joy and displayed no surprise at the fact that her daughter-in-law had borne a child two years after Ram Autar's departure from the village. Going from house to house, she collected old baby clothes and money, and when her well-wishers tried to explain, with the aid of calculations, that under no circumstances could the child be Ram Autar's, she showed no signs of enlightenment. It was the first of *sarh* when Ram Autar went away, the same day she slipped and fell in the new English-style toilet of the yellow house. And now it was *chait*, and during the month of *jeth* she had suffered heatstroke and narrowly escaped death. That was also when the ache in her knees got worse. "The village medic is a bastard, he mixes chalk with his medicines." Then, assuming an idiotic expression she shifted from the main question and continued to babble foolishly. Was there anyone who had enough of a brain to force this old woman to see sense, to make her accept what she had decided not to?

After the birth of the boy she wrote to Ram Autar: "Ram Autar — after love and kisses, may it be known to you that all is well here and we pray to Bhagwan for the best for you — and a son has been born to you. So consider this letter a telegram and come home soon."

People were certain that Ram Autar would burn with rage. But their gratification turned out to be premature because a letter from Ram Autar arrived in which he expressed great joy and happiness at the birth of his son. He also mentioned he would be bringing socks and undershirts for the child. The war was over, he wrote, and he would be home soon. The old woman sat majestically on her mat all day long with the baby propped up on her knees. What better way to spend old age? All the work was being taken care of, the merchant's interest was being paid regularly, and her grandson played on her knees.

Well, people conjectured, when Ram Autar returns, then we'll see what happens. And Ram Autar was coming back from a war which had been won. He was a soldier, after all, would his blood not boil? Everyone waited with bated breath; the servant class, which had sobered somewhat due to Gori's betrayal, now felt invigorated at the prospect of a murder or two that would be committed as honour was avenged.

The boy was nearly a year old when Ram Autar finally came to the village. There was jubilation among the servant class. The cook poured extra water in the pot so the food could simmer at leisure while he was out enjoying the long-awaited spectacle; the washerman removed his pot of starch from the fire and placed it on a ledge in the wall, and the water-carrier set the water bucket against the well.

As soon as Ram Autar appeared, the old woman ran to him, clasped her arms around him and began to wail. But in the very next instant she deposited the boy, who was all smiles, into Ram Autar's arms and beamed, her tears forgotten. Ram Autar looked about him sheepishly as if the boy were indeed his. Then, going to his suitcase, he rummaged hurriedly through his things. People were sure he was looking for a dagger. But when he took out some red undershirts and yellow socks from the suitcase, the collective male ego of the village suffered a deadly blow. What a fool! The bastard thinks he's a soldier! What a eunuch! And the daughter-in-law? Her head-covering drawn about her closely like a new bride's, she came forward meekly with a brass container filled with water, sat down at Ram Autar's feet, took off his smelly boots, washed his feet, and then sipped a few drops of the water.

People did their best to explain the situation to Ram Autar. They taunted him and called him a fool, but he only laughed as if understanding nothing. As for Ram Rati, it was time for him to bring his bride home, so he left. Ram Autar's actions provoked anger rather than surprise. Our father, who generally didn't take much interest in matters concerning the servant class, was also compelled to take note; he too was perplexed and decided to reason with Ram Autar.

"Look here, man, haven't you come back after three years?"

"I am not sure, sir . . . perhaps that is how long it has been."

"And the boy is a year old?"

"He seems to be a year old, sir . . . .he is so naughty, the little devil." Ram Autar was blushing.

"Calculate, you fool!"

"Calculate, sir?" Ram Autar murmured in a sickly tone.

"You damn fool, how did that happen?"

"I do not know, sir . . . it is Bhagwan's gift."

"Bhagwan's gift, you fool? This child cannot be yours."

Abba finally succeeded in overwhelming him with arguments which proved that the child was a bastard, and Ram Autar showed some signs of comprehending the truth. Then, in a stifled voice, speaking like a man half-crazed, he protested, "I gave the strumpet a good beating."

"You're a damn fool! Why don't you throw the strumpet out?"

"No, sir, I cannot do that," Ram Autar stammered fearfully.

"Why not, you idiot?"

"Sir, where will I get three hundred to spend on the family during the wedding?"

"Why should you spend a penny on them? Why should you have to suffer the consequences of your wife's misconduct?"

"I do not know, sir . . . .that is the custom in my family."

"But the boy is not yours, Ram Autar — it's that bastard Ram Rati's." Abba exclaimed in exasperation.

"So what is the difference, sir? Ram Rati is my brother, sir, his blood is the same as mine."

"You're a stupid fool!" Abba was losing patience.

"Sir, when the child grows up he will help out," Ram Autar tried to explain in a pleading tone. "He will contribute his two hands, sir, and he will be my support in my old age." Ram Autar lowered his head with these words.

And who knows why, Abba's head, like Ram Autar's, was also lowered, as if thousands of hands were bearing down on it . . . .these hands were neither legitimate nor illegitimate; they were only hands, living hands that wash away the filth from the face of this planet, that carry the weight of its aging.

These tiny hands, dark and soiled, are illuminating the earth's countenance.

*Translated by Tahira Naqvi*

# Aunt Bichu

WHEN I saw her for the first time she was seated in the ground-floor window of Rahman Bhai's house and was cursing and swearing. This window, which overlooked our courtyard, was kept closed as a matter of principle since there was always the possibility of coming face to face with women who observed purdah. Rahman Bhai was in the employ of nautch girls. No matter what the function at his house, a circumcision ceremony, *bismillah* or wedding, Rahman Bhai always succeeded in getting one of these women to dance at the celebration; Waheeda Jan, Mushtari Bai and Anwari were able to grace a poor man's house at least once with their presence.

But he treated the young girls and women in his neighbourhood with the utmost respect. His younger brothers, Bundu and Genda, on the other hand, were always getting into trouble because of their philandering. Still, his neighbours did not look upon him favourably. He had established illicit relations with his sister-in-law while his wife was still alive. This orphaned girl who had no one in the world to call her own except her sister, was forced to live in her house. She took care of her children and other than nursing them herself, she did everything for them, including cleaning their soiled clothes and washing their filth.

And then one day a woman from the neighbourhood saw her nursing the baby. The secret was out. People suddenly realized that half the children in that household resembled their aunt. Rahman's wife may have castigated her sister in private, but in public she would never admit to any wrongdoing on per part. She always said, "Whoever accuses a virgin of such things will be punished by fate." However, she was constantly on the lookout for a groom for her sister. But who would want to have anything to do with this worm-eaten kabab? In one eye she had a white speck the size of a penny, and because one foot was smaller than the other, she walked with a limp.

A strange kind of boycott had come into effect in the neighbourhood. If someone needed Rahman Bhai's services he was simply given an order along with, "Have we not given you permission to continue living here?" And Rahman Bhai quietly gave in because he considered this indulgence an honour.

For this reason Bichu Phupi sat in Rahman Bhai's window and hurled insults from there. The others were afraid of Abba; who wanted to tangle horns with a magistrate?

That day I discovered that Badshahi Khanum, whom we called Bichu Phupi, was my only real aunt, my father's real sister, and this long-drawn out tongue-lashing was aimed at members of our family.

Amma's face was ashen. Cowering, she sat fearfully in her room as if waiting for Bichu Phupi's voice to strike her like a bolt of lightning. Every six months or so Bichu Phupi stationed herself in Rahman Bhai's window and bellowed at us. Reclining in a chair slightly out of her view, Abba would appear to be totally immersed in his newspaper during her tirade.

Occasionally he sent up one of the boys to her with a message, refuting something she had said. A new burst of anger followed as a result. All of us would abandon our games and congregate in the verandah to hear our dear Bichu Phupi swear and curse. The window at which she sat was filled with the weight and expanse of her body, and she resembled Abba so much, it was almost as if it were he up there, without his moustache, a dupatta covering his head. Unruffled by the force of her diatribe, we continued to stand around and gape at her.

Five feet, six inches in height, thick wrists with joints like a lion's, hair white as a heron, large teeth, a voluminous chin, and her voice — God be praised! It was only one octave lower than Abba's.

Bichu Phupi always wore white. The day her husband, Uncle Masud, made a play for the cleaning girl, Phupi smashed all her bangles with a piece of stone and removed the coloured dupatta from her head. From that day onward she referred to her husband as 'late' or 'dead'; the refused to allow hands and feet that had known the touch of a cleaning woman's body to come into contact with hers.

This unhappy event took place when she was quite young so she had been suffering 'widowhood' for some time. Uncle Masud was also my mother's uncle. There was somthing strange in all of this. Before they were married, my father was my mother's distant uncle. (In those days my mother was petrified of him.) When she found out she was about to be engaged to him she sneaked some opium from her grandmother's purse and swallowed it. Since the amount she ingested was very small, she recovered after a few days of discomfort. Abba was in college in Aligarh at the time.

he was in the middle of exams when he heard what had happened and, dropping everything, he dashed to my grandfather's house. My grandfather, who was also Abba's first cousin and good friend, pacified him with great difficulty and tried to convince him to return to college. Hungry and nervous, Abba paced up and down not far from my mother's bed. Through the curtains, her eyes half-closed, my mother saw the shadow of his broad, overbearing shoulders shaking with anxiety.

"Umrao Bhai, if something happens to her . . ." the giant's voice broke.

Grandfather burst out laughing. "No, no, dear brother, don't worry, she will be all right."

At that moment my little innocent mother became a woman; fear of this giant-like man vanished from her heart forever. For this reason Bichu Phupi used to say, "The woman is a sorceress. She had illicit relations with my brother, she was pregnant before she got married."

When my mother heard these insults being uttered in the presence of her grown children, her face crinkled up and she began to cry. Seeing her weep like that, we forgot all the harsh treatment meted out to us and felt almost maternal towards her. But as for Abba, these foul remarks only made the lights in his eyes dance like fairies. He would send up Nanhe Bhai with an affectionate message for Bichu Phupi:

"Well, Phupi, and what did you eat today?"

"Your mother's liver!" she would exclaim, burnt to a cinder by his response.

Abba would send her another message. "Why Phupi, that's why you have haemorrhoids in your mouth. Take a laxative, I say, a laxative."

She would then begin cursing my older brother with the malediction that his virile body be picked by crows and vultures; she pronounced the curse of widowhood upon his bride-to-be who sat in some room, God knows where, dreaming about her bride-groom- to-be. And through all of this, her fingers stuffed in her ears, my mother would chant the incantation, "You are Might, You are Mighty, rid us of this calamity."

After a short while Abba would give Bichu Phupi another push and Nanhe Bhai would ask, "Aunt Bad-shahi, is Auntie Sweepress well?" And we would wonder fearfully if Phupi was now going to leap at us from the window!

"Go, you son of a snake! Don't quibble with me or else I'll crush your face with my shoe! This old man hiding inside, why is he sending out the boys? If he is a true Mughal I challenge him to come out and face me himself."

"Rahman Bhai, O Rahman Bhai, why don't you give this wrinkled old hag some poison?" Scared out of his wits Nanhe Bhai said what he had been instructed to by Abba. But he had no reason to be afraid because although he spoke them, everyone knew the words came from Abba. That is why the pain of sin would not be Nanhe Bhai's. Nevertheless, addressing such rude remarks to an aunt who resembled Abba so closely made him break out in a cold sweat.

What a world of difference there was between my father's family and my mother's. My mother's relations lived in Hakimun Gali, while my father's family held residence in Banon Kathre. My mother's forefathers traced their roots to Salim Chishti. By calling himself his *murshad*, the follower, the Mughal emperor had found the way to salvation. They had lived in Hindustan for hundreds of years; their complexions had become darker, their features had lost their sharpness, and their temperaments had mellowed.

My father's ancestors on the other hand, arrived with the last of the troops. Mentally, they were still riding in battle. There was fire in their blood, their features bore the sharpness of a sword's edge, their complexions were fair like those of the British invaders, their statures reminded one of gorillas, their voices thundered like a lion's roar, and their hands and feet were as wide as boards.

And my mother's kinsmen — they were of delicate built, of artistic temperament, and soft-spoken. By profession they were usually hakims or maulvis, which is why their street had come to be known as Hakimun Gali. Some of them had begun to take an interest in business and had turned to professions like gold-lace weaving and perfumery. Because most of my father's relatives held posts in the army, they considered these jobs to be low-class and unsuitable for men. It is true that my mother's people had not developed an interest in any of the competitive sports like wrestling, swimming, arm-wrestling, or fencing. And *pachisi*, a favourite in my mother's family, was viewed by my father's side as a game fit only for eunuchs.

It is said that when a volcano erupts, the lava flows into the valley. Perhaps that is why my mother's family was inevitaly drawn to my father's. Answers to how and when this connection began can be found in the family records, but I don't really remember much. I know that my paternal grandfather was not born in Hindustan and both my maternal and paternal grandmothers were from the same family. But there was one younger sister who was married to the Sheikhs. Perhaps my mother's people had cast a magic spell on my father's family which is why they gave their daughter to 'low class commoners' as Bichu Phupi liked to call them. While she swore at her 'late' husband, she also heaped curses on her dead father who had ground the Chughtai name in mud.

My aunt had three brothers. Two of them were older than her, one younger. Since she was the only sister, she became wilful and headstrong, always getting her way, always forcing her three brothers to do her bidding. She was raised like a boy, rode horses, could use the bow and arrow, and was quite adept at fencing. Although her body had expanded to look like a mound, she still stuck out her chest proudly like a wrestler when she walked. (Of course her chest was the size of four female chests.)

Abba used to tease Amma: "Dear, would you like to wrestle with Badshahi?"

"May I be saved from punishment!" Amma would lift her hands to touch her ears, and mutter. But Abba immediately sent off Nanhe Bhai with the challenge.

"Phupi, will you wrestle with my mother?"

"Yes, yes, why not? Go tell your mother to come here. Tell her to prepare herself and come right away. If I don't make her look like a fool don't call me Mirza Karim Beg's daughter! If you are your father's son, bring her to me, bring that daughter of a maulvi to me ..."

Clutching the folds of her wide-legged shalwar in one hand, Amma would hastily retreat into a corner.

"Aunt Badshahi, Grandfather was illiterate, wasn't he?"

Perhaps a long time ago Amma's great-grandfather had given Abba's father a few lessons. Abba distorted the facts to provoke Bichu Phupi.

"That man? What could that butt-wiper teach my father? That caretaker who was raised on our crumbs?" This was a reference to the relationship between Salim Chishti and the Emperor Akbar. The Chughtai's traced their roots to the family of Emperor Akbar, who had endowed Salim Chishti, my mother's ancestor, with the title of spiritual leader. But Phupi said, "Nonsense, utter nonsense! Spiritual leader indeed! He was a caretaker at the mausoleum, just a caretaker."

She had three brothers, but she had fought with all of them. When she battled with one, she reviled them all. The oldest was a devoutly religious man; she referred to him as a beggar and a vagrant. My father was a government official so she called him a traitor and a slave of the British (because the British had put an end to Mughal rule.) But for that she would have been in Lal Qila now, drenched in rose attar, a queen, instead of ending up with her 'late' husband whom she accused of belonging to that class of weavers who had a perchant for soupy dal. Her third brother, my youngest uncle, was a scoundrel and a villain. The policeman used to appear at our door nervously to check up on his whereabouts because he had committed innumerable thefts and murders and was a drunk and a debauchee. Bichu Phupi referred to him as a dacoit, a title that was rather insipid when set against the colourful background of his career.

When she squabbled with her husband, however, she would say, "May your face burn! I'm not helpless and alone, I'm the only sister of three brothers. If they hear of this you will not be able to show your face to the world. As a matter of fact, if my youngest brother finds out he will take your intestines out and place them in your hands. He's a dacoit, a dacoit! And should you escape his wrath, my magistrate brother will make sure you rot in jail — he will force you to grind grain for the rest of your life. And if by some chance you slip through his hands, the oldest, who is so pious, will put a curse on your afterlife. Look here, I'm a Mughal woman, not some Sheikhani or a common worker's daughter like your mother." But Uncle Masud knew that he had the sympathy of the three brothers, so he listened to the stream of abuse with a quiet smile. It was this very smile that my mother's relatives had used to torment my father's family for years.

On every Eid day my father went directly from the mosque to Bichu Phupi's house with his sons to hear her curse and swear. On their arrival she hastily withdrew into the inner room and from there, hurled insults at my sorceress mother and her villainous brother. She sent out her servant with sweet vermicelli, but pretended it was from a neighbour.

"There is no poison in this, is there?" Abba would tease. And right away my mother and her family would be torn to pieces. After partaking of the *sewayyan* Abba gave her *eidi* which she would immediately throw on the floor, saying, "Give this money to your wife's brothers who have lived on your scraps." Abba would leave quietly. He knew that as soon as his back was turned she would pick up the money, press it to her eyes, and weep for hours.

Secretly, she would send for her nephews and give them *eidi*.

"Bastards, if you breathe a word of this to your father or mother I'll cut you up into little pieces and feed you to the dogs." But Abba knew how much she had given the boys. If for some reason he was unable to make it to her house on Eid, messages followed one after the other. "Nusrat Khanum (my mother) is widowed at last. Good, I'm glad, I'm so relieved." Insulting messages would pour in all day and then in the evening she would make an appearance at Rahman Bhai's window and start swearing at us from there.

One day while eating *sewayyan* Abba felt nauseous and threw up, probably due to the heat.

"Badshahi Begum, please forgive and forget — my time has come it seems," he groaned. Without wasting a second, her veil thrown carelessly over her face, beating her chest with her hands, Bichu Phupi was at our door in no time. But when she saw Abba laughing mischievously she turned and stormed out of the house, leaving a trail of insults in her wake.

"Because you are here, Badshahi, the angel of death has taken off in fear," Abba said. "I would certainly have died today if you hadn't come."

I cannot tell you what kind of maledictions fell from Bichu Phupi's lips. As soon as she saw that he was out of danger she said, "God willing, you will be struck by a bolt of lightning, you'll take your last breath in the gutter, and there won't be anyone around to carry you to the grave."

Abba gave her two rupees and teased, "We must pay our family entertainers for their buffoonery."

Momentarily befuddled, Phupi blurted out, "Give the money to your mother and sister!" And immediately thereafter she slapped her face and said, "*Ai*

Badshahi, may your face be blackened — you're digging your own grave!"

Actually Bichu Phupi was at daggers drawn only with Abba. If she met Amma by herself somewhere she would draw her close and hug her, lovingly saying, "Nacho, Nacho," and ask, "Are the children well?" She completely forgot that the children she was inquiring after were the offspring of that unfortunate brother she had cursed all her life. Amma was also her niece. What a rigmarole it was! By some odd coincidence I was my mother's distant cousin as well, and by that token my father was also my brother-in-law. There's no doubt that my mother's family caused my father's family much grief, but it was really disastrous when Bichu Phupi's daughter, Mussarat Khanum, fell in love with my mother's brother.

This is what happened. My mother's grandmother, who was also my father's aunt, fell sick and when everyone thought she was about to die, members of both families arrived to tend her. Uncle Muzaffar, my mother's brother, came to nurse his grandmother, and Mussarat Khanum arrived with her mother who was there to minister to her aunt.

Bichu Phupi had no fear in her heart. She knew that she had trained her children to hate and despise her side of the family, and Mussarat Khanum was too young anyway; only fifteen, she still slept with her mother and as far as Bichu Phupi was concerned, was still a baby.

But when Uncle Muzaffar lifted his limpid brown eyes and saw Mussarat Khanum's delicate form, he could not tear his gaze away from her.

During the day, while the elders slept, tired from a full night of waiting hand and foot on Amma's grandmother, the faithful young sat at the sick woman's bedside, keeping less of an eye on her and more on each other. When Mussarat Khanum extended her hand to remove the cold compress from the old lady's forehead, Uncle Muzaffar's was already there.

The next day the old woman suddenly opened her eyes. Shaky, using the pillows to lift herself, she sat up slowly and immediately summoned the whole family. "Call a maulvi," she ordered.

Everyone was perplexed. No one could understand why she wanted the maulvi at this time. Did she want to get married on her deathbed? Not a single person had the courage to question her command.

"Marry these two right away." Everyone was dumbfounded. Who were 'these two?' Just then Mussarat Khanum fainted and fell to the floor. Alarmed, Uncle Muzaffar quickly ran out of the room. The thieves were caught. The ceremony took place. Bichu Phupi was stunned.

Although nothing untoward had happened — they had simply held hands briefly — the old woman thought they had exceeded the limits of decency.

And now Bichu Phupi exploded. She attacked without the aid of horse and sword and laid waste the path before her. Her son-in-law and daughter were banished from the house that very moment. Since they had nowhere to go, Abba brought them to our place. Amma was beside herself with joy in the company of such a beautiful sister-in-law, and *walima* celebrations were held with great pomp.

Bichu Phupi didn't see her daughter's face again and announced that she would henceforth hide her face from her brother. She was already estranged from her husband and now she turned away from the rest of the world. What was it but a poison that had invaded her heart and head? Her life threatened her like a viper.

"The old hag played this little game so she could ensnare my daughter for her grandson," she kept saying; she might well have been right because the old lady lived for another twenty years.

Brother and sister never reconciled. When paralysis struck Abba for the fourth time and the end seemed near, he sent for Bichu Phupi.

"Badshahi, I'm taking my last breath. Come now if you want to fulfill your heart's desire."

Who knows what arrows were concealed in this message. The brother sent them and they pierced the sister's heart. Trembling, beating her chest with her hands, Bichu Phupi appeared at the door she had abandoned for a lifetime and thundered into the house like a white volcano.

"Badshahi, your prayers are being answered." Abba was smiling despite his pain, and his eyes were still youthful.

Although her hair was all white, Bichu Phupi suddenly looked like the little Bichu who used to throw a tantrum and force her brothers to give in to her every request. In her eyes, usually vicious like a lion's, was a fearful, cowering expression; large tears rolled down her marble cheeks.

"Bichu, my dear, scold me," said Abba lovingly. Between sobs my mother begged Bichu Phupi for curses.

"O God, O God," she tried to roar, but her voice quivered and broke instead. "O God, bless my brother with my life . . . Dear God, in the name of your beloved Prophet . . ." She began weeping like a child who is frustrated because he cannot remember a lesson correctly.

Everyone grew pale. The earth seemed to slip from under Amma's feet. O God! Not a single curse fell from Bichu Phupi's lips that day!

Abba was the only one who was smiling, smiling the way he used to when he heard her swear.

It is true that a sister's curses cannot harm her brother, for they are dipped in mother's milk.

*Translated by Tahira Naqvi*

# Lingering Fragrance

IN THE growing dusk of the room, a faint shadow was advancing ... tip-toe ... towards Chhamman Mian's bed.

Now the shadow was standing with its face towards the bed. Instead of a pistol, the hand probably held a dagger. Chhamman Mian's heart pounded. Toes stiffened. The shadow bent over his feet. But before the enemy could strike the fatal blow, Chhamman Mian had pole-vaulted to the other side and grabbed the assassin's throat.

"Cheeeeen !" A faint squeak was uttered by the shadow. Chhamman Mian dashed the wily opponent to the floor.

Tinkling of bangles and anklets sent Chhamman Mian hurtling towards the light switch. The assassin disappeared under the bed.

"Who the hell ... ?" Chhamman demanded.

"I ... Haleema."

"Haleema ? What ... what the hell are you up to ?"

"No ... nothing."

"Who sent you here ? Dare lie and I'll pull out your tongue."

"Nawab Dulhan," the voice was tremulous.

"O God ! Pyari Ammi is after my life." His imagination was going wild. For several days Ammi had been giving him strange looks and whispering to Nayaab. Nayaab is a witch, she really is. Bhaijan too had been smiling at him insidiously. It's a bloody conspiracy. Not unusual among nawabs. Several times, granduncles had tried to poison Abba Huzoor. Hired goondas to do the job. Wanted to get their dirty hands on the property and devour all of it. Rifaqat Ali Khan was given poison by his own real uncle, administered by the hand of his favourite *kaneez*. To hell with such deadly property and possessions.

Pyari Ammi probably wants it all for her favourite son. After all she has brought her brother's daughter into the house as the daughter-in-law. No wonder she is after my blood.

Chhamman Mian had no love for property. Beating, torturing, squeezing labour for *lagaan*, auctioning their cattle—such displays of power made him sick.

But . . . O God! If our own mother turns into a deadly enemy . . . no one can be trusted As it is she does nothing but admonish me all the time. "Don't do this . . . don't do that. Don't read so much, play so much, live so much!"

"Where is the knife ?" Propped up on his elbows Chhamman was peering underneath the bed.

"Knife?"

"Hands up!" Chamman used his special detective voice.

"Wha-at ?" Halima trembled.

"*Ullu ki patthi*. Hands up!"

When she lifted her hands her dupatta fell aside. Great embarrassment and lowering of arms.

"You rascal . . . I said hands . . ."

"Why . . . Oh!" she chirped.

"To hell with your 'Why . . . Oh!' Where's the knife ?"

"What knife ?" Irritably spoken.

"What were you holding?"

"Nothing ... I swear."

"Why ? Then why did you come ?"

"Nawab Dulhan sent me," she whispered, eyes lowered, fidgetting with the bead strung on her thin wire nose-ring.

"Why ?" Chhamman was scared.

"To rub your feet." She leaned on the bed.

"*La haul walaquwwat* * ! Now scram !"

He was unnerved by the mischief in her eyes.

Haleema's face contorted,lips trembled. Thump ... she sat down on the carpet, buried her face in her hands, and burst into tears.

"Haleema ... please. Haleema, don't. Please go. I have an early class ..."

More tears.

Ten years ago, Haleema's tears had fallen at the same rate. Her father was slumped on his stomach coughing up blood and chunks of pink flesh. She was clutching him to her little bosom. Then they all wrapped Abbu in white sheets and took him to the hospital. People never return from hospitals, she learnt. The same rate of tearfall was  recorded on the day her mother dumped her beside Nawab Dulhan's bed, filled her empty bags with grain, and left, with never a backward glance at her weeping child.

She grew up in the courtyard of the servants' quarters, nourished on scraps from people's dirty plates. She was never permitted to crawl on the dirt stretch which separated the lowly quarters from the plinth of Nawab Dulhan's verandah. Playing with the

---

* An exclamation corresponding to, "Get thee behind me, Satan !"

filth and dirt with her playmates—the shit-eating chickens and new-born puppies—Haleema had a steady growth and a nondescript childhood.

Shameless, wretched child, she continued to defy mortality. Nayaab Bubu's ten or twelve year old Jabbar used to beat her to pulp. Sometimes he touched a pair of red hot tongs to her soles, squeezed an orange peel into her eyes or thrust a pinch of snuff up her nose. For a long time, Haleema sat patiently and sneezed like a toad, while the household collapsed with laughter. The bullying continued unabated, when she was sent to the door to hand over or receive something; a pinch, a jerk at her nose-ring, a yank at her braid. A rascal, Jabbar. Nawab Saheb's favourite — his own life-blood.

Doesn't make a darned difference, whether or not a maid enters wedlock. Not a single peacock's feather is added to her cap. Nawabzadis would rather be seen dead than allow a maid to sit with them. Two words spoken by the qazi do not have the power to bore a hole in granite, or solve the question of basic survival.

In the mahal, Nayaab Bubu had a very special status. She played her cards carefully and, instead of becoming the Begum's hated co-wife, became her bosom confidante. Her magic stick wielded over the Nawab compelled him into writing a sizeable share of the property in Jabbar's name. Jabbar, her beloved son. All the servants of the household were terrified of him. He swaggered around the house in imported trousers and a *boski* shirt. Supreme Lordship of the Servants, although a chauffeur in name. Bubu inside and Jabbar outside—a pair of millstones. Anyone who dared come between them was instantly pulverised.

And Haleema was still crying.

Chhamman Mian's reprimand devastated her. When he tried to console her she became uncontrollable. When he held her ice-cold hands to pull her to her feet, she clung to him like a vine.

God ! Those daring winter nights ! Deafening thunder-claps. Haleema on Chhamman's inexperienced hands. Cricket buddies had whispered so many ways of laying a girl. But call it misfortune or blunder, Chhamman had always dismissed sex talk as nonsense. He was intimate with only two things, cricket and books. Despite the biting cold, Haleema had scorched him like a brush with live coals. His hands were stuck to her as if she were moulded from glue.

Suddenly a knife seemed to probe his brain. He sprang away from Haleema, trembling with anger.

Storm creating havoc outside, Haleema's tears doing the same indoors !

"Haleema. . . please . . . don't !" He was squatting before her crying form.

What he really wanted was to put his head on her bosom and cry his heart out. But he was afraid that the head and the bosom would be glued together. Wiping away her tears with his kurta, he helped her up and, before she could anticipate his intention, he had pushed her out of the door and bolted it from inside.

Sleep had been banished by the force of Haleema's tears. For the remainder of the night, Chhamman Mian shivered in his quilt and cried tears of poison. Outside the frustrated wind lashed through the trees, groaning and moaning in despair.

Finishing her *farz namaz*, Nayaab Bubu raised her hands in prayer. Folding the corner of her *janamaz*, she got off the divan and tip-toed towards Jabbar's room.

Softly opening the door, she peered at her son's handsome sleeping form and tears of maternal pride filled her eyes. Inside she saw the tell-tale signs of Gultaar's dalliances with Jabbar. Gultaar, Chhamman Mian's and Jabbar's father's special maid, left mementoes of her nocturnal visits behind. Today there was her dupatta visible from under the quilt. One day this fool's indiscretions will slice off her nose. She pulled out the dupatta. May God protect Jabbar from the evil eye. A spitting image of his father !

Suddenly it struck her. A father's maid was like a mother. Right ? Best take a *fatwa* from the *alim* Saheb. One shouldn't lose out in both worlds—this one and the hereafter. How could she blame the wretched Gultaar ? Diabetic old Nawab versus this flower of manhood. How she had cried last night. The boy had become so careless. Didn't give a damn that the door was ajar. Had Bubu not been such a light sleeper, any passer-by would have witnessed their love-play. May God protect everyone.

Nayaab Bubu had negotiated the purchase of two proper maids for her Jabbar. Unfortunately, one died of small-pox and the other ran off with the sweeper's son. The harlot ! She had dealt a hard blow. Maids belonging to noble families did not display such depravity.

Many times she wanted to ask Begum for Haleema, but could not muster up enough courage.

"Haleema is marked for my Chhamman." Begum's word was law. Today her persistence will be rewarded. In any case Jabbar did not care for meek, sickly females. Like his father, he went for red-hot peppers !

Muttering under her breath she climbed up to the

terrace. "What ?" Her heart stopped beating. Haleema was fast asleep, snuggled in Sarvari's quilt. With the toe of her sandal, she kicked Haleema's anklet and pulled the quilt right off the sleeping girl.

Haleema woke up in a panic and started pulling out her dupatta from under the sleeping Sarvari.

Eagle eyes darted back and forth over Haleema's body. Like a thief she sat with her eyes glued to the pattern on the faded quilt, counting the stitches of the quilting with her finger.

"Well . . . ?" Bubu placed her hands on her hips. "Damn it . . . what did I tell you ?"

"Yes . . . Bubu."

"What . . . ?"

Haleema remained silent.

"Say something, you bloody mute."

"His legs were not hurting." Haleema hung down her head.

"Hunh!" Bubu swung around in disgust, her fingers moved faster on the beads in her hand. What a stroke of luck ! Her heart was all spring ! The lineage would now depend entirely on Jabbar. Her own Jabbar. It is God's will. It is not as if the older son was at fault. That wretched girl, Sanobar. God had given her a short lifeline, that's what. At barely fourteen years of age, she was gifted to the older Sahibzada. What a lovely child Sanobar was. Very frail. If only she had parents to take care of her ! In the normal course she would have left her father's house and, with the music of the shehnai ringing in her ears,would have set her delicate foot on her husband's threshold. The mingling of two hearts, and a new world would have been created.

Sanobar loved playing "Brides". Often she would

sit down, pretending to be the bride, surrounded by a cluster of maids. Beautiful child. Small bones, taut body, tiny hands and feet, pearly teeth, and the large eyes of a devi. How she had begged the Begum to bestow her on Jabbar. But Begum was her usual obstinate self. This maid was a gift from her *maika*, she had brought her for the older Sahibzada.

Who says Sanobar's "wedding" was fake ? Bubu was the maid of maids. She was perfectly aware that every girl had a secret desire to become a bride. And a maid had the same feelings as her mistress. Woman first, maid second. During the early evening she had sent Sanobar to the bath. When she emerged, she dressed her in a peach coloured outfit. She had plucked the henna from the bus with her own hands. Sanobar's palms and feet had turned a glorious red. Touching her hair with a fragrant oil, she had twisted it into braids. Friends whispered secrets in her ears and teased her all evening. When Hashmat Mian, Chhamman's older brother, picked her up and took her to his bosom, poor Sanobar had drawn a little ghunghat over her face.

Having seen the face of Hashmat Mian, poor Sanobar, at the age of fourteen had stared at the angel of death. Within the year she became pregnant. The sickly, frail child lay on her stomach all day, puking. Allah, Allah! On such occasions how much fuss is made in normal households. Every member of the clan outdoes the other to please the newly pregnant bride. In prepregnancy days Hashmat used to dance to her tune. For every kiss he used to bend his knees and grovel. Now he was showing the first signs of revulsion.

The mahal tradition was that when cattle became heavy with child they were despatched to the village.

As soon as they were relieved of the calf and the milk started flowing, they were summoned back. Maids received identical treatment. Pregnant ones were packed off to the village. There they delivered the brat and there it was left to grow or die. They returned, empty-handed, to the mahal so that the Begums would not be disturbed by the sound of crying babies.

How pathetically the wretches would wail and cry. Like animals they groaned for their young. Breasts filled up with milk, causing intense pain. Often they would burn with high fevers. Sometimes one of the Begums' babies was brought in for suckling. How they would enjoy the pleasures of taking the baby to the breast. But such delights were ephemeral. Ladies of noble birth cannot be expected to breed like animals, just to give their maids the pleasure of suckling! Once their impotent grief had spent itself they were once again put back to work.

Sanobar asserted her will. Refused to go to the village. Bubu tried to reason with her but she fell at the Begum's feet. Bubu had seen too much of life. She hated all maids, hated her own existence. Mostly hated, but was there a streak of love somewhere ?

Sanobar's time in this world was up. She refused to leave and her presence kept souring Hashmat Mian's mouth. If anyone tried to reason with her, she would be ready to gouge out their eyes. One day she suddenly started lashing out at the young man. Sahibzada's blood boiled over. His exasperated kick landed squarely on her stomach and Sanobar was thrown into a running drain. For three days she brawled like a buffalo. To call a doctor for her would have been unthinkable. People have such evil tongues and bad intentions. On the third day, in the darkest corner of the servants' quarters, Sanobar took her last few tormented breaths.

Doubtless, Sanobar was a practitioner of black magic, a real-life sorceress. Four years had passed since Hashmat Mian's wedding but the bride had shown no signs of pregnancy. All types of treatment had been tried. Charms, talismans, offerings at mazars, lamps at mandirs; nothing worked. True or false, the gossips maintained that Sahibzada had kicked a full term pregnancy in the womb, hence his impotence. Day and night Dulhan Begum threw hysterical fits. At the slightest excuse she ran to her parents' house. Her cousin, a renowned doctor, was treating her . . . in more ways than one, it was rumoured.

Nayaab Bubu sighed. Dipped her elbow to test the water before carrying the pitcher to Nawab Begum for her morning wash.

At first Nawab Begum had hated the very existence of Nayaab. But after she fell at her feet and professed that as Nawab Dulha's servant, she was equally devoted to serving Nawab Dulhan, the latter showed some signs of relenting. Nayaab assured her that since she had not been bought from the marketplace, she could not be treated like a harlot. Blood of noble generations was coursing through her veins and arteries. Begum had no option but to accept. What the hell! All men of the family tasted a morsel here and there. To give her credit, Nayaab had always remained within limits. She never permitted herself to give credence to a single word of the Nawab's sweet talk. When the Nawab started his affair with Munawwar Mirza, she joined the Begum in the opposition front. Instead of celebrating Begum's impending disinheritance, she cried tears of blood. Her bond was with the Begum and Nawab. Who the hell was this bloody usurper, conniving at the family property ? Men were like gusts of wind, changing direction from moment to moment.

Begum and Nayaab, two teammates, planned a careful strategy. A rakhi tied by the Begum on Tarahdar Khan's wrist pledged them to a brother-sister relationship for life. Tarahdar took Munawwar and departed for Paris. After consigning Munawwar to hell, she proceeded to decorate Begum's bridal bed with her own hands. While slipping on flower bracelets and anklets on her hands and feet, she slipped two words of advice into the Begum's ear . . . how to make the Nawab happy. That night, alone, in the darkest corner of the servants' quarters, she held Jabbar to her bosom and kept an all-night vigil.

To this day, Nayaab had not discontinued her little personal services for the Nawab Begum, not once.

Seeing her downcast look, Begum puckered her brow. "Is all well ?"

Haltingly Bubu related the details. The ground underneath the Begum's feet slipped away. Jabbar was dispatched with the car to fetch Hakim Saheb.

"Nothing to worry about," Hakim Saheb assured them. "The boy is young and inexperienced." He promised to send a "tonic" with complete instructions for the Sahibzada. "It is possible, huzoor, that he may have felt some revulsion. Sometimes the "presentation" does not whet the appetite. That does not mean that the digestive system is defective."

"I had a premonition that the girl was somewhat . . . you know . . . thin, frail, sickly. If you take my advice let Baqar Nawab have her. Hashmat Mian has an eye on the Nawab's English bloodhounds. He will gladly agree to barter the dogs for the girl." Bubu started massaging Begum's feet.

"Heaven forbid ! I would rather poison the wretched girl than hand her to that leper. He is rotting from head to foot."

Never before had the family witnessed such a massive setback. A maid visits the master and returns safe and sound in the morning.

Usually the young masters would take the sexual initiative, without considering the delicacies of distribution and propriety. To prevent rivalries between brothers, the elder Begums made a just division of flesh. Having done that they were assured that each would respect the other's property rights. These domestic dispensations of justice were a hundred per cent legal and binding.

"I am sick of this boy. Eighteen years old and no flirting with the maids. My brothers started at age eleven or twelve. Sixteen, seventeen, and they were stomping and fuming for the kill. Nayaab, did you make sure that she bathed properly? Or did you send her to his bedroom stinking of ginger and garlic?" Nawab Begum was agitated.

"Begum, you still consider me a novice ? How many maids have these hands prepared for the bedchamber? I swear by Imam Husain that he who sees the naked heel of my 'handiwork' won't bother to look at a *pari* from Mount Caucasus. What about Hashmat Mian ? Was ready to fall into the trap of that damned foreigner. Wasn't it my handiwork on Sanobar that saved his skin ?" Bubu was offended by Begum's scepticism regarding her special skills.

"Begum, your son is the flower of youth. But these

are hard days. Recently, Afzal Nawab paid a heavy price for two slave girls. What happened ? The police came and camped at his doorstep. Paid no heed to his assurances that he was looking after these two destitutes as a charity in the name of God almighty. He offered them a generous helping from his coffers. To what avail? The girls were removed to some home. 1500 rupees down the drain. No chance of getting a new maid."

This news created the kind of stir that even a Third World War may not have. Rumours began to hiss and crawl in every corner of the mahal like a clutch of snakes from an open pit. Whoever learnt of it, (and how fast it moved from mouth to ear) pounded his breast.

"God, O God! Poor Chhamman Mian." When he got the news, Afzal Mian headed straight for Chhamman's room, flapping his pyjamas and chewing his tobacco.

"How was I to know ? So this is your inclination, is it ? Had I known why would I have put your Bhabhi's noose around my neck ? Never mind, darling, I am still yours." A few years ago he had fallen head over heels in love with Chhamman. But when Nawab Saheb loaded his pistol, he sobered up. Chhamman Mian hated him.

"Shut up. I have no such taste or inclination. It's just that I don't like such things. Not permitted before marriage."

"But, Sarkar, a maid is permissible before marriage."

"Wrong. Not admissible."

"That means that all our ancestors were fornicators ? Only you are the true adherent of faith?"

"It is my belief . . ."

"Your belief, shit ! Have you ever studied the rules of Din?*

"No. But this defies all reason."

"To hell with your reason. No solid facts. All airy nonsense."

"It is a crime in the eyes of law."

"Who cares for the law of the kafirs ? We only accept the word of God. We treat our slaves like our own children. Nayaab rules the household, her son lacks nothing. Look at the maids—fed with the best grains, they are bursting with health. And if you were handed starved and shrivelled goods . . . my boy, take Sarvari. She's been fattened perfectly."

"Hush !"

"What the hell is going on ?"

"Nothing. Please stop gnawing at my brain."

"Fine by me. If you like being the butt of everyone's jokes, who can stop you. And by the way, Sarkar, in case you didn't know, your fiancee . . ."

"I have no fiancee."

"Well, fiancee-to-be, then! Hurma Khanum is becoming too friendly with that bastard, Mansur."

"So . . . What am I to do?"

"Shall I tell you? I am going towards Sadar—I will send the bangle-vendor. Make sure to wear glass bangles right upto your elbows. What else ?" With his mouth full of betel juice, he let out a roar of laughter.

"Illiteracy . . . damned illiteracy !"

"Our venerable ancestors were illiterate, were they ?"

"Must have been. How do I know ?"

"Nonsense from a convoluted brain. The elders must have thought about this matter carefully before

* Tenets of Islam

establishing the tradition. To this day we respect their guidance and adhere to it. This is the best way of preventing young men from falling into worse habits. They become responsible, remain healthy . . ."

"Ways of legitimizing fornication."

"Your words are reeking of *kufr*. Insulting the faith."

"Don't talk about faith.This is its only tenet etched on your heart."

"You are insolent and stupid. To hell with you !"

At night when dinner was served, Nayaab Bubu, with elaborate ritual, presented Hakim Sahib's concoction in a gleaming silver spoon. Already Chhamman had torn up the instruction sheet without reading it and had given hell to Sarvari. He felt like drowning himself in the biggest serving dish on the table. He dashed to the ground the inoffensive silver spoon and stomped out of the dining room. The whole bloody world had branded him impotent, sexless.

So far all the books in his library had used the words "fornicator" and "adulterer" for men who slept with women outside the sanctified bonds of marriage.

Outside the house the wind was raging like a mad demon. The frail branch of a tree was continually tapping on the window-pane, as if seeking refuge from the terror outside. It was a long time before Chhamman fell asleep.

Cool drops of water on his feet woke him up. His heart was pounding.

Haleema's sobbing face was resting on his feet. He quickly drew up his legs.

Again those anguished tears. This girl had teamed up with the enemy. These people would not rest until they destroyed him. Alas !

"Now what is it ?"

"Am I so repulsive that I can't even touch your feet ?" Haleema's voice was choked.

"Stop talking nonsense. Go away."

"I won't. What do you take me for ? I admit I am a maid but I'm not a leper. The entire mahal is cursing the day of my birth. Everyone is laughing at me because I repulse you. I'm not worthy of you. Tomorrow Sarvari will replace me in your service."

"I will kill her. I don't want service."

"You will get used to it. Hakim Saheb says . . ."

"Hakim Saheb is an asshole."

"What should I do ?"

"Go to sleep, it's very late."

"Early or late, what do I care ? Do me a favour. Give me a lethal poison."

"Why should I ? And don't you dare say that again. Suicide is a sin against the Almighty."

"Then shall I go and burn in Baqar Nawab's fire? The man has leprosy."

Another flood had started.

"Baqar Nawab ? Who is talking about that bastard?"

"I am. You get Sarvari. And in exchange for a pair of English bloodhounds . . ."

"Stop this at once!"

"Baqar Nawab is diseased all over. The sweepress was telling Bubu. How Bubu hates me. Jabbar ! My repulsing his advances was a slap on her face."

Haleema's explanation finally began to make sense. Trembling with remorse and anger, Chhamman Mian looked at her. He wanted to dry her tears. But the thought of touching her was terrifying. Once his hand felt her face would he ever be able to withdraw it ?

"Do you want to marry me ?" he asked.

"God !" Haleema could hardly speak. "Hurma . . . everyone knows Hurma is your childhood fiancee."

"And you . . .?"

"I am your maid."

"Let us suppose you are my maid. Your mother was not. Your father wasn't the son of a maid. You are a Saidani, Haleema, your father was a farmer. Haleema, listen." Both her hands were in his. "I will tell Pyari Ammi. I won't marry Hurma, I will marry you."

"Marry !" Haleema flung both his hands aside with an electrical impulse. "Tauba, Tauba ! Remember Ulfat ? Sadiq Nawab wanted to marry her . . . and what did they give her ? Poison. Bari Begum's orders. How she writhed in pain for three or four days. As if the breath was stuck in her throat, refused to let her die." Haleema put both his hands on her neck.

Exactlywhat he was afraid of, happened. Haleema's body was made from glue. Chhamman's hands got stuck.

"Go, go. . . Haleema . . . my dear . . . dearest." He enfolded her in his arms.

"How cold, these little hands."

"So warm them. . ." She undid his kurta buttons and placed her cold palms on his thumping heart. Two sobbing, inexperienced children immersed themselves in each other. The breeze outside was swaying gently like the pleasure-filled gait of a new bride!

Everything Chhamman did was a bit out of the ordinary. Everyone laughed at him. Toys are meant to be played with, they shouldn't become objects of worship. Begum had sighed with relief when, the next morning, Bubu offered her respectful salaams with a meaningful glance at Chhamman's bedroom. Eight o'clock and the door was still bolted from inside.

When Chhamman left for college, Begum saw, with her own eyes, the proof of the night before. Immediately, she offered two *rakat* prayers of thanks-giving. Haleema was a little feverish. She lay face down in her servants' chamber all day. Bubu cracked dirty jokes each time she passed by. The mahal was buzzing, "Chhamman Mian has accepted Haleema." Other maids were green with envy. Lucky Haleema ! What an innocent, handsome groom. Privately, they always referred to their masters as grooms . . . it made them feel good.

Girls had always made Chhamman Mian nervous. But Haleema had opened up a new channel of com-munication. He became good for nothing else. A free period, and he was seen running home. Friends drop-ped in on Sundays and holidays, and Chhamman was making excuses: "I have to study." And how did the study session go ? Head on Haleema's lap. Kiss stop at every full stop.

"Illiterate. Good for nothing. If only you had stu-died a bit you could have transcribed my notes." And Haleema scratching ABCD on the floor with a piece of charcoal.

"Can you fill ink in my pen?" Ink on her hands, mouth, nose, dupatta. Topped off with tears ! A pro-per idiot !

The mahal had superb arrangements. Sons were allowed to stay in a separate enclosure, off the main building. Maids were not expected to do any other work. But Haleema had been trained by Nayaab. She insisted on washing Begum's hands and feet. Never shirked small chores like cleaning and replenishing Begum's paan-dan.

"Go, look after your Chhotey Sarkar." Begum tried to dissuade her from personal service, but she never looked up from massaging Begum's legs. After all, it could not be denied that her beloved son never hesitated to kiss the servant's feet.

Everything was made ready for the "new couple". New clothes, jewellery; almost like a separate existence. A small kitchenette was handy for trying a favourite recipe. Each day the *malan* appeared with her basket of fresh flowers. But Chhamman Mian disliked seeing the flowers sprinkled on the bedsheet.

"Very cruel of our bodies to crush the flowers." He gathered them all into Haleema's lap.

Nayaab Bubu's parrot-like recitation was nauseating." The moment she pukes, she will fall from grace. People can't even stand their own wives, let alone a maid with morning sickness." Chhamman's devotion to Haleema, however, did not leave her entirely untouched.

"I am thinking of arranging the nikah during the month of Khali. These days Feroza Khanum appears slightly peeved." Nawab Begum was now satisfied with Chhamman Mian's manhood.

"To hell with gossips, but I hear Hurma Bitiya has become too liberated." Bubu interposed.

"May live coals burn the tongues of gossip-mongers, but I hear he is a friend of Arshad Mian's. Constant visitor to that house."

"God ! Who told you?"

"Tarahdar Khan's wife. She is a regular visitor. She is related to the seamstress who teachers *sozankari* to Mariam Bitiya. With her own eyes she saw them play with a racket and ball. . . ."

"God forbid that it be an impediment to Chhamman Mian's education, but if you take my advice . . . the sooner the nikah . . ."

"But he runs a mile each time I broach the subject. 'Haleema', he says, 'Haleema or no one'. I have given him my ultimatum. Utter such nonsense again and I swear you will see my dead face."

"Gibberish and rot, Begum, Nawabs and their protestations! Hunh! Never a connection between word and deed! Just keep a close watch. Within a week he will be fine. The girl is already looking sickly."

No secret of the mahal could be hidden from Bubu. Whether it was the buffaloes or the mice, whoever was pregnant, Bubu could tell immediately. By the redness of their faces she could declare that the chickens were ready to lay.

"Pyari Ammi! Is Haleema going to the village?" Chhamman Mian blurted out. Haleema had been crying for the past few days.

"Yes, my love; Nayaab will go along with her. And you know what? I have sent a special message to Ammi Huzoor to send your favourite lime pickle."

"But . . . Pyari Ammi, why are you sending Haleema? Who will look after my clothes?"

"Sarvari, Lateefa."

"If Sarvari or Lateefa touch anything in my room, I will slice them to bits. But why. . . why are you sending Haleema away?"

"Our decision. Who the hell do you think you are? Interfering in domestic matters. . . ."

"But . . . Pyari Ammi . . ."

"Mian! We are still alive. Do what you wish after thrusting us into the grave." Pyari Ammi's eyes were emitting sparks. "Even your father doesn't dare interfere in domestic matters. Have you ever suffered in the past? In all matters concerning maids, Bubu has the last word."

"Pyari Ammi, Haleema is my life. God! She is not a maid ... daughter of a Syed. With loving care, you selected her for me. Now you are tearing off the flesh from raw nails. Why? What have I done?" He wanted to say all this and more, but his throat was choked with tears. Without a glance to the right or left, he walked out of the room.

Haleema was angry with the unending flow of her tears. She wanted to celebrate these last few farewell days. Only four more days to go. Who could predict the future? Four precious days. With great care she had prepared four outfits. Perfume made her stomach heave, but she forced herself to sprinkle fragrance in every fold of the bed. Each strand of her hair was washed and wafted over the smoke from fragrant herbs. Hands and feet were touched up with fresh henna. Dozens of glass bangles were slipped over each wrist, because Chhamman Mian enjoyed breaking bangles. No matter how many he broke, thank God there were always a few left as mementoes of her "married status".

"Not sad about going away"? Chhamman Mian asked, seeing her flushed with happiness. His heart was heavy.

"No." Bubu had strictly forbidden tears.

"Why?" Mounting anger.

"Soon; I will be back soon."

"How soon? A few days?"

"Six-seven months."

"Six months!"

"Shh, softly."

"I will die . . . Haleema . . ."

"God forbid. May all your troubles fall on my head." Haleema warded off the evil spirit. "My beloved husband! Don't let such words escape your lips. God in his mercy will let me return to look after you. Everyone doesn't die. With Sanobar it was different. The older master kicked her womb. O God!" She bit her tongue, clamped her mouth shut with her hand.

"Child!" Chhamman quivered.

"No . . . no, Chhotey Mian!"

"Swear by my soul." Placed her hand on his chest.

"No . . . no. . . no!"

"You liar!" Lighting the lamp he looked at her with probing eyes. Like a criminal he sat with his hands folded in his lap.

His child . . . a real live human being! What was he to do? Leap with joy? Touch the sky and sweep all the stars into Haleema's lap?

"When?"

"Six months." Bashfully spoken.

"My result should be out by then." Chhamman was thoughtful.

And Haleema was thinking about the village. How would the child's crying ever reach his ears? If he was shameless and hard like his mother, he Might survive among the other maid-children, never to be recognized by his father. Grow up to become a servant . . . iron clothes, polish shoes. If it was a girl, she would be given the ultimate honour of rubbing someone's feet . . . to be sent, later on, to the village, to pay off her debt to life.

But Haleema's tongue was clipped to her mouth. Bubu had said, "If you dare incite our Sahibzada, I will slice you into feed for the street dogs."

"Haleema . . . you are not going to the village."

"Please . . . my innocent Sarkar."

He did not permit her to speak any further.

Bubu says men are repulsed by pregnant women. What kind of a man was he? Showering the same kind of love on her as he did on the first night.

Next day Chhamman Mian bunked college. A one-man delegation knocked at all doors.

"Bhaijan — why is Haleema being sent to the village?"

"Tradition of this mahal."

"She is not cattle. She is the custodian of my child!"

Bhaijan's face flushed with anger. "Shame on you for this stupid remark. How dare you utter such nonsense in my presence?" He walked off in a towering rage. Never before had men interfered in the domestic politics of the mahal. Whenever they considered it propitious, Pyari Ammis provided healthy maids for their sons, who massaged their feet and did whatever else was required of them. The moment they were declared a "health hazard" they were sent along with other goods and chattel to the village to be "repaired". No person in his right mind ever got emotionally tangled with a maid.

"Afzal Bhai, please tell Pyari Ammi not to send Haleema to the village." He begged his cousin.

"Are you mad? A pregnant woman — bloody injurious to health. Don't get so worked up. You'll need a new arrangement." He laughed shamelessly. And what about your nikah to Hurma in November?"

"I won't marry Hurma! If Haleema goes to the village that will be the end of my studies", he announced.

Begum's blood vessels were ready to burst. "How dare he? If *he* can be obstinate so can *we*! Now Haleema will stay here only over my dead body. Nayaab. . . not tomorrow or the day after—take her away *now*. I swear by the Holy Prophet . . ."

"Najam Bitiya is planning to go to Europe after her delivery?"

"Why do you take her name? May god keep my daughter healthy." Najam was Chhamman Mian's sister.

"Amen! But she won't take the child, will she? And it is not advisable to send Dulha Nawab alone. If that wretched foreigner gets her hands on him, we are doomed."

"God, Nayaab! What are you saying?"

"There are only a few days between Haleema and Najam Bitiya's deliveries. Even if it is a week — no matter."

Begum had begun to understand.

"Najam Bitiya will be saved the bother. When she goes to London, Haleema will continue to nurse the infant. The child will get clean, hygienic milk."

Begum remained silent.

"What if she is not looked after properly in the village? As it is, she appears half dead. Here she will stay before my very eyes. I will feed her nourishing food. And we would have given in to Sahibzada's insistence."

"Precisely what I don't want." Begum appeared firm but her voice betrayed a slight softening of attitude.

"Up to you. All I wanted was for the matter to blow over in a couple of days. Mian will tire of it. We will have had our way and the burden of the favour can be offloaded on to him."

When Nayaab became pregnant with Jabbar, Farhat Nawab cooled off fast. When a woman becomes pregnant, the man loses interest. Law of nature.

But Chhamman Mian was giving the lie to the law of nature and to Nayaab Bubu. He was mad enough to have clutched to his bosom what should have remained grovelling at his feet. Such heroics had never been displayed by any Nawabzada, even for his lawful Begum. All day long his nose was buried in books about pre-natal care and child-raising; all his pocket money was wasted on buying vitamins and tonics for the maid.

Haleema pricked her finger with a needle. She was sitting in the courtyard embroidering Chhamman Mian's kurta. She knew why she was being allowed to stay on, but she did not want to shatter Chhamman Mian's dreams.

Chhamman Mian was panic-stricken. Never before had he seen a pregnant woman at such close quarters. He had heard that Najam Baji was pregnant. But she was always moaning, her enormous form wrapped up in numerous shawls. He was worried about Haleema. What if she burst open like a frog? When he didn't get his answers from his books, he ran all the way to Farkhunda Nawab's house.

Farkhunda Nawab was ostracised by the family because, many years ago, she had burnt her fingers in an abortive love affair. But her husband, Ashraf, was a police officer. Everyone needed to stay on his right side, so Farkhunda could not be ignored or annoyed. The ladies were especially jealous of her. She was very learned. Her son, Naeem, was a close friend of

Chhamman.

Chhamman had no clue that Farkhunda Nawab had been invited by Pyari Ammi to give her advice regarding the bride's jewellery. She reassured Chhamman that she would look up Haleema when she dropped in on Friday.

From the car she walked directly towards Chhamman Mian's rooms.

She scolded Chhamman for his nervousness. "Haleema is fine! She won't burst. Don't feed her so much fat. Milk and fruit should be sufficient."

When she was leaving, Haleema said, "Tasleem Phupijan!" She had pulled her dupatta over her face.

"May god give you a long life, my little doll!" So saying, she rushed out of the doll's house.

Later, when Pyari Ammi displayed the bride's jewellery, she was very quiet.

"Don't sit there like a mute — say something."

"Times are changing, Bhabijan. Hurma is a nice girl, but . . ."

"I know . . . she is fashionable, and the jewellery is old-fashioned. Never mind. I'll order the latest styles from Bombay. Let's talk frankly . . ."

But Farkhunda sat quiet, evidently ill at ease. Then came a string of excuses. A meeting at the club . . . etc., etc. After she left Begum and Bubu had the pleasure of tearing her to shreds.

When Nayaab went to show the jewellery to Hurma, she heard that Feroza Nawab had gone to a friend's house, and that the girl was playing tennis.

Hurma entered, stamping her feet. Nayaab opened the jewellery box.

"Jewellery, Rani Bitiya. Make your choice!"

"Why should my choice be necessary for Haleema

Bi?" she asked, vigorously brushing her short hair.

"God forbid! Haleema is a maid."

"I see. But the child is Chhamman Mian's isn't it?"

"Child!" Suddenly Bubu was hot around the ears.

"Farkhunda Khala was saying . . ."

"Oh no, Bitiya . . . I mean . . . Tauba! Tauba! You are as prickly as a thorny bush! You mother's absence from the house gives you no right to make fun of an old woman. If she was present would you dare fling your shoes in my face by behaving like this?"

Bubu swept out of the house in great indignation.

How the rascal jumps around! Placing his hand on her taut silvery stomach, Chhamman Mian was marvelling at the miracles of nature.

"Why are you so cold, Limoo?" When he was overwhelmed with love for her, Chhamman switched from Haleema to Lima, from Lima to Limoo. He wrapped her lovingly in a quilt. Burying his face in her body, he took several deep breaths. How fragrant Limoo is! Like a fully ripe mango. Ever inviting. A bowl of cool water, full to the brim, drink from it every day and the thirst is everlasting. It was selfish of him to make so much love to her. She will wilt away with excess. No . . . from now on he won't touch her. If only he could make time stand still! Don't look ahead, don't look back. Darkness has been left behind . . . but what lies ahead? Who can trust the future?

"God's curse on her. How Haleema has betrayed us!" Begum dipped her finger in honey and thrust it into her newborn grand-daughter's mouth.

"Nayaab, your mouth is a pit of coals. You said they will deliver together. Najam has been crying since morning. Doesn't want to start the baby at her breast. And your Haleema! No sign of delivering. You promised to send Haleema's baby to the village and hand her Najam's for nursing. Now what?"

The world can stop rotating, but Nayaab's word, once given, could not be belied. That cheap Haleema, how dare she defy her prediction?

Haleema was squeezing oranges. Chhamman Mian would soon return after winning the match. Bubu glanced at her like an eagle sizing up its prey before pouncing on it. Today she was full of venom.

"Haleema!" Her voice was cruel. Haleema trembled.

"So? What have you been harbouring?" Her eyes scorched Haleema from head to foot.

"Speak, bastard, whose is it?" As if it was the first time she had seen her swollen stomach.

"This orange . . . ?"

"No, wretch, this melon." She whisked at the full term pregnancy with the end of her fan.

Haleema was dumbfounded! No one had ever remarked on her pregnancy. She stared, open-mouthed.

"Will you speak or shall I take my shoe to your face? Bastard, whose is it?"

When Gori Bi, the maid of Manjhley Nawab, had asked Nayaab the same question many years ago, she had flung the reply right at her face!

Haleema's tongue was frozen. If someone had cut her into little bits, she would never have uttered Chhotey Saheb's name. His sin was her sweetest benediction.

"Why don't you say something, you damned wretch?" A resounding slap landed on her left cheek. A gold ring tore her flesh and drew blood.

Chhamman Mian was scoring hit after hit. The

entire field resounded with applause. When he lifted the silver cup in his hands, he felt as if Haleema's taut silver stomach was throbbing.

By force of habit he came running to the room looking for Haleema. When he got no response, he ran across, drenched in sweat, into Pyari Ammi's room.

"Where did you get this lota? It is quite unique."

"Bubu, this is a cup, not a lota!"

"Phone Hakim Saheb, my love." Pyari Ammi was groaning. "My legs are getting stiff again."

"I will. Bubu , ask Haleema to take out a cotton kurta. It is very hot."

When he returned after phoning, Bubu motioned with her hand, "She is sleeping."

"My clothes . . ." Bubu nodded her head.

When he came out after his bath, Sarvari was drawing the cord in his pyjamas.

"I am asking about Haleema and you are talking bloody nonsense." Chhamman growled.

"Allah! How do I know? Must be in the servants' quarters." Sarvari was dolled up from head to toe.

"Servants' quarters? Get her here." He snatched his kurta and threw it across the room.

"You heard me, witch. Go! Run!" He yanked the pyjama from her hand. Sarvari giggled.

"Bubu sent me."

"Sent you ? Why ?"

More giggling.

"*Ullu ki patthi.*" Chhamman raised his racket. With great coquettry, Sarvari left the room, tinkling her anklets and jangling her bracelets.

For five or ten minutes Chhamman was very agitated. Wrapping a towel around his waist, he flipped the pages of a magazine. After fifteen minutes he became restless.

"Anybody there?" This was his typical way of calling for Haleema. Once again, Sarvari descended, armed with the apparatus of heavy flirtation.

"Tell me the truth, witch." He caught hold of her braid and gave it one twist around his wrist.

"You are killing me ! Oh God ... please! There ... there in the servants' quarters."

Chhamman let go of her braid. Trembling from head to foot, he thrust his feet into a pair of slippers and ran out.

"Where are you going, Mian ? Don't. This is not the time for men to go." Sarvari ran after him. But Mian did not hear a single word. Met Nayaab in the verandah.

"Bubu, get the lady doctor."

"Oh God, Chhotey Mian ... your clothes. You bastard!" she yelled at Sarvari. She was sending Lateefa, but Sarvari fell at her feet.

"Bubu, let Jabbar take the car. Telephone won't do."

"Whatever for ?"

"Haleema ... !" His throat was dry.

"Haleema? She doesn't need a doctor. She ... needs a memsaheb from London! Shameless corpse. These niceties have given a long rope to the maids. Go, Mian. There was a phone call from your friend, Naeem Saheb. He is having a birthday party. Sarvari, miserable wretch, take out Mian's special churidar-pyjama and sherwani." She started to walk away.

"What had I come to say, Mian? You made me forget. Your Pyari Ammi is not well. On your way to Naeem Saheb's, look up Hakim Saheb. I'll ask Jabbar to get the car." Walked away quickly before he could open his mouth.

Bewildered, Chhamman returned to his room. Then got up with a start and threw on a few clothes. How many times had he seen a maid's death ! For months his dreams were haunted by Sanobar's corpse. Haleema is like a flower. Anaemic. Tubercular. He ran to his elder brother's room.

"Bhaijan !"

"What ?" He was engrossed in a game of chess with his friend.

"I have to talk to you." With trembling hands he tugged at his sleeve.

"Wait a minute. What a superb move ! Watch us. Well, Mian Qudoos. Save your castle, otherwise. . . ."

"Bhaijan." Chhamman felt death all over him.

"Sit for a few minutes. Your move, Mian Qudoos."

Twenty minutes passed. Twenty decades for Chhamman.

"By the way, congratulations ! What a superb cup." He looked back at Chhamman and spoke with warmth.

"Bhaijan . . . Haleema . . . please call the doctor !"

"She will be called if necessary."

"No, Bhaijan. This will kill her. Please *do* something."

"Let her die then. Am I God to prevent the inevitable? And you? . . . Shamelessly blubbering for a slovenly maid. Have some decency, man. She is a bloody whore. Don't indulge in her whims. With a bastard in her stomach, is she a whore or a nun ?"

"Bhaijan . . . I . . . Bhai . . ."

"Stop stammering. Without a nikah a woman is a harlot, a whore, an adultress. She should be stoned in the market-place. Better dead than alive. The world would become a cleaner place."

"I share her blame."

"So? What do I care? Go and repent. Don't waste my time !"

Hellishly difficult. Reasoning with such a bloody blockhead. If it were anyone else Chhamman Mian would have broken his jaw. But he had always respected his older brother. Childhood habit. Gulping down his rising blood, he strode back.

Like a maniac he banged his head at every door. Begged his father, but Gultaar had taught him such a lesson, that at the mention of the word, "maid" he jumped three feet in the air.

"How dare you confess your dirty deeds with such shamelessness? First you poke your nose in the shit-drain, then you want to drag your family into the same mire."

Chhamman rubbed Pyari Ammi's feet with his eyes. But she managed to throw a hysterical fit. Why hadn't she lost her hearing before such evil words struck her eardrums ? Why didn't blindness strike her before she saw the dawning of this disastrous day?

He sank to his knees before Chacha Abba. "*La haul wala quwwat*! Let her die, the dirty rag. Don't *you* worry. I will give you my Mahrukh. A real fire-cracker ! Shame on you, boy. . . dying for a sickly maidservant. Your indiscriminate reading of worthless books has resulted in this."

People were laughing openly, joking. The target of their jibes was sitting on the cold and moist floor which skirted the servants' quarters. Chhamman Mian was crying. An eighteen year old crying like an infant, whimpering like a child.

Abba Huzoor was furious. If Pyari Ammi hadn't

gone into a state of hysteria, he would have skinned
the boy with his own knife. Traitor. The day he heard
that his beloved son had successfully copulated with
the maid, his mutton-chop whiskers had ridden up
and down with an irrepressible grin. How disgrace-
fully the older son had let him down. If the younger
hadn't performed, who would have inherited the vast
family fortunes?

Never had such melodrama been witnessed. Servants were tittering, maids were giggling. In the darkness of a semi-room, on a rough bed of jute string,
Haleema was cooing like a pigeon. Her palms were
bleeding from the tightness of her grip on the rough
hemp.

"Sarvari, you wretch ! He is sitting on the damp
floor. He will catch cold. Oh ... Oh." If only these
painful contractions would stop ... for one moment
... she would make him swear by her head to get up
from the wet floor. But ... but ... before God Almighty, she held nothing ... nothing against him.

Excruciating waves of pain were racking her large,
shapeless, sweat-drenched body. She had bloodied
her lips, so that no sound reached Chhamman. Her
shrieks of pain would have driven him mad. But the
soundless waves were registering on his heart.
Chhamman was almost delirious with fear. He
wanted to lift a stone and break open his skull ...
perhaps the steaming tension would be released. Suddenly he heard his name uttered in an agonizing
shriek. He was yanked out of his depression. He
hurtled towards his cycle and, in his mud-splattered
clothes, dashed out of the gate, barely missing a head-
on collision.

"My son!" Regaining consciousness, Begum

started beating her chest.

"My God, Chhamman, is all well ?" Eyes shot red, covered in slime, Chhamman was crying like a baby. "Phuppo ... Phuppo. ..."

"Is she ... ?

"Dead. Dying. No-one listens to me. No-one."

"You are stupid. I asked you to inform me. Let me call an ambulance. No-one has the stamina to fight with your elders at the mahal."

"I will phone." Ashraf lifted the receiver.

"I was playing my cricket finals. When I returned, I discovered ... Phuppo, she will die. Maybe she is dead already. ..."

"No ... she won't."

When Farkhunda Nawab's car, followed by the ambulance, entered the mahal, the commotion that ensued was deafening. Begum Sahiba threw another fainting fit. Nawab Saheb came snarling towards the door with his revolver loaded. On seeing the police car behind the ambulance, he turned right back. The family had never seen such public insult; not even when Manjhley Nawab's property was confiscated by the court.

Farkhunda Nawab looked neither to the left nor to the right. She marched straight in the direction of the servants' quarters.

Chhamman Mian swooped up the bleeding Haleema in his arms. In the mahal, the mourning-carpet was spread out. Miraculously, the Begum rose from her fainting fit and started on a litany of curses.

The next day, with a stroke of his pen, Chhamman Mian abdicated his right to the family property. It wasn't a fortune that he had earned by the sweat of his brow... so who cared ? Whatever Abba Huzoor dictated, he wrote—most willingly.

Chhamman Mian now lives in a dirty old house in a narrow gali. It is said that he teaches cricket at some school or another. Attends college in the evening . . . Often he is seen on his bicycle dressed in worn-out cotton trousers and an old shirt. In the basket attached to the handlebars, among the fruit and vegetables, sometimes one may see a child, sitting quietly, with large limpid eyes.

What a story ! Lost his entire family for nothing. All this education for nothing. They say he has a woman in his home. Who knows whether he has married her or not. God! What bad days have befallen us!

*Translated by Syeda Hameed*

# Glossary

| | | |
|---|---|---|
| *Adab* | : | respectful greeting |
| *adwan* | : | the strings at the foot of a bedstead by which the cross-strings are tightened and braced |
| *alim* | : | learned individual |
| allopath | : | practitioner of modern medicine |
| *almirah* | : | cupboard |
| *amar bel* | : | clinging vine |
| *anna* | : | fraction of a rupee |
| *arti* | : | ritual performed during Hindu prayers |
| *ayat* | : | verse from the Quran |
| *Ayat-ul-Kursi:* | : | an ayat in the Quran |
| *babua* | : | doll |
| *basant* | : | the season of spring |
| *Begum* | : | Madame |
| *behan* | : | sister |
| *Bharata Natyam* : | | classical dance of south India |
| *bismillah* | : | a ceremony to mark a child's first reading of the Quran |
| *boski* | : | a heavy material, similar to linen |
| *brinjal* | : | aubergine |
| *chait* | : | twelfth month of the Hindu calendar |

| | | |
|---|---|---|
| *chal* | : | cluster of dwellings; neighbour-hood |
| *charpai* | : | bed made with jute rope |
| *chauthi* | : | fourth day after a wedding |
| *chillas* | : | forty-day observance |
| *chranti* | : | disparaging colloquialism for Indian Christians |
| *churan* | : | powdered condiments, said to help digestion |
| *churidar pyjama* | : | tight, calf-hugging pyjamas, gathered into folds at the ankles |
| *dacoit* | : | armed robber |
| *devi* | : | female deity |
| *dhoti* | : | loincloth |
| *Diwali* | : | Hindu festival |
| *dupatta* | : | scarf worn across the bosom and over the shoulders by women |
| *Eid* | : | Muslim festival following 30 days of fasting |
| *eidi* | : | money given to younger people during the festival of Eid |
| *farz namaz* | : | essential prayer |
| Fatima Zehra | : | the Prophet's daughter |
| *fatwa* | : | verdict |
| *feringhi* | : | foreigner |
| *galli* | : | narrow lane |
| *gharara* | : | formal wear of Muslim women, resembling ankle-length culottes |
| *ghee* | : | clarified butter |
| *ghunghat* | : | veil drawn over the face and head |

| | | |
|---|---|---|
| *Gita* | : | a religious book of the Hindus |
| *goondas* | : | ruffians |
| *gurdhani* | : | a sweet made with sugarcane |
| | | |
| *Haj* | : | annual pilgrimage of Muslims to Mecca |
| *hakim* | : | practitioner of traditional medicine |
| *halwa* | : | traditional dessert |
| *havan* | : | sacred Hindu ritual around a fire |
| *hukkah* | : | hubble-bubble |
| *huzoor* | : | milord |
| | | |
| *inshallah* | : | the will of God |
| | | |
| *jaali karga* | : | lacy material |
| *jahannam* | : | hell |
| *janam* | : | birth |
| *najamaz* | : | prayer-mat |
| *jeth* | : | the second month in the Hindu calendar, corresponding to May-June |
| *jinn* | : | djinn |
| *jora* | : | ensemble |
| | | |
| *Ka'aba* | : | House of Abraham around which Muslims walk seven times in fulfilment of Haj |
| *kabab* | : | meat cutlets |
| *kafir* | : | non-believer |
| *kajal* | : | kohl for the eyes |
| *kaneez* | : | female servant |
| *karakuli* | : | fur cap |
| *karga kurta* | : | lacy smock |

| | | |
|---|---|---|
| *katha* | : | saga |
| *khachar-khachar* | : | messy |
| *khali* | : | the month between the festivals of Id-ul-Fitr and Id-ul-Zuha |
| Khatau | : | brand name of a popular cotton voile |
| *kheel* | : | puffed rice |
| *kholi* | : | a small room |
| *kibla* | : | direction in which Muslim prayers are offered |
| *kismat* | : | fate or destiny |
| *kufr* | : | heresy |
| *kurta* | : | smock |
| *lagaan* | : | interest or rent or revenue from land |
| *lakh* | : | a hundred thousand |
| *lota* | : | metal vessel for water |
| *mahal* | : | castle |
| *mahasabhi* | : | member or sympathiser of the Hindu Mahasabha, a staunch Hindu political party |
| *maika* | : | maternal home |
| *malan* | : | female gardner |
| *malida* | : | a cake made of pounded meal, milk, butter and sugar |
| *mandir* | : | Hindu temple |
| *mangal sutra* | : | black beads worn around the neck by Hindu women as a symbol of marriage |
| Manipuri | : | style of dance originating in Manipur, a state in north-east India |

| | | |
|---|---|---|
| *mannat* | : | a promise or vow |
| *Marwari* | : | person from Marwar, in west India |
| *masa* | : | unit of weight |
| *mashallah* | : | by the grace of God |
| *Maulvi Saheb* | : | Muslim priest |
| *mazar* | : | shrine |
| *mehr* | : | a Muslim woman's dowry, promised by the husband at the time of marriage |
| *mem* | : | lady with a fair complexion (coll.) |
| *mughlani* | : | female descendant of the Mughals |
| *muhalle wale* | : | neighbours |
| *mujra* | : | dance |
| *murshad* | : | disciple |
| | | |
| *naika* | : | coquette |
| *nautch* | : | dance |
| *Nawab* | : | member of the nobility |
| *Nawabzadi* | : | daughter of a nawab |
| *neem* | : | tree of the species, *Azaradichta Indica* |
| *niaz* | : | offering of food and alms in the name of the Prophet |
| *nikah* | : | Muslim wedding ceremony |
| | | |
| *paan* | : | betel leaf |
| *paandan* | : | container for paan |
| *pachisi* | : | a form of chess |
| *paisa* | : | money |
| *pandit* | : | Hindu priest |

| | | |
|---|---|---|
| *Pandus and Kurus* | : | two mythical warring factions, brothers of the same father, in the well-known Indian epic, the *Mahabharata* |
| *papad* | : | crisp chips made with lentils or rice |
| *pari* | : | nymph |
| *Pathan* | : | tribal name for people belonging to the north-west frontier province of Pakistan |
| *Pathani* | : | female descendant of the Pathans |
| *pulao* | : | entree of rice with meat |
| *purdah* | : | the custom of veiling |
| *qamis* | : | smock |
| *qawali* | : | group singing in praise of Allah; a Sufi tradition |
| *qazi* | : | one learned in Islamic law |
| *qorma* | : | traditional meat dish with gravy |
| *Qureshi* | : | descendant of the Quresh tribe of Saudi Arabia |
| *rakat* | : | the divisions of the Islamic prayer |
| *rakhi* | : | string tied around the wrists of brothers to commemorate the rights of sisters |
| *roti* | : | unleavened bread |
| *sarh* | : | month in the Hindu calendar |
| *Sayyedani* | : | female descendant of the Prophet |
| *seh-dari* | : | a room with three doors |
| *sehra* | : | a veil of flowers worn by the bride and groom at their wedding |
| *sewayyan* | : | sweet vermicelli |

| | | |
|---|---|---|
| *shab-barat* | : | Muslim festival celebrated on the fourteenth day of Shaban |
| *shalwar* | : | long, loose pyjamas, caught at the ankles, worn by men and women |
| *shalwar qamis* | : | ensemble |
| *shehnai* | : | wind instrument |
| *Sheikhani* | : | female descendant of the sheikhs |
| *sherwani* | : | formal long coat worn by men |
| *Sindhan* ` | : | a woman from Sind in Pakistan |
| *sindhur* | : | vermilion, worn by women in the parting of their hair to signify marriage |
| *Sozankari* | : | special embroidery |
| *Swami* | : | guru |
| *talaq* | : | divorce |
| *Tarakh!* | : | sound of a slap |
| *Tauba!* | : | God forbid! |
| *Teej* | : | a festival during the month of May in west India, when many young girls are given away in marriage |
| *tola* | : | unit of weight |
| *ullu ki patthi* | : | common abuse, roughly corresponding to, "You idiot!" |
| *walima* | : | party given by the bridegroom the day after the wedding |
| *wazifa* | : | repeating a daily prayer |
| *Yalamu Mabain* | : | words from the Quran |
| *zamindar* | : | landlord |